To Fran -

May all your dreams come true!

Make a Wish

Stories Written for Real People Where They are the Star

By

Marlayne Giron

Marlayne Giron

Psalm 45:1

Make a Wish

Cover design by Marlayne Jan Giron
Interior design by Marlayne Jan Giron

Published in the United States of America by:

CreateSpace
7290 B. Investment Drive
Charleston, SC 29418
USA
www.createspace.com

ISBN-13: 978-1456437336 (CreateSpace-Assigned)
ISBN-10: 145643733X
BISAC: Inspirational / Fiction / Christian / Short Stories

FORWARD

I have personally gotten to witness the affect these stories have had upon the recipients. Many of them have come to me and told me how touched and blessed they were by their own wish story and how it has impacted their lives. They said that their story was the best gift they have ever received and many read them on a daily basis. I also have been personally blessed by Marlayne's writing and I believe you will as well. – Mary Fields

Dedicated to:

My "sissy", Mary - my muse, champion and greatest cheerleader. I'm so glad we met. This book would not exist without you and your belief in me.

INTRODUCTION

The "wish fulfillment" stories that you are about to read had a very innocent beginning. A good friend of mine, Henry, who has been a quadriplegic since the age of 14 (and is now in his early 50s at the time of this writing), was really down in the dumps. He had been stood up for a fishing trip and because of his condition; he is subject to the schedules and whims of others. He wouldn't get out of bed, wouldn't do anything and his wife Vicki had given up trying to coax him. Henry and I had become good friends ever since Vicki reviewed my book, The Victor, on her blog.

I had already spoken with Henry several times before this so I was distressed when I heard how low he was feeling. But what could I do? I lived on the west coast and he lived on the east coast. How could I possibly cheer him up? Then a light bulb went on over my head and I thought, "*I can write him a story*"...and that's exactly what I did. I wrote "A Gift for Henry" in about one hour and then emailed it to them that night. The first thing the next morning I checked my email to see what the response was. Well...it was amazing! Vicki had written me and told me that they had wept for 20 minutes after reading it. That it had truly been inspired of God because of the details I put in that I were not aware that were perfect for Henry. Such as the smell of orange blossoms being his favorite, how he was always trying to wiggle his toes to see if they had started working and that all he wants to do when he gets to heaven is to run, run, run for the Lord.

All of these stories were written as gifts for others either because I was inspired to do so or because they were requested. Some are deeply emotional, heartfelt and inspirational while others are just fun.

Each story is preceded by a brief paragraph which gives a little bio on the person for whom it was written and why. Each person appears in their own story as the "star".

If you would like your own story, all you have to do is contact me via email and... "Make a Wish"!

Marlayne Giron
thevictorbook@sbcglobal.net

Contents

CHAPTER ONE
"A Gift for Henry"

Below is Henry's personal account of the accident that resulted in him becoming a quadriplegic (yes he typed it himself):

SEPTEMBER 16, 1972 is a day that I will relive for the rest of my life. It happened at the Withlacoochee River in Florida, about two miles from my house. It was around 2:30 in the afternoon and I was 14 years old.

I had snuck away from the house on my bicycle when I was told I could not to go swimming that day. I met two of my friends on the way to the river as planned, where we had swam many times before. If only I had known what was going to happen that day, I would never have gone! When we got there, there was a man, his wife, and their two daughters swimming.

We put our bicycles down, took our shirts and jeans off that we wore over our swimming trunks, and headed down to the river edge and dove in. The water was cool and the current was flowing as usual. We swam back to the river bank and got out of the water. We decided to climb a tree which leaned over the water. We had dove out of that tree many times in the past.

I was the first to climb the tree and dive into the water, followed by my friends. We all swam back to the bank and got out. We climbed the tree again but this time we did a canon ball, swam back, got out again. Then one of my friends asked the other if he wanted to dive off his shoulders. He said yes, so he squatted to let him get on his shoulders and then stood up so he could dive into the river. After he dove in he swam back and as he was getting out he slipped back into water because the bank was getting very slippery. I ran and did a cannon ball again off the bank and as I was getting out, I too noticed that it was not so easy. I slipped a few times before I was finally able to climb back up on the bank. The wet clay was sticking to my feet so I rubbed my feet on the ground and removed most of it. My friend asked if I wanted to dive off of his shoulders and I said, "Sure, why not".

So as he squatted down I climbed onto his shoulders and then he stood up so I could dive into the water.

Just as I was ready to dive, ***IT HAPPENED!!*** *My right foot slipped off his shoulder and I fell straight down on top of my head and rolled off into the water. I knew immediately that something was wrong. First of all, there was a tingling sensation all over my body, as though a thousand needles were sticking me! Secondly, I could not move anything. I tried so hard, but nothing would move. I KNEW I WAS IN TROUBLE. My body was not responding no matter what I tried. I was in the fetal position (*where your arms and knees are drawn up to your chest*), floating face down in the water, drifting along with the current. I could not see anything but the black water as the river towed me further and further away! You cannot imagine everything that was running through my mind all at the same time! But the main thing that I was thinking was, "I NEED TO BREATHE!" All of my thoughts changed from what was wrong with me to, "I am going to drown if I do not breathe NOW!!!" I could not hold my breath any longer (*your body will take a breath whether you want to or not, IN or out of water*). I knew that if took a breath my lungs would fill up with water, but I HAD TO BREATH!! I was so terrified by now because I just knew I was going to DIE!!*

*Just as my body forced me to take a breath, which would have been nothing but water, my friend grabbed me and turned me over. I was finally able to take a breath of air, which felt like I had waited an eternity for! My friend swam back, with me in tow, to where my other friend was waiting to help pull me out of river that had almost taken my life!!! The family that was there swimming took me to the nearest hospital where they said I was now a quadriplegic (*you are paralyzed from the neck down and cannot feel anything*) and would never walk AGAIN!! The doctors said I would probably not make it and if I did I would be a vegetable for the rest of my life! Many times my family was called by the doctor who said I wouldn't live through the night. I did die three times but God brought me back! Everyone* *wondered "Why did God let this happen?" But God's wisdom is far greater than ours and out of this tragedy came faith, hope and inspiration! God was there all the time. God had other plans for my life, that plan was for me to serve Him! God is using me in so many ways it is amazing!*

People used to shy away from me because of my condition, but now they are drawn to me like a magnet. For example, the longest I have been able to "witness" to someone was over two hours and had him in tears! If I go anywhere with my wife to whom I have been married to for twenty-two years, someone will approach me and I just have to testify. I have given my testimony in church and spoken to the teen youth group, and it has changed so many of their lives. I will praise God one glorious day, with no wheelchair, handicapped van, horrible muscle spasms, or confinement. I will be free, all because of our precious Lord and Savior Jesus Christ!!! Even though we suffer and are tried in this life, the next life will be unbelievably satisfying beyond belief.

I was hurt thirty-seven years ago and I am not a vegetable, I've lived longer than the fourteen years the doctors had predicted that I would in nineteen-seventy-two. I have graduated high school, gone to college, got married, and I have three kids and four grand kids; all because God had a plan for my life.

May God bless each and every one of you; don't despair at your own circumstances, God has brought me through so many things in my life time and I give all the Praise and Glory to Him! Amen.

"A Gift for Henry"

Henry awakened with a start, his heart pounding and looked around. For a few seconds all he could do was to stare at the vista which greeted his eyes and then it hit him like a ton a bricks…he was sitting up for the first time by himself since the accident. He opened and shut his eyes slowly several times, the amazing view never changing and then slowly, as if he were afraid he would shatter and break like glass, he bent his neck down and looked at his lower half. Instead of thin, atrophied legs that ignored all of his mind's commands, there were two tanned and muscular limbs. Holding his breath…he did something he hadn't been able to do in decades…he wiggled his toes.

A shout of pure joy issued from his mouth, so loud it even scared himself. "YAHOOOOOO!" Then he did something else he hadn't done in years…he pinched himself… as hard as he could, right above the hips in the "tickle spot" and practically doubled over with mixed joy and disbelief.

"Vicki!" he shouted, wiggling and wiggling his toes more violently. "Will you look at this? Just look!" There was no answer. It wasn't until he found himself standing and then jumping up and down with glee that he really noticed and took stock of his surroundings. The sky was the deepest blue he had ever seen but there was no sun. Instead an incredibly pure and blazing glow of light originated from everywhere. In every direction that he looked he saw the loveliest terrain he had ever laid eyes on. Majestic mountains with craggy peaks (but no snow); fields of wildflowers broken only by gurgling brooks which fed into crystal clear lakes; wide open undulating plains of the greenest grass he had ever seen. No buildings, no bugs (except butterflies), the most delicious smell of orange blossoms permeating the air and a hint of lilting music that seemed to come from everywhere.

"VICKI!" he shouted again, frustrated that his wife was not there to share the experience with him and validate that it was all real.

"She'll join you later," responded a deep and profoundly gentle voice. Henry whirled around and instantly fell onto his face upon recognizing who had spoken to him. "Henry, please rise," said the man, lifting him gently onto his feet. "I want you to enjoy this time I have given you on your feet, not your face."

At His touch, a surge of strength flowed through Henry's entire body that was electrifying. He felt like he could run all the way to China and back again and not even get winded. Jesus smiled a crinkly smile at him and pointed off into the distance. Henry followed with his eyes and saw the most gorgeous tree he had ever laid eyes on. It was indescribable but even from this distance he could tell it was laden with flowers and fruit; somehow he knew that this is where the lovely perfume was emanating from.

Henry looked back into the face of His blessed Redeemer, his eyes filling with tears and his heart welling with emotion so strong he felt it would burst with joy. Jesus laid his nail-pierced hand upon his shoulder and Henry felt a thrill pass through him.

"Run, Henry!" Jesus smiled broadly. *"Run!"* Despite his desire to not leave his Savior's side for even a moment, it had been as though the words were more of a command than a suggestion. The next thing Henry knew his legs were pumping, his arms were flailing and he was racing like a Cheetah through the fragrant grass towards what he knew was the Tree of Life, closing the distance faster than he dreamed could be possible. As he ran, tears of joy flew back in the wind – and a howl of laughter and sheer joy erupted from his throat. He was running. *HE WAS RUNNING!!*

He exulted in the sheer joy of feeling his once dead limbs alive and thriving again. Oh… if only the dream would never end…if only he would never have to wake up…but wait…he had pinched himself…and *it had hurt. What was going on?* He came to a stop just before the tree, amazed that he wasn't even breathing hard. Maybe he wasn't dreaming…maybe he was…

"You're not dead, Henry" whispered the voice of Jesus quietly in his ear as if The Master were standing just behind him.

"And you're not asleep either. This is my gift to you for now…unwrap it and take it out whenever you feel the need and know that one day soon, it will be yours to enjoy for eternity with all your loved ones who have trusted in Me."

Henry hung his head and wept, his shoulders heaving with gratitude. The Lord's voice interrupted his thoughts again. "I have one more gift for you before you leave…if you'll accept it…"

"Lord," sobbed Henry. "It is enough that you suffered, died and rose for me and have allowed me to live a life, though broken physically, that has been abundant for you. I will accept whatever gift you want to give me but what can I do in return for you?"

"You have been giving me the best gift for many years, Henry…*You*." Replied Jesus, and suddenly Henry turned around to find Jesus standing before him again only he wasn't dressed in his "typical" biblical clothes but in hip-waders and carrying two fishing rods. "I once told Peter, Andrew, James and John that I would make them fishers of men," he continued with a broad smile that lit up everything about Him. "But today I think that you and I will just go fish for trout in that stream over there. I can guarantee a good catch but as for you …well today you'll have to clean and fry them up. Deal?"

Henry's mouth just hung open and then he bellowed with laughter. "Deal!" he exclaimed.

Epilogue: Henry will still fall into occasionally depressions. About a year after I wrote him the first story I found out from Vicki again that he was in another one of his black moods. Wouldn't get out of bed for a couple of weeks, wouldn't see anybody, and wouldn't do anything, just sulked. It's understandable being in his position. I would probably be a lot worse if it were me. I found out late one night of the latest bout and despite the fact that I was tired and wanted to go to bed I got hit with another inspiration. Again, I typed it up and emailed it off. Then I contacted Darlene, his long-time friend and good neighbor (for whom I wrote "Three Wishes"), and asked if she would buy a German Chocolate Cake (his favorite) and deliver it the next day for me. Henry read his story and got out of bed in time to enjoy his cake.

"An Arse-Whoopin' for Henry"

Henry stared up at the ceiling in a glum, dark mood. He didn't know exactly what it was that was making him feel like this, all he knew is that he didn't want to do anything. He didn't want to get out of bed; he didn't want to watch television, he didn't even want to get onto the computer. His wife Vicki had tried several different things to try and snap him out of it but nothing had worked so far so she had let him be, praying and hoping that the funk would clear and he would back to his old self again.

Even the delivery of Mrs. Field's birthday cookies from his author friend and adopted "mom", Marlayne, had done nothing to lift the black mood. Yup. He was one unhappy dude at the moment and he didn't care. He felt weary of life; he was sick of being stuck in his wheelchair and dependent upon everyone else for absolutely everything. He was just going to lay in bed and wait…wait for what…he didn't know.

Suddenly the felt a presence in the room.

"Henry!" said a none-too-pleased voice.

Henry craned his neck around as best he could and felt his heart begin to race.

"Just want do you think you're doing, laying in bed most of the day and moping?"

Henry's mouth opened and shut several times but no words would come out. What do you say to a question like that when it comes from the mouth of the Son of God?

"Uuuuuuhhhhhhhhhhh," was all he could manage. Jesus bent over his bed and looked him deeply in the eyes.

"Do you believe that I love you?" He demanded.

Henry nodded his eyes wide.

"Do you believe that I work all things together for good for those who love Me?" came the second question. Again Henry nodded.

"Where is your faith, Henry?" the words stung deeply but they also ignited a fire in his breast. He had allowed the devil to beat him down so that he would be rendered useless for his Lord. What had he been thinking?

"Your friend, Marlayne, prayed for you tonight and I am come in answer to that prayer." Jesus informed him. "Now…no more self-pity and succumbing to depression and despair! I have work for you to do before I return!"

"Yes sir!" Henry replied, almost saluting. Jesus' face became less stern and his cupped his hands upon Henry's cheek with infinite tenderness.

"I love you, my son." He said with a beatific smile. "Never forget that. I have entrusted much in you. Do not give up."

"Yes, Lord!" Henry gulped, feeling ashamed but at the same time encouraged.

"Vicki!" he yelled, giving Jesus a relieved grin. "Come and get me out of bed; I've got to be about my Father's business!"

CHAPTER TWO
"Three Wishes"

I met Darlene through a comment she left on my web page about "A Gift for Henry". Henry and Darlene knew each other in high school had lost contact for decades. Coincidently enough, they found each other again shortly after I came into the picture through Facebook. What was even more amazing was that they only lived 4 miles away from each other!

Darlene had lost her beloved husband, Stevie, due to congestive heart failure a few years ago. He had died in her arms. Heart problems ran in his family and Stevie knew that would not live a normal life span on this earth. Henry asked me to write her a story just like the one I had done for him. I knew how painful the holidays were going to be for her so I wanted to do something to let her know that God saw her hurt and pain and that He cares. Three Wishes is God's special Christmas gift to Darlene and is one of my favorite "wish fulfillment" stories.

"Three Wishes"

Darlene regarded the Christmas decorations in her local grocery store glumly. She hated this time of year. Absolutely hated it! All it did was accentuate the sadness that she always carried in her heart like a heavy lead balloon. As a kid she had enjoyed the holidays as much as anyone else but all that had changed three years ago when her husband, Steve, had died in her arms of heart failure. She sighed, fighting back the tears that welled up in her eyes and threatened to spill down her cheeks. She wasn't going to cry in the check-out line! Not in front of all these strangers!

The box boy stuffed the last of her groceries into the bag and Darlene hurried out, her head down, her shoulders beginning to shake. She got into her car, her hands trembling with the grief she tried to suppress and yet couldn't. She let her head drop onto the steering wheel and allowed the tears to come. She missed him. She couldn't help it. Even after a few years, there was still a big hole in her heart that just wouldn't heal.

Oh, Stevie…she thought to herself, not for the last time. *If only we had had more time together…if only your heart hadn't been sick…if only…*

Darlene violently brushed the tears from her cheeks and started the car. She didn't want to go down that road again. She had to get home, unload the groceries alone without help and get some dinner for herself. The very idea depressed her beyond belief.

She turned the key in the ignition and maneuvered out of the parking lot. She made to turn right, but the car suddenly had other ideas. It turned left. It shocked her so much she just gaped. Then the gas pedal depressed itself and the car began speeding up and driving itself. Darlene sat back and watched in shock as the car continued to steer, turning down streets she was unfamiliar with, stopping and starting without assistance from her, and wondering where on earth her car was taking her and why. For some reason she felt no panic but a few times she caught the shocked glances of people in other cars as she half-heartedly smiled and waved at them as her car turned a corner without her assistance. Once or twice she gripped the steering wheel and tried to steer the way she wanted to or to brake but the car was completely unresponsive. *Why fight it?* She thought to herself and sat back to watch what would happen. A half hour passed, then 45 minutes; soon the car was on the main highway heading north. Before she knew it, she had nodded off to sleep.

She awoke when the car came to a stop, not remembering what had happened and wondering if she was asleep, dreaming she was awake. She looked around and found herself and her car in a tiny driveway in front of a little cottage, brightly lit with cheerful Christmas lights and a wreath on the door. There was nothing else in site. She got out of the car feeling stiff from her unexpected nap. She went up to the door of the cottage which was bright red, and knocked. Hopefully whoever lived there would let her use the phone or give her directions on how to get back home before the milk spoiled. She knocked twice.

"Come in, Darlene!" said a voice that made her heart skip a beat. A voice she had not heard in years but a voice that was dearly beloved and familiar all the same.

Heart pounding, she walked into the little cottage. There was a fireplace with a cheery fire crackling away, a Christmas tree with ornaments that looked strangely familiar and her favorite Christmas music playing on the stereo that she hadn't played in years because it had hurt too much to listen to it.

"Welcome, home, sweetheart!" said the voice again and Darlene felt arms wrapping around her like a warm cocoon.

"Stevie?" she sobbed, turning around to face what must surely be a dream or a ghost. "Is it really you?"

"Yes, dear," he responded with an apologetic smile. "I'm sorry we had to bring you here the way we did and that it took so long but I hope the memory we make will all be worth it to you."

"We? Memory?" Darlene repeated, completely bewildered. She stepped back out of Steve's arms for a moment and rubbed her eyes, unable to believe she was seeing what she was seeing. Steve stepped forward again and gently took her hands into his.

"I'm sorry I ruined the holidays for you," he said, he eyes truly sorrowful. "I didn't want to leave you at all, you know, but my heart wasn't made to last as long as everyone else's. Can you forgive me?"

"It's just that I miss you so much." Darlene said, the tears spilling down again. "I have wished so often that I could just have you with me just one more time, just a little bit longer…"

Steve took her face gently into his hands and smiled at her. "Wish granted," he whispered and embraced her again. This time Darlene did not pull away. She melted into his embrace and allowed herself the luxury of breathing in the scent of his hair and his clothes without all the medicinal smells that he had used to carry later in life when his heart began to fail. After a few moments, Steve parted and led her back to the rear of her car with a smile, reaching for one of the grocery bags.

“Here, let me help you with that.” He said, hefting it up easily.

“No! I’ll get it!” Darlene protested, falling back into the routine of doing most of the lifting herself because of his weak heart.

“Not necessary!” Steve said, grabbing both effortlessly. “No more bad heart!” He led her into the tiny but charming kitchen and took the groceries out one at a time. Instead of the dull, boring regular items she always got, she stared in amazement as Steve pulled out the favorite beverages, foods, and treats they used to share one at a time. It was a gourmet feast and it was already prepared and hot.

Together they sat down at the table where candlelight glowed and ate and talked for hours. Then they cuddled up onto the couch together in front of the fire and the tree, listening to soft Christmas music together.

“I don’t want this moment to end.” Darlene said at last, somehow knowing the moment for her departure was soon approaching. Steve laid a gentle kiss on her forehead and held her close.

“Do you remember our last moments together?” he whispered. Darlene choked on her sobs, the raw wound opening up again.

“Of course I do! How could I ever forget a moment like that?” she said, her heart aching. Steve held her closer and looked deeply into her eyes, his face serious.

“Darlene, I always knew I would not live very long and have a normal life span. I also knew it would be unfair to whoever I married and my kids because of it but I was selfish and asked God to grant me three wishes: 1) That I would be able to marry the woman I love, 2) that I could be a father (no matter how they turned out), and 3)…” Steve paused, his own eyes filling with tears.

“Three?” repeated Darlene, wondering what it could be. Steve sighed deeply and held her closer.

“…that when it was finally my time to leave this earth and

go to heaven, I would die in the arms of the person who loved me best in this life...*you.*

"God gave me all three of my wishes and now He has granted this one for you. He has given you one more wonderful memory...a little more time...just a taste of the joy of our being reunited in heaven so you can still go on with your life in this world and grieve a little bit less, knowing how well I loved you and how I still love you and that I'm waiting for you. The time is growing short when we will be together again forever but until that day comes, I want you to live each day knowing that I'm still loving you and caring about you. Try to find joy again in the little things again and I'll be right there, sharing it with you. Can you do that for me?"

"I'll try." Darlene smiled weakly, wishing she could stay in that little cottage with him forever.

"Now lay your head on my shoulder and go to sleep," said Steve, holding her close. "And when you wake you'll be back to your regular life but remember that you always carry my love and my heart inside your own."

"Okay," whispered Darlene, clutching him tightly. "I'll remember. I promise."

"That's my girl," Steve smiled, caressing her head until she fell asleep.

Darlene awoke with a start and looked around her. The cottage was gone and so were the tree, fireplace and Steve. She was back in her little home but there on the table was the most beautiful arrangement of snow-white and deep red flowers she had ever seen. She picked up the tiny envelope and withdrew the little card that had Steve's handwriting on it and instead of crying...she smiled.

P.S. – Yes – Darlene got this bouquet shortly after I sent her the story.

CHAPTER THREE
"The Magic Quill"

Mirriam is a teenaged, homeschooled, Christian blogger and she is a very fascinating girl! She and I share a common love for all things Tolkien, especially Lord of the Rings. I thought I was really into it but she puts me to shame. She has taught herself the two forms of Elvish created by J.R.R. Tolkien and can both read, write and speak the fictional languages quite well. She has quite a few blogs where she reviews books and has a lot of blog followers. One of her blogs featured pictures of gifts she had gotten at Christmas and one of them was a quill and ink set that she thought looked "very elvish" and it became the inspiration for her wish fulfillment story that was created as a surprise for her. When I found out she was coming up on her 16th birthday, I decided to gift her with my collection of vintage J.R.R. Tolkien novels that had sat collecting dust in my garage, unlooked at, and unappreciated for decades. I knew if anyone would appreciate them it would be Mirriam. I packed up 3 large boxes full and shipped them off to her. Her mom took pictures as she opened them. I finally got to meet her and her mom in Atlanta airport last June on my stop over to Richmond, Virginia. She's a wonderful girl.

"The Magic Quill"

Mirriam sat on her bed with one of her two best friends, Keaghan, staring at the blank parchment before her. The blank page stared back at her as if it had just won a "stare out" contest. Her most newly acquired treasure, a genuine fountain pen was poised just above the page, waiting for the words to flow out of her.

"C'mon, Mirriam!" encouraged Keaghan. "You've never had problems writing before now! What's going on?"

Mirriam closed her eyes and set the quill down carefully so as to not drip any of the black ink on herself or anything else.

She had gotten the gift little more than a week ago for Christmas but couldn't seem to bring herself to start writing with it. It was such a special gift and so "Elvish"; it could only be used for a very, very special story; especially since she had also purchased some really expensive vellum paper that looked like real parchment. It couldn't be just any old story…

"Just start writing *something*!" whined Keaghan, becoming exasperated.

Mirriam sighed and put the glass quill onto the page and began to write: *Lothlorien was aglow with golden afternoon light…*

Suddenly both Mirriam and Keaghan gasped aloud; their eyes widening in wonder. Instead of black ink flowing in shaky print onto the vellum was a gorgeous script with letters of living light that blazed and glowed across the page in a foreign language that seemed somewhat familiar to Mirriam.

"Look!" shrieked Keaghan, pointing to the bedroom wall. A portion of Mirriam's bedroom wall had completely faded away (or become invisible) but instead of looking at her neighborhood, she was staring at the limbs of a giant Mallorn tree. Keaghan nudged her in the ribs, still gaping. "Write some more!" she hissed. Shockwaves of nervous excitement running through her veins, Mirriam again began to scratch out whatever words came into her mind. She wasn't sure, but she could feel magic crackling in the air.

…the flet upon which Earwen and Keaghan sat was crowded with the company of other woodland elves, their bows and quivers at the ready as orcs marched under their position, completely unaware of the doom which waited to rain down on them from above…

Mirriam and Keaghan looked up and watched in amazement as the walls of her home completed melted away into nothingness only to be replaced with a 360 degree view of the most amazing golden forest they had ever laid eyes on from a vantage point that was at least 100 feet above the forest floor. Mirriam tucked her long hair behind her ear to get a better look and felt something strange. She gazed at Keaghan's face whose eyes were practically bulging out of her head in mixed wonder and terror.

Mirriam felt her ear and practically dropped the bow in her left hand. *Her ear was pointy*! An elf directly to her right turned round slightly and gave her a warning look. Not a surprised look at seeing a total stranger crouching next to him but a warning look as if to say: *CONCENTRATE!*

The signal was given and all the elves surrounding Mirriam and Keaghan stood as one and began shooting arrows upon the unsuspecting orcs.

"Earwen!" hissed an elf behind her. "Let fly!" Without a second thought, Mirriam stood, renocked her arrow and sent it flying into the neck of a large black orc. The sudden onslaught was almost over before it began. The entire company of orcs lay dead upon the footpath below. Their attack had been so swift and deadly that not one of them had been able to shriek, sound a warning horn, or escape. Their war party had been decimated by the elf-arrows of the Galadrim.

"Well done, Earwen!" said the elf behind her, squeezing her shoulder. Mirriam turned about and her mouth fell open. Standing at least a full head taller than her was someone she had never thought to see in real life, *Legolas*.

"Is that who I think it is?" whispered Keaghan in her ear. Mirriam nodded, unable to tear her eyes away from the finely chiseled face and striking blue eyes of the elf-prince. Legolas smirked at her and waved a hand in front of her face so as to wake her from her trance.

"Awake, Earweeeennnn," he murmured, leaning in closer. A lightning bolt of electricity jolted up her spine, freeing Mirriam from her trance. "Time to go! The lady Galadriel and Celeborn are waiting for our return."

"What do we do now?" hissed Keaghan, grabbing onto Mirriam's arm. Mirriam finally looked at her best friend. Her hair was now down below her waist but enough of it was tied back for her to see that her ears were pointy as well. Mirriam stifled a giggle.

"Just do what I do," she whispered, shouldering her bow. To her amazement, Legolas reached back and clasped hold of her free hand and held it for the duration of the trek. With mounting excitement, she followed Legolas' lead down the stairs from the flet to the footpath where the orcs lay dead. She plucked her arrow from the neck of her one kill, wiped the black blood off onto the grass and put it back in her quiver.

Legolas studied the helmet and iron collar for a moment then flipped the body over.

"You felled the leader, Earwen," he commented with a congratulatory nod in her direction. "Not too bad for your first day out but my count is 13." Mirriam found herself grinning at him, his comment familiar and humorous. It was strangely reminiscent of the rivalry between he and Gimli in the Lord of the Rings on the number of enemy combatants they each had killed in the war of the Ring. The forest was quiet now except for the cry of birds and the subtle sound of a quill still scratching on vellum which only Mirriam seemed to notice.

She and Keaghan followed the line of woodland elves as they made their way back to Caras Caladon to report to Galadriel of their success. Every chance she got, Mirriam would steal a glance at Legolas as well as her own body. She was clothed in the grey cloak and golden/brown attire of the Galadrim that blended into the colors of the forest and her legs were clad in knee-high, kid-skin leather boots. Her friend, Keaghan, was similarly attired with long hair, pointy ears and a bow and quiver that had gone unused. It took the better part of the day and was nightfall before they reached the gigantic Mallorn tree where the Lady Galadriel and Celeborn ruled the golden realm. Silver lanterns lit up all over the forest illuminating their way and the welcoming cry of the Galadrim reached their ears as they made the long climb up to the top flet.

Legolas and the other elves of their warband stood at attention and then bowed with respect as the Lady Galadriel appeared before them. Legolas stood forward, bowed and laid the iron collar and helmet of the orc that Earwen/Mirriam had shot at the feet of Galadriel. She regarded them for a moment then lifted her golden head with a beatific smile.

"Whose arrow felled the Captain?" she asked, looking from one glorious elven face to another.

"Earwen," spoke up Legolas, since Mirriam found herself tongue-tied in apoplectic glee. Her arms was already black and blue from the nonstop pinching she had given herself throughout the trek to Caras Caladon, unable to believe she was inside Middle Earth in a story of her own creation. She could still hear her quill scratching on the vellum but it seemed like the sound was more inside her head than in her ears now.

Galadriel turned her liquid eyes upon Mirriam/Earwen and smiled. "Well done, Earwen, elven daughter," she said, her voice as beautiful as a bell. She laid her hands upon Earwen's shoulders in blessing. "You are the first daughter of the Galadrim to wield bow and arrow to successfully slay our avowed enemy. For this I have a special reward…"

Mirriam cast a quick glance over her shoulder at her best friend, whose face was a study in shock, wonder and disbelief. She turned back to face Galadriel and Celeborn who held forth a wooden box with a silver leaf upon its lid. Mirriam lifted the lid and inside found a crystal ink bottle which was filled not with ugly black ink but a brilliant light which pulsed and glittered in her upheld hand.

"Mithril ink," Galadriel explained, turning it this way and that so it caught the light. "With this ink you will be a mighty story teller and whatever you write shall come to pass."

Tears welled in Mirriam's eyes and a sob caught in her throat. She was speechless and received the gift with shaking hands. She bowed again in thanks to the Lady Galadriel and Celeborn and turned to face Legolas who still stood behind her. In his eyes was great pride and something else Mirriam couldn't quite put her finger on.

"I am so proud of you, beloved," he said, caressing her cheek with his warm hand. The quill scratching in her head came to an abrupt halt the moment his arms went about her.

"Mirriam! *Mirriam*! Wake up! Are you okay?"

Mirriam turned her head to face Keaghan, completely disoriented. The room slowly stopped spinning and she looked down at the page before her. The ink was now just an ordinary black but the parchment was filled with Sindarin Elvish script that not even she could translate if she spent 50 years trying.

"Who wrote all this?" she asked Keaghan, holding it up in wonder.

"You did!" exclaimed her friend. "You just sort of went into some kind of trance and began writing as if you were possessed or something!"

Mirriam stared down at the page of strange writing again until she got to the last line which suddenly began to waver and change before her eyes until the Elvish script became English.

"...for when thou dost set nib to the page; the magic shall be renewed."

"What does it say, Mirriam?" asked her friend, unable to read a single word. Mirriam closed her eyes and hugged her legs, her heart and lips remembering again Legolas' kiss.

"*Earwen*," Mirriam corrected her, opening her eyes and smiling at her best friend. "My name is Earwen and *I am a shield-maiden of Lothlorien*."

CHAPTER FOUR
"In the Land of Milk & Honey"

Wendy is a dear friend and fellow Messianic Jew who longs with all her heart to live in Israel or to make what is called Aliyah but is not permitted to by the government because of her belief in Yeshua (Jesus) as Messiah. When she heard of my other stories, she asked me to write one for her and "In the Land of Milk & Honey" is the result. She told me that after she read it she wept for half an hour.

"In the Land of Milk & Honey"

Consciousness came slowly…lazily…gently. The bird song somehow sounded different, the air heavier and sweeter. Wendy opened her eyes slowly and beheld dappled sunlight filtering through a canopy of grape leaves, laden with heavy purple-black grapes.

She turned her head to the side and looked about her "room". It was simple and yet beautiful. Pure white blankets glowing with the morning sunshine lay upon her. A wooden table, elegant in its simple beauty held a bowl of fresh fruit, and a pitcher of iced tea and a glass.

With a sudden intake of breath, Wendy sat up and looked through the transparent walls of her Sukkoth booth. In the distance were rolling hills of vineyards and orchards and to the other side in the distance, the lake of Galilee. She suddenly knew why the air felt heavier and sweeter…the presence of Yeshua.

How had she come to be in this place; the land where her heart beat like a drum with joy and all her senses were awakened as if from a deep stupor? Y'israel. She stood slowly, hesitantly to her feet noticing at once her white linen frock, glowing as if it possessed a light of its own. On her feet were hand crafted sandals. The morning sun was rising higher and with it came a breeze smelling of roses, bay laurel and the fresh scent of the sea.

She stepped outside her Sukkoth booth into a garden which surrounded it. It was humming with bees and fluttering butterflies, busy collecting nectar from the numerous blossoms. With pounding heart; afraid to wake up from what must surely be a dream, she slowly climbed the nearest hill, breathing deeply in and out as if each breath were nourishment. She stood and faced the holy city, Jerusalem and was stunned. It was not as she remembered it at all. The Dome of the Rock was gone, and in its place stood a gleaming temple of gold and alabaster. The filth of the Arabic section of the old city was gone, replaced by avenues of trees and streets that glistened like gold in the early light.

"Do you like it?" spoke a familiar masculine voice. Wendy closed her eyes and inhaled sharply. It was the voice of her beloved…and it was not in her head but in her ears.

"Yeshua…" she breathed, holding up her arms; tears welling up and spilling down her cheeks from underneath her closed eyes. She fell slowly to her knees. "Yeshua?"

"There is a question in the saying of my name, beloved," came the response. "You are wanting to know if you may stay here always?"

"Yes," whispered Wendy, barely able to breath or speak.

"My precious child," responded the Master, gently enfolding her in His embrace. "There is no such thing as time where I am concerned; for I live outside of it…and you with Me. Where I am there you are also…and my eyes and heart are ever upon this place, so in a sense…you have never left Israel and it has never left you. The body which you must inhabit within the human time domain is limited but not your heart or your soul. One day time will cease to exist and both body and soul will be reunited with Me in this place that remains the apple of my eye. Can you endure until that "time" and do the work I have set before you?"

"Lord, you know my heart and soul's desire…I will always gladly serve you."

Yeshua smiled upon her and in the instant she beheld that smile she felt the sight, sounds, smells and "feel" of the land implanted indelibly upon her mind and heart. From that moment on, wherever she placed her feet, Israel and Jerusalem went with her and before her. A precious secret to enjoy; just between her and The Redeemer as well as the hope of the real reward yet to come.

"Now, come…" Jesus said, holding out his warm brown hand to her. "Let us enjoy this day together and converse to our heart's content. What would you like to do first?"

CHAPTER FIVE
"More Than a Memory"

Michele is the sister of my first love, Barry. Barry died of a brain aneurysm when I was 22 and he was 25 back in 1982. After his death I "adopted" his mom (Ruth) and father (Al) and had dinner with them every Sunday for a few years until Ruth and Al moved up to Oregon to be closer to their daughter, Michele, in 1991. Barry and Michele's dad, Al died in 1994.

Even though I have only seen Michele less than a hand full of few times, we have come to accept each other as "sisters" because of our mutual love for her family and especially Barry. He has been gone for so long that there is barely anyone remaining in her life that ever knew him; making his existence in the past that much more unreal. Her own children never got to know their wonderful "Uncle Barry". So it was with sheer panic in December of 2008 that I realized that I had lost her mom's mailing address and phone number and was desperately hoping that I would get her annual Christmas card so I could tell her that my book, The Victor, was going to be published. In it was a special dedication to Barry that I had put in there more almost 30 years ago.

I received her annual Christmas card and fired off a letter to her the next day asking her to call me because I had something important to tell her and Michele. To my relief I got to speak with Ruth on 12/15/08 and let her know that the story I had worked on for so many years was going to be published. Ruth sounded like her old sweet self but much more frail. I promised to send her a copy of the first book off the press as soon as I got it. In early January 2009 I mailed a copy of The Victor to Ruth who was now living with Michele and a few weeks later I got an urgent email from Michele asking me to call because she had lost my phone number. With dread I called and Michele told me the news which just broke my heart. Ruth had died about a week earlier and my book had arrived on the day of her funeral. I couldn't help but burst into tears. Ruth had been like a second mother to me and she had never even gotten to see the book dedicated to her long gone son, Barry, who I had loved dearly.

In August of 2008 I got to see Michele for perhaps only the third time in my life but it was just like being with family. We talked for hours and reminisced. Michele is the only member left of her family but like me, we hope to all be reunited again. This story is my gift to her.

"More Than a Memory"

The rain was coming down in heavy drops and in only moments, Michele's hair and clothes were drenched. Living in Oregon for years, she never carried an umbrella (only the tourists did) and put up with the constant rain like everyone else without one.

Now rivulets of cold rain water were beginning to run down inside her collar and drench her from the inside out. She needed to take cover. To her right was a revolving door leading into a Starbucks and without a second thought she ducked in for a quick respite and her favorite hot drink, a white chocolate raspberry latte, to warm her up.

The site that greeted her eyes paralyzed and completely disoriented her. She blinked, rubbed her eyes and shook her head, her mouth gaping as her surroundings refused to change back into reality. Before her was the living room of her Huntington Beach home the way it looked when she had lived there with her brother, Barry in their teen years. Immediately tears sprang into her eyes with the familiar ache that clutched her heart.

"Is that you Michele?" sang a voice from the kitchen. The beloved voice of her mother sent a thrill through her heart and her voice caught in her throat. Had she fallen unconscious? Was she having a dream? Having received no response, Ruth poked her head through the doorway. "Cat got your tongue?" she grinned at her dumbstruck daughter.

Michele's mouth moved but no sound would come out as she stared at the face of her dear mother who had passed away just under a year ago. At that moment a figure walked up behind her and pinched her in the ribs, making her scream. She whirled around and standing there alive and as if he had never aged, was her brother Barry.

He grinned at her and gave her a bear hug but there was no feedback from the hearing aids he used to always wear. He stepped back and pointed at his head with a lopsided grin. "I hear great now!"

Michele's eyes traveled hungrily up and down the length of him. Same wavy brown hair, twinkly eyes, mischievous grin, dimples and plaid flannel shirt with the sleeves rolled up as if 25 plus years had never passed. The tears now spilled down her cheeks unabated and a sob of joy caught in her throat. With a look of understanding compassion on his face, Barry enfolded her into his arms and let her sob. Michele could barely hear the familiar footsteps behind her on the floor and then her mom's arms were about her.

"Al, just don't sit there watching the game, get in here!" Ruth yelled. At that, Michele pulled back and turned around to see her father stride towards them, his arms held out wide. She flew into them, crying even harder.

"There now," soothed her mom in her wonderful accent. "Do you really want to spend your entire visit with us crying? You're scaring Sonny!"

"Meooooww!" agreed the gorgeous Himalayan cat, entering the room. This was all just too much!

"I don't understand!" was all Michele could manage, shaking uncontrollably. Al, Ruth, Barry and even Sonny all stared at her in sympathy. "Am I dreaming or dead?"

"Neither!" chorused all (except Sonny) in unison.

"This is a gift, sis," explained Barry gesturing to the family dinner table laden with a Thanksgiving turkey and all the fixings. "The Lord thought you'd enjoy one more day and meal with us all together again."

Michele clutched at her heart. It was all too much to take in and yet she couldn't deny it was what she had secretly longed for more often than she could say but there was still something missing. A lot of "something's"; as if on cue, the doorbell rang.

"I'll get it!" cried Barry with a wink in his sister's direction, bounding over to the door. He opened it up to reveal Michele's husband, Dave, and all their kids.

"Uncle Barry!" they all shrieked, not the least bit shocked or bewildered. Barry hugged and pounded Dave on the back with glee and hugged each of Michele's kids in turn as if he had known them all his life. They in turn hugged his neck with equal glee and then everyone circled around the table and grabbed each other's hands.

"Barry, would you lead us all in thanks to the Lord?" smiled Ruth, winking at Michele.

"I was hoping you'd ask!" Barry grinned. At that everyone bowed their heads as Michele's beloved brother led them all in a prayer of thanksgiving for a reunited family that was separated only by the very thinnest veil of eternity.

CHAPTER SIX
"Tea Rooms & Romance"

Hannah is also a teenaged, homeschooled teen blogger whose heart's desire has been to marry a Japanese husband who loves the Lord when she comes of age. She and Mirriam are good friends so I thought it would be fun to include her in on the story that Hannah requested. She loved it so much that she just couldn't stand not knowing what happened next and asked for a "second chapter" which I was happy to oblige her with. After that, she and two of her friends (who I have also written stories for) picked up the baton (so to speak) and continued their wish stories, expanding them into feature length novellas.

"Tea Rooms & Romance"

Hannah looked wearily out the window of the Boeing 747 window. The excitement and thrill of flying to Japan on an exchange student program had already worn off and been replaced by jet lag, flying fatigue and a bit of anxiety. It seemed like she had been trapped in her tiny coach seat for a week although it had only been 9 hours. Her back was stiff, her legs cramped and all she wanted to do was to climb into bed and sleep!

Her host family, the Nakaguchi's promised they would be waiting for her at the gate with a big sign that had her name in English on it but now she was worried because at the last minute her flight had been canceled due to mechanical difficulties and she had been forced to board another carrier to make it to Tokyo on the same day. She had not been allowed to use her cell phone to call ahead and forewarn them about the change in airline and arrival gate. If she hadn't felt so exhausted she would have been freaking out in panic. She couldn't read or speak Japanese and her flight was arriving at a completely different terminal than what her host family was expecting.

She shut her eyes and prayed again. *Please, dearest Lord, help me to find my host family. Please send an angel or something to guide me!*

Two hours later the flight finally set down in Tokyo and along with all the other travel-weary passengers, Hannah lugged her carryon luggage down from the overhead compartment, almost decapitating a little Japanese man in the process when it fell out of her grip.

He let loose with a stream of angry Japanese, scolding her. Hannah felt like crying. Going to Japan for an entire year had been such a dream for her but it was starting off like a nightmare!

She finally made it off the plane and into the terminal. The outside air within the airway between the terminal and the airplane was hot and very humid. In the space of just a few moments, she had sweated through her clothes. *OMG!* She had been warned about the humid weather in Japan but nothing could have prepared her for walking into what felt like a sauna!

She reached the terminal and looked around hoping that by some miracle God had communicated to the Nakaguchi's her new arrival status. She saw signs but none of them were in English and none had her name. Her heart sank. She turned to take a 360 degree look around and lost her balance as fell over someone.

"Ouch!" she cried out, feeling a sharp pain in her ankle. She looked down and could already see it starting to swell and turn blue. *Great, just great. First the plane change and now this! What else can go wrong?*

"Please excuse me!" cried a young masculine voice. The next thing she knew, she was being gently lifted to her good foot by a total stranger. "I apologize for making you to trip!" he continued, helping her to balance on her good leg. Hannah suddenly came eye to eye with a strikingly handsome and young Japanese man. His mouth fell open in surprise and shock for a moment and then 5,000 years of ingrained Japanese politeness came to the fore. He bowed briefly then helped to maneuver her over to a seat in the terminal. Then he knelt down and propped up her injured ankle onto her suitcase so it was elevated.

"One moment, please!" he said, bowing again. He raced off to a local concession stand and came back with a towel filled with ice cubes. He laid it gently upon her ankle. Stealing glances at her every few moments, he set about to arrange her luggage neatly around her then he stood and bowed again. "I humbly beg forgiveness, Miss American," he said, turning red. "I did not attend to cause you injury."

Miss American? Hannah giggled despite the pain. "Uh, it's okay…it was an accident," she said, peering at her now bloated ankle and wondering how on earth she was ever going to find her host family now. She tried calling them on her cell phone but she had never used the international features before and needed her guide sheet on all the numbers to dial. She looked at the chagrinned young man and suddenly noticed how handsome he was. He stuck out his hand to her, American style.

"Akihiko," he introduced himself. "It translates as *bright prince*."

Hannah blushed deeply and shook his hand. "Hannah….uhhhh….just Hannah." She said, wishing she had an exotic meaning for her name as well. *Bright prince!!!!*

Akihiko smiled at her and Hannah felt her heart skip a tiny beat. "Is there anything more I can to do you?" he asked in his faulty English. Hannah stifled another giggle, tempted to tell him that no, a twisted ankle was sufficient, but then she thought better of it.

"Yes, Akihiko," she said, nodding earnestly. "Could you help me find my host family?" She then explained to him as simply and as clearly as she could what had happened with the plane change and how she was supposed to have been in a different terminal 1 hour from now to meet them. Akihiko nodded every now and then, making mental notes in his head. When Hannah was done, he stood up and flung his arm across his chest in a knightly salute.

"Never fear!" he intoned with a solemn face that made Hannah want to giggle some more. "Akihiko is here! He will save your day. Wait here!" With that he ran off and rounded up several airport employees. One went down to baggage claim to get the rest of her luggage so they could help her through customs and the other ran for a wheelchair. In no time at all, Hannah found herself being wheeled through the terminal at breakneck speed with Akihiko half riding/half pushing from behind while barking a stream of orders in rapid-fire Japanese.

With Akihiko's help and that of the kind air terminal employees, Hannah was fast-tracked through customs and then they were speeding on their way to the other terminal to meet up with the Nakaguchi's before they ever knew what had happened!

She and Akihiko actually came up on them from behind. The entire family was there, the two parents, daughter (who was the same age as she) and son who was a few years older.

"Mr. Nakaguchi!" Hannah called from her chair, waving her arms. "I'm over here!"

The entire family turned around in shock and gaped at her, wondering where she had come from and why she was in a wheelchair. Of course, being Japanese they wouldn't think to even ask such intrusive questions but merely bowed in greeting before turning to Akihiko.

"Konnichiwa, Akihiko!" exclaimed the brother of the family, a grin spreading from ear to ear. They bowed to another and then clasped hands like they were old school chums (which they were). He and Akihiko obviously already knew one another and began jabbering away in Japanese. The other family members listened politely and *oohhhhed* and *aw-soooed* every once in a while, nodding as they looked from Akihiko to Hannah as he explained what had happened.

Finally Mr. Nakaguchi turned his full attention to Hannah. "Welcome to Japan, Ms. Hannah." He said, bowing slightly. "Akihiko has apprised us of everything. It was good that it was he whom you ran into; he is a long time friend of my oldest son,

Kamiko. They were classmates and lives with his family near our apartment."

"Oh!" said Hannah, unable to think of anything else to say. She looked over at Akihiko and found him looking right back at her with a curious look on his face. *Awkward pause.*

Taking the silent cue, everyone took a hand in picking up her luggage with Akihiko pushing her wheelchair like a proud tour guide.

They negotiated their way out of the concourse and then to a long black limousine that was large enough to fit everyone. Feeling solely responsible for Hannah's injury Akihiko took it upon himself to help her get in and then when they arrived to help her get out; half-carrying/half-walking her to the elevator that led to the Nakaguchi's apartment. To her amazement, he even held her fully in her arms while the Nakaguchi's daughter, Hitomi, helped to carefully remove her shoes before entering their home.

Hannah hopped inside on her one good leg until she found a chair to sit on. From that moment on, the entire family took charge. Hitomi and Kamiko brought all her luggage into the room she would share with Hitomi who unpacked everything for her, putting her clothes, shoes, and personal hygiene items away as unobtrusively as possible. Hannah was absolutely mortified but there was nothing she could do about it until she could walk again. Once unpacked, she was led back to her room and shown the blow up air mattress they had gotten especially for her.

Exhausted she crawled into bed and slept for the next 12 hours.

The next evening she woke up feeling completely discombobulated. Her body clock said it was morning but the window in the room showed a dark night sky. She looked over at the Tatami matt next to her where Kamiko was sleeping; her mouth slightly open. The alarm clock was in Japanese but it looked like it was 2am. It was going to be a long night. Suddenly she was struck with inspiration.

She got out her cell phone they had placed near her (along with the directions on how to call international) and dialed the number of her friend Mirriam.

It should be the early afternoon and Mirriam should already be home and done with school…

"Hello?" answered her friend's voice on the other end.

"Earwen!" whispered Hannah, trying not to wake Hitomi up.

"Hannah?"

"Yes."

"So you got into Japan okay? What time is it there now?"

"Two am."

"Jet lag is awful isn't it?" Mirriam responded compassionately.

"I can't talk long because Hitomi is sleeping," Hannah whispered, glancing over at Hitomi who showed no sign of waking up. "But I just had to tell you…I hurt my ankle but I think I've met my Prince Charming!"

"*Shut UP!*" squealed Mirriam, knowing how Hannah had always longed to meet and marry a Japanese Christian man. The sound carried well out of the earpiece and Hitomi stirred.

"Gotta go!" whispered Hannah. "Just wanted you to be the first to know! I'll email you later all the details!"

The next morning (for real), a doctor friend of the Nakaguchi family came over and inspected her swollen ankle which was now a nice black and blue color. His gentle prodding evoked a few squints of pain but he seemed satisfied that it was nothing more than a sprain. He wrapped her ankle up tight, told her to ice it regularly then left bowing.

Hitomi helped her over to the low table where the family sat politely waiting for her. She sat cross-legged since she still couldn't kneel on the ankle and smiled thanks at all of them. They smiled back then bowed their heads and said grace over their meal. The Nakaguchi's were one of the few Christian Japanese families that had opened their home to exchange students from America. The prayer was in Japanese but at everyone said "Amen" in English.

Hannah was famished; she looked at the food before her; a bowl of brown rice and hot Miso soup and of course, tea.

Just as they all finished their meal there was a polite knock at the door. Kamiko got up with a barely suppressed grin and opened the door. In the doorframe stood Akihiko.

He entered the room bowing to all but his almond brown eyes were fixed upon Hannah. She felt her cheeks begin to flame. Hitomi took her arm with a smile and helped her to their room, closing the Shoji screens behind them.

"Akihiko has asked if he may take you to a traditional Japanese Tea Room for your first day," she explained, trying to hide her grins. "I think he is smattered on you."

Hannah burst out giggling but quickly clapped her hand over her mouth. "I think you mean smitten." She grinned.

With Hitomi's assistance Hannah got cleaned up and changed her clothes. The doctor had left both crutches and a wheelchair for her use. She hobbled out on the crutches while Akihiko carried the wheelchair out the front door. Armed with her camera, guidebook and purse, the family bowed and waved goodbye as Akihiko helped her into her chair.

It was all happening so fast her head was in a whirl. He maneuvered her and the wheelchair into the elevator then out to the street where he took her to a local train station. Hannah should have felt nervous, after all, Akihiko was practically a virtual stranger, but it all seemed fine somehow and she had God's peace that passed understanding. Soon they were both on a bullet train and speeding into the Japanese countryside.

They arrived hours later and she soon found her wheelchair being guided towards an old Japanese tea house that had a gorgeous view of Mount Fuji. It had dark wood walls and a green tiled roof. She left the chair outside and Akihiko helped her into a small room with Tatami mats. They made her as comfortable as possible and then the ceremony began.

A beautiful geisha sat down inside the room and played a traditional Japanese song upon her Shamisen. Another geisha entered the room, sliding the shoji screens aside silently, and carried in a tray that contained the tea implements: the *chashaku* (tea scoop), *sensu* (fan), *chasen kusenaoshi* (whisk shaper), *chasen* (bamboo whisk) and *fukusa* (purple silk cloth) as well as the green tea powder.

Hannah watched in wonder at the elaborate preparations to prepare a simple cup of tea and could feel Akihiko's eyes upon her the whole time. It was not proper to speak during the ceremony so they both sat in silence. The hot tea was first passed to Akihiko who after sipping, turned the bowl three times in his hand then offered it to Hannah.

She accepted with a shy bow and sipped the slightly bitter, hot liquid. Once the ceremony was completed Akihiko helped her back into her chair and took her further into town to a noodle house where they could talk freely and eat. They spent the rest of the day together and when the sun began to set, they boarded the bullet train again back for Tokyo. They reached the Nakaguchi home by 8pm where the entire family greeted her at the door and assisted her in. Once she was settled in a chair, Akihiko clasped her hand in his, placing a small parchment wrapped gift in her hand.

"Thank you for accompanying me today." He said, smiling shyly. "I leave you now in the good hands of the Nakaguchi family. I hope to see you again many times before you return to America." With another bow to her and the rest of the family he showed himself out of their apartment.

Hannah looked down at the little bundle in her hands and carefully unwrapped it as Hitomi looked on. Inside was a delicate gold necklace upon which hung letters in Japanese

"What does it mean?" asked Hannah turning to Hitomi.

"In your language it means *Destiny*." Hitomi replied.

PART TWO (By Special Request)

"No way!" squealed Mirriam's voice over Hannah's cell phone when she had finally gotten a moment to herself to call her best friend. "He gave you a gold necklace that said "destiny"??! *Hannah!"* she continued in her best Darth Vader impression. *"He is your DES-TIN-EEEEE!!"*

Hannah giggled, the whole experience from the moment she had gotten off the airplane up to now had been rather surreal and it was just now starting to hit home that she may have, indeed, met her "Mr. Right".

"Did he try to kiss you or anything?" Mirriam interrogated, wanting to know every last teeny tiny detail.

"Of course not!" Hannah replied shocked. "No one kisses me until I'm married! Not even on the cheek! That reminds me, I need to call my parents and let them know I got here safely."

"Are you going to tell them about *HIM*?" Mirriam asked.

"Well yeeeeeeeeeeeeeeeeeeeeees," replied Hannah, wondering how she was going to break the news to her parents about Akihiko.

"Well tell me ALL about it after you do!" Mirriam said. "I have to get going and update my blog now. This author I know put me in a "wish fulfillment" story and I want to blog about it."

"What's that?" Hannah asked, curious.

"I'll send you the link over email." Mirriam replied mysteriously.

"Okay, bye!" Hannah said then dialed her parent's house. She had sent them a quick text message that she had gotten there okay but knew they would want to talk with her too.

"Hi Dad!" she said when he answered the phone.

"Hanny!" he exclaimed, overjoyed at hearing her voice. "How was your flight? Did you get to catch up on your sleep? How are you liking Japan?"

"The flight was long and uncomfortable, I'm not quite caught up on sleep yet and I *LOVE* Japan!!" (Of course she didn't say *why...*)

"That's wonderful, honey. We're very proud of you. I bet by the time you get back you will be fluent in Japanese!"

"I hope so..." Hannah hemmed, trying to think of an appropriate way to broach the subject. "Uh, Dad, I have something rather important to tell you."

"So soon? You've only been there a few days," he replied. "What could have possibly happened in that short time already?"

"I think I may have met...uhhhh...ummmmm...HIM."

"Him?" repeated her dad. "Who-him?"

"Him-*him!*"

"Honey, you're losing me. Give me a hint here," said her dad, completely lost.

"Daaaaaaaaaaaaaaad, you're not making this easy." Hannah moaned. "Remember all those talks we've had about when I get old enough for boys to take an interest in me?"

"Yes," came the reply. "Are you trying to tell me that there is already someone interested in you in Japan after only 2 days?" His voice was incredulous. Hannah then described everything that had transpired from the plane change up to the present moment, leaving nothing out. When she was done the silence on the other end was almost deafening.

Then her dad cleared his throat. "Well, Hanny, I trust you to live and abide by the morals and guidelines we discussed and agreed upon together. If I didn't trust you, I wouldn't have agreed to let you go to Japan. I'm glad you have been open and forthright with me and I have no doubts that you will act responsibly. Mom and I love you very much; and all the animals here send their greetings. Have a great time, soak up all the local flavor and come home safely to us. Oh, and don't forget to bring your siblings souveniors!"

"Okay, dad!" Hannah said, relieved. "I promise to keep things appropriate. I'll bring everyone back some great souvenirs."

"That'll be great, honey. Goodbye and keep in touch and take good care of that ankle."

"I will, dad. Love to you and mom."

Hannah hung up the phone and fell over onto her side with a big sigh. Well that was over with and it went better than she had expected. Now she could move forward with a clear conscience.

Akihiko called upon the family the next day and spent the day with all of them and especially his school buddy, Kamiko, but his brown almond eyes constantly flitted back to Hannah, causing her to blush with pleasure constantly. Just as he was bowing and saying his goodbyes, he finally turned his full attention upon Hannah.

"Please excuse my forwarding," he said, with a formal bow, confusing his English words. "May I ask the pleasure of accompanying you to a Kabuki performance?"

"Kabuki?" exclaimed Hannah, unable to suppress the joy in her face. She had always longed to see a real Kabuki play but there was no such thing back where she lived. The closest she could get to seeing such a thing would be to rent a National Geographic DVD or something similar.

"I would like to escort you to see a performance of Kanadehon Chūshingura at the National Theater this coming Saturday. May I have your permission to do so?"

"Oh! I would LOVE to!" Hannah exclaimed, reminding herself not to jump up and down on her injured foot. "Thank you!"

The smile that spread over Akihiko's face went from ear to ear and he almost seemed relieved. He bowed low and to Hannah's amazement and shock, lifted her hand and kissed the top as if he were a knight in medieval England. A thrill raced up Hannah's arm, then neck and through her hair. She could almost swear that every strand was suddenly standing on end as if electrocuted! She could hardly wait to tell Mirriam!! *Kabuki and a kiss on the hand in the same day!!!*

Hitomi was almost more excited than Hannah was. To see one of the most famous Kabuki plays at the National Theater was no small deal. She took Hannah shopping the next day to find a suitable dress to wear (one could not go to the National Theater in blue jeans and cotton shirt!) she explained. They found a lovely pale pink dress with cherry blossoms printed on it that was both modest and very feminine.

The morning of the play, they both got up early and Hitomi fussed over her, styling her hair up in a French chignon and placing delicate pink enamel combs on either side. They had become as close as sisters in one week. Hannah wore no makeup or jewelry except for the beautiful "Destiny" pendent Akihiko had given her. When the doorbell rang signaling his arrival, she found herself hardly breathing she was so excited. By now she was able to walk unaided and with only a slight limp but he treated her like fine porcelain, tucking her arm into his and steering her in the right direction with his hand on the small of her back.

They arrived at the National Theater (where Akihiko's uncle worked who had arranged for the last-minute tickets). Hannah couldn't believe how incredible and imposing it was. Because of Akihiko's uncle their seats were fabulous, 5 rows back right in the middle. Because the programs were written in Japanese, Akihiko explained the plot of the play.

"Kanadehon Chūshingura or the "*Treasury of Loyal Retainers"* is famous story of the Forty-seven Ronin who track down their lord's killer, and exact revenge upon him before committing seppuku as required by their code of honor upon the death of their lord," he whispered as the curtain went down and the lights dimmed. The music began and the actors (all male) took their places upon the stage.

Hannah had a difficult time understanding everything that was going on but midway through the play she ceased to care because all she could think about was Akihiko taking her hand in his and holding it throughout the duration of the play.

CHAPTER SEVEN
"Butterfly Kisses"

This story was written for Donna, a friend of Henry's. Here is her introduction: *My daughter, Violet, was born 8/6/75. She was beautiful. We spent most of our time together. She was very smart in school, got good grades and attended nursing school the last two years of high school. She was my best friend.*

Violet got married on Valentines' day 1993 and died March 31, 1993. She wasn't 18 yet but told me she always wanted to marry on Valentine's Day and didn't want to wait for another year after she turned 18 in August. So I signed the papers she needed to marry. She and her husband were very happy for the final month of her life. They had bought our house in Oak Hill and were still there waiting for our home in Jackson to be ready. I was there when she passed. She had come home the night before and talked with me since I always waited up for her to come home. She worked at a nursing home as a nurse's aide, and she said she was hungry and then she would go to bed. Her husband had fallen asleep on the couch and she didn't want to wake him. The next morning my husband came to me and said her husband couldn't wake Violet up for school. She had 10 more days to go. She was on the floor beside the bed (she would sometimes lay on the floor if her back hurt). When I got hold of her leg to shake her she was cold. I gave mouth to mouth and screamed call 911! But my baby was gone.

After 3 long months the doctors could find no reason for my daughter's passing. So I will never know why. When she was little I used to pack her around on my hip until she was 6 or 7. She was small and I loved holding her.

She was beautiful, kind, smart and taken way too soon from this earth. I miss her dearly and I will for as long as I live. I pray the good Lord reunites us one glorious day.

"Butterfly Kisses"

Violet approached the Savior, her heart full with the need to ask something of Him. Although she had been exulting in the joys of Heaven for what seemed like only moments, she somehow knew that significant time on earth had passed and that a major milestone was approaching. He turned and gazed upon her with His wondrous eyes of love and smiled. His eyes and smile never ceased to move her soul deeply. She could feel the love pouring forth from Him as if she was the only soul in all of heaven and He had eyes for no one but her.

"Come here, beloved." He said, holding out his arms to her. Violet ran forward and threw herself into His embrace.

"Oh Master!" she said, her heart bursting with joy at His touch.

"I know why you are here," He said, stroking her hair, his voice soft in her ear. "I have been expecting your visit."

"It has been almost 17 years on earth, Master; would it be alright if I visited just this once? It would mean so much to her!"

The Savior drew back and looked down upon her with infinite compassion. "Just this once, beloved," He agreed.

Upon the utterance of His words, Violet found herself standing in the familiar kitchen of her mother's home. It was late evening and Donna was standing at the sink doing the dishes when suddenly her shoulders slumped in abject sorrow. Her head bowed, heavy with the all too familiar grief. Although time had softened the pain slightly, she still suffered in silence the knawing ache of sorrow and longing…she missed her daughter so.

Violet's soul clenched with sympathy for her mom. *If only she knew! If only she could but experience just a moment, just a second of what heaven was really like and know how soon they would be reunited when all her tears would be brushed gently away by the Master's own hand!*

Violet slipped her arms about her mother's waist and laid her head upon her shoulder. "It's okay, mommy," she said, "don't cry!"

So gentle was the embrace, so soft was her voice that it took Donna a moment to even realize that she was not alone anymore. For a moment she was taken back in time to a season of her life when her daughter's love filled her world with sunshine. She twirled around and stared in shock and unbridled joy.

"VIOLET!" she shrieked, dropping the dish in her hands onto the floor. Her arms flew about her daughter and the tears she had swallowed down for almost 17 years poured out like a cleansing river. Violet stood there, content to let her mom vent her sorrow; knowing the tears would bring healing. She rocked her gently back and forth and cooed soothingly in her ear as if she were the mom and Donna were the child, patting and rubbing her back. In a few minutes Donna quieted down and she stepped back to let her eyes drink their fill of her long-missed daughter.

Violet smiled at her; a smile of pure radiant joy. "Don't cry for me anymore, mommy," she said, plucking a Kleenex from a nearby box and dabbing at her mom's eyes. "I am *so happy* in heaven! You just have no idea how incredible it is! Our Savior's peace and overwhelming love permeates every fiber of your being there!"

"How…what….*are you real?* Am I dreaming all this?" choked Donna, clutching her daughter's hands; never wanting to let go. She was more beautiful than she remembered and glowing with a soft light that surrounded every inch of her.

Violet smiled. "No, mom, this is not a dream. I asked the Master for permission to pay you one visit before we are reunited in heaven together. I have waited for this moment since the day I came home!"

"Home?" Donna repeated, not understanding.

"Yes, our heavenly home." Violet clarified. "Now, I get to spend an entire day with you, what would you like to do?"

Donna was at a complete loss for words or ideas. *One day? That was it? Shopping? NO! Eating out? Another dumb idea.*

Earthly food probably tasted like dirt compared to what Violet was getting in heaven...HEAVEN FOR GOODNESS SAKE!

"Let's just sit here and talk!" suggested Violet. Donna nodded dumbly and allowed her daughter to lead her out the front door to the porch swing. They sat together side by side and rocked. Violet laid her head on her mom's shoulder while hugging her arm against herself.

Donna closed her eyes and listened to the music of Violet's voice as she talked on and on about being in the presence of their Lord and all the famous people in the Bible she had met as best she could in human terms. As she spoke, Donna felt every hurt, every wound dissolve away and thoroughly heal from the inside out as if every syllable were a balm sent straight from heaven. The ache she had borne since the day she had seen her daughter's lifeless body on the floor disappeared for here she was; more beautiful than ever and telling her about the wonders of heaven. Exquisite peace flowed over her soul like a cool river filling until she felt she would burst with joy. What a precious gift the Lord had given her in this beautiful girl; however brief on earth; she knew now they would have each other for eternity and for the first time since that awful day, eternity seemed more real than life here on earth.

Donna suddenly opened her eyes when she realized that Violet had stopped speaking. Hours had passed in what had only seemed like a few minutes.

"Mommy," she said, gently removing her arm. "It's time for me to go but I have one last gift for you before I do."

Despite her disappointment Donna did not feel sad. She smiled at her beautiful Violet, wondering what could possibly be any better than the day they had just spent together in each other's company. Violet grinned at her in a delighted, mischievous way and clapped her hands together, just once.

Suddenly a cloud of butterflies flew up and surrounded them both; all different colors and sizes. They whirled about, alighting then taking flight again while mother and daughter gasped and laughed in sheer delight. Then as Donna watched, utterly charmed, the butterflies began to rise higher and higher in a spiral with Violet floating upwards with them, waving her goodbyes with a magnificent smile.

"I'll see you soon, mommy!" she called, her voice as clear as a bell. "Every time you see a butterfly from now on, just know that it's me blowing kisses to you! Don't forget!"

"I won't, dearest one," breathed Donna, clutching her now whole and healed heart with joy and gratitude. "I love you!"

"...and I love you!" came her last words on the soft summer wind.

CHAPTER EIGHT
"No Ordinary Day at the Mall"

Hannah is a home schooled teenaged Christian blogger and she requested a wish story in which she would meet her future "Prince Charming". She couldn't give me any specifics other than to say that she always imagined receiving loads and loads of flowers. Here is what she writes as the intro for her story:

"Every girl has a wish. Whether they are young or grown, we all make wishes. Its starts with our first lonely star we see in the night sky and it continues ever after. Candles on a birthday cake, the wish bone from the Thanksgiving turkey, hands on the Yule log, cloudless nights, coins in a fountain, and whenever you catch the clock at 11:11. All of these are opportunities for wish making. I believe I have made the same wish ever since I watched Prince Charming carry Cinderella off to the castle (excusing the occasional "I wish someone would give me a piece of chocolate" wishes). There may have been times when they were more specific, and perhaps there are still times when they are. All the same, this wish is one belonging to a sixteen year old girl who desires nothing more than to meet her very own prince and be carried away as his. The following story is the fulfillment of this wish. I know God has chosen him, and that he is somewhere out there, perhaps wondering if he'll ever find me. I want nothing more than to hand over a pure heart when he finally does, despite the loneliness in waiting. But when the time comes, I know every second will be worth it. I'm Hannah and my kindred spirit is Haley. This is my wish. It is 11:11, and I shall leave you to read..."

"No Ordinary Day at the Mall"

Hannah and Haley sat in the food court of the Mall St. Matthews, people watching and sipping their diet sodas. They had had a successful day of shopping, having spent hours in clothing boutiques. They had each purchased 2 pairs of jeans and a cute top (matching of course) after long and considered deliberation.

"What about him?" asked Haley, indicating a tall young man walking through the mall with a sports bag in his arms.

"Too skinny," concluded Hannah and Haley together in unison. They looked at each other, giggled and made the "owie-owie jinx" symbol. One after another they looked at prospective love interests only to find a major flaw (either evident or just made up for fun) in each one. They had come to the mall that day to see a special event. An author of a medieval fantasy/fiction called *"The Victor"* was supposed to appear at the Barnes & Noble later that day to do a book signing. They were saving the rest of their cash for later when they would get an autographed copy of the book. The mall had gone all out and decorated the area in front of the bookstore with medieval banners. Their attention was suddenly drawn to the opposite end of the mall where they saw the crowds of shoppers hurriedly parting like the red sea to make way for what had to be the last thing they ever expected to see in a mall corridor. A man on a runaway horse…in a full suit of armor!

"What the….?" exclaimed Hannah and Haley together, eyebrows on the rise. The horse was coming straight at them at full gallop. It too wore armor and had gold and azure trappings that hung from the reins and which flew behind it. It whinnied loudly but instead of feeling terrified, Hannah felt a thrill go up her spine. Her breath caught in her chest.

"Boy whoever manages the mall must really like this book to hire someone to do this!" yelled Haley, springing up to get out of the way of the charging horse. Hannah remained rooted where she stood, a strange feeling coming over her. The mall about her began to spin and she felt herself becoming increasingly dizzy and disconcerted. Just as her knees buckled and gave way, she found herself scooped up into the saddle by the knight. His charger wheeled around and she held on for dear life as it reared and let out a loud neigh. At that moment, everything disappeared" the mall, the shops, even her friend Haley. She found herself clinging with all her might to the back of a mail clad knight on the back of a white horse that was now galloping on sod under a canopy of arched trees to a distant hill upon which stood a lofty castle.

What did they put in my diet coke? She wondered. She looked down at herself and instead of blue jeans and a t-shirt found herself in a gorgeous, dusty lavender gown of velvet, with a silk chemise that streamed back in the wind. Her hair flowed out behind her but she didn't dare let go her grip to touch what surely must have been a circlet with attached veil upon her head for fear of falling off. The white horse snorted and the knight slowed down to give the animal a rest.

"Easy, easy…Glimraith" soothed the male voice inside the helmet. It was deeply masculine if albeit tunnel-ish sounding. He patted the magnificent beast and twisted about in the saddle, lifting the visor to reveal a pair of striking blue eyes. Hannah blinked, her mouth dropping open. If the eyes alone were any indication of what the rest of him looked like (they were fringed by jet black lashes) she was in for quite a treat when he took off the rest of the plumed helmet.

"Are you injured, milady?" he said, his black brows knitting together in concern. Hannah shook her head and shut her mouth so as not to look like an idiot with her gaping mouth.

"Forgive the manner of my coming to fetch thee," he continued in a gentle baritone. "But my quest was in earnest. We must make the Keep before sunset and the day is already far gone."

"Keep?" replied Hannah, puzzled, still trying to figure out where the mall had gone.

"The Court of St. Matthews…" clarified the knight, dismounting with ease. "Since you have naught but your gown and eventide is fast descending, you shall no doubt be warmer if thou ridest before me."

With his assistance, Hannah scooted forward until she was sitting in the saddle. The knight remounted with ease behind her, drew his large black woolen cloak about both of them and urged the horse onwards into a fast cantor towards the magnificent castle which grew larger with every league they covered. Cottage fires in the surrounding village began to light as a deep purple dusk settled about them. Hannah closed her eyes, thoroughly confused but strangely at ease. The strong arms of the knight were about her and his body heat and cloak kept her warm. She had no clue what or how this was happening but instead of feeling panicked she had a strange sense of déjà vu and anticipation. She glanced down at her clothes and marveled at the gorgeous silver stitching all over the front of her bodice and the pearls which glimmered here and there. They arrived at the castle, now lit from within by torch and candlelight. The white horse clattered over the cobblestones, across the drawbridge and into the main courtyard. The knight (whose name she still didn't know) dismounted and before she could blink had grasped her about the waist and gently lifted her down. To Hannah it seemed like the entire process was in slow motion. She felt his strong hands about her waist and was unable to tear her eyes away from his as she slowly slid down and finally landed on her feet. She swayed for a moment, a wave of dizziness coming over her again. Apparently time travel made her seasick. Her knees buckled but he was attentive to her every need and without a word scooped her up in his arms and carried her into the castle. He seemed to know his way around without even looking. His eyes never left hers the entire time until the moment he carried her into a gorgeous chamber room and set her carefully upon her feet, keeping his hands about her waist until he was sure she would not tip over again.

"Milady," he said, bowing over her hand and kissing it gently. "I will attend thee later, in the meantime, make thyself ready for a feast for it is to be held in thy honor," he said.

Hannah finally found her voice. "My honor?" she repeated. "Please," she said, grasping his arm as he turned to go. "How did I get here? Where did the mall go and my friend Haley? My mom and dad are going to freak if they don't hear from me soon! And…and… what is your name anyway?!!" Her voice began rising in near hysteria. At first she thought she was just daydreaming but now it was looking like she had actually gone through some kind of time domain transference of some kind with no clue of how to get back to her real life.

The knight paused, regarding her with deep concern. He removed his plumed helm and Hannah gasped at the sight of his handsome face. His eyes were the deepest blue she had ever seen and his hair, whiskers and brows ebony. His finely chiseled face was both beautiful and incredibly masculine at the same time. The kind understanding smile he bestowed upon her made her heart feel like it was melting into a molten hot puddle of mush. He took both of her tiny hands into his and held them both up to his lips.

"Fear not, beloved," he said, his voice soft and very reassuring. "All will be well. Tonight is for thee but on the morrow all will return to what has been. Can you not be content to simply enjoy what has been given thee and let tomorrow worry about itself?"

Hannah nodded, falling under the spell of his eyes and voice once again. A smile creased his face making her heart skip a beat.

"I shall leave thee to thy maid servant and return for thee later," he said, gently brushing her cheek with his fingers. The heavy oaken door closed slowly behind him and Hannah sighed…finally turning around to take in her room.

"O...M…G!!!!" she squealed out loud. It was the most exquisite room she had ever seen in her life. The stone walls were covered with gorgeous tapestries all in shades of dusty blue, lavender and moss green. The canopied bed was covered in a deep midnight blue velvet coverlet embroidered with silver thread, pearls and gemstones with curtains that matched but what really caught her attention was the multitude of vases filled with flowers in complimentary colors and the candles which glowed on every available surface. It looked like an enormous valentine in jewel tone colors. *If only Haley were here!*

"OMG, HANNAH!" screeched a familiar voice. Hannah whirled about and found herself facing her best friend, similarly attired in an emerald green velvet gown and matching headdress, her hair longer, thicker and curling all the way past her waist. "Can you believe all this??!" The girls grasped hands and jumped up and down for joy.

"Did you see *him?"* Hannah asked, meaning the knight.

"Only a glimpse but ohhhhhhhhhhhh boy, Hannah!" Haley giggled, her eyes alight. "An honest to goodness knight in shining armor!"

"He told me to get ready…ready for what?"

"Birthday celebration?" Haley guessed, taking her friend over to a gorgeous dressing table where brushes and beautiful bejeweled combs awaited her. Hannah sat down and allowed Haley to comb out her long tresses. The girls then changed into their banquet clothes, red for Haley and a gorgeous pale pink for Hannah with matching veil that drifted down almost to the floor like a cotton candy cloud.

A knock came upon the door and with a wink, Haley went to answer it like a good lady-in-waiting. Hannah could hear her gasp of awe even from where she stood on tip toe, trying to get a glimpse of the knight whose name she did not know. He entered the room and it took her breath away. He wore a dark blue tunic edged in gold with knee high kid-skin boots and a black cape clasped at the throat with a golden chain. From his waist hung a magnificent sword but what really caught her attention was his face and eyes. He had eyes for no one but her and he walked forward bearing a bouquet of reddish/black roses wrapped with a red organza ribbon. Their sweet smell filled the room.

He went down on one knee before her and presented the roses to her. Hannah took them, trembling then gave them to a waiting Haley who put them into a nearby pewter vase. The knight arose and tucked her arm through his.

"Shall we?" He said, with a deliciously handsome smile. Hannah nodded and allowed him to accompany her through numerous hallways and corridors with Haley right behind grinning like a Cheshire cat. When they got to the main ballroom both girls almost *(almost)* screamed with excitement. Beauty and the Beast, Cinderella and Sleeping Beauty had nothing on this castle. The ballroom stretched up above their heads four stories high with large leaded glass windows that let in the full moon and stars. Candles and torches flickered everywhere and the room was filled with Lords and Ladies in the most gorgeous clothing and jewels they had ever seen. Upon their entrance everyone turned around and welcomed Hannah, Haley and her knight with warm applause. Then the music started.

The knight put his arms about Hannah, prepared to lead her into a waltz. Hannah froze, terror seizing her heart.

"Wait!" she hissed, "I don't know how to waltz!" The knight grinned at her and pulled her closely against him.

"Trust me," he murmured. The music began and Hannah found herself being swept about the room as if she had grown wings. She closed her eyes and let the music and her handsome knight take her away. She was barely aware of the other couples spinning about them on the floor except for every now and then when Haley would come flying by in the arms of a good looking young courtier. The evening passed swiftly. Hannah and her knight waltzed together and also with the other couples in group dances. They broke for a late dinner and sat side-by-side at a long table, sharing a trencher while acrobats, jugglers and jesters performed for their pleasure. The food was nothing like the fast food Hannah and Haley were used to at all but was rich, flavorful and creatively presented. Not sure what to do, Hannah allowed him to select morsels for her and had to stifle an embarrassed giggle as he even peeled a large purple grape for her with his fingers and popped it into her mouth with a grin. She never wanted the evening to end but eventually found herself yawning with exhaustion.

"Come," said her knight, standing to his feet and offering his hand. Hannah stood up and put her hand back into his. His fingers closed about hers gently and possessively. They felt so warm as they wrapped about her own. They walked together and soon she felt his arm slip about her waist and draw her close to his side. She leaned her weary head upon his breast and stumbled suddenly with exhaustion. It had, after all, been *quite* a day. She felt his arms go under her legs and he lifted her effortlessly into his arms to carry her the remaining distance back to her bedchamber. He carried her through the door and laid her gently upon the bed, covering her and removing her slippers.

Just before he left the chamber, he lifted her palm up to his lips and kissed it gently, his eyes looking deeply into her own which were heavy with sleep.

"Fare thee well, my love," he whispered, a hint of sadness in his eyes.

"Wait!" said Hannah, struggling to remain awake for one more moment. "You never told me your name!" She saw his lips move in reply but could hear no sound. Sleep overwhelmed her like a wave at sea, sweeping her away from him upon its' irresistible tide.

She awoke the next morning back in her own bed with the sun streaming in her window and birds singing outside. She sat up on her elbows and wondered to herself if it had all just been a dream or some kind of magic spell. She shook her head…*it must have just been a dream*... she concluded with a sinking sad feeling and then she froze. Upon her dresser sat a pewter vase and in it was the gorgeous dark red rose bouquet the knight had brought to her the night before. She flew out of bed and gazed at them, blinking in wonder and disbelief. Sitting propped up next to them was an elegant piece of parchment paper with script flowing across it.

"Dearest beloved..." it read. *"...wait for me!"* And below this he had written his name…

CHAPTER NINE
"Clay in the Potter's Hands"

The story below was requested by Donna's close friend, Marian. Donna is currently in ICU on a ventilator and quite depressed. *Donna is an artist, very bright, outgoing, and very creative. She has had a difficult life involving divorce and has a son in his 20's who has a hard time with her chronic illness issues. Donna has severe osteoporosis from steroid use in treating her allergies, asthma and lung conditions. She is in her early 50s. She also has a lot of pain due to osteoarthritis/osteoporosis and Sequelae. I think her dream would be to have shop when she could work as an artist and sell her artwork/crafts. She draws/paints beautifully and is incredibly creative with decorating and crafts. She makes her own greeting cards when she feels up to it.*

"Clay in the Potter's Hands"

The sound of the respirator constantly filled Donna's ears morning, noon, and night; making it difficult to sleep well. Her chest hurt actually her *entire body* hurt and life looked very, very bleak and hopeless. Donna glanced out her door at the nearby nurse's station, wishing she could trade places with any of the people she saw standing there instead of having to be tethered to a machine simply to breath. How she longed to be free of her chronic illnesses and to just live and be creative with the gifts God had given her.

It seemed like her life was in a wasteland of limbo and she was worried about her son who had had to put up with a mom who, through no fault of her own, had been chronically ill with respiratory issues most of his life. Now all the medication she had taken to help her in the short term was taking a toll on her body in the long term.

A single hot tear of frustration rolled down her cheek, instantly dried by the air of the ventilation mask. At that moment she felt a gentle hand brush her cheek and remove the mask. For an instant she panicked, knowing that the removal of the mask spelled big trouble but when she looked up to see who had removed it, her heart nearly stopped. *It couldn't be. Was she dreaming? Did she just die?*

The figure half sitting on her hospital bed smiled at her and that smile sent waves of glorious, intense love flowing over her like a mighty river. His eyes gazed upon her with a brilliance of pure, unadulterated love and total acceptance.

"Take my hand, Donna," said the Savior, reaching for hers. She didn't think twice but laid her small cold hand inside that of her Redeemer's. It was warm and the touch of His hand upon hers sent a thrill coursing up her spine. "Come with me," he said, standing. Donna stood, unable to tear her eyes away from His face, drowning in the pulsating waves of love that flowed outwards from Him and surrounded her in a warm cocoon.

Suddenly she found herself in a different place. She was in an art studio – a studio that made her pea green with envy for it was everything she had always imagined for herself had she been healthy and rich enough to afford it. It was filled with glorious light and had everything an artist would ever want or need.

"This is all for you," said the Lord, putting his arm about her shoulders and turning her about so she could see everything.

"Lord," said Donna, totally confused. "Did I just die? Am I in heaven?"

"No," He smiled at her. "This is just a little vacation." He gestured to all the art supplies. "Enjoy yourself and make something for Me," He said, giving her a wink then disappeared. Donna stood in slack jawed amazement and regarded her surroundings again, walking to and from the drafting table and then from shelf to shelf to inspect everything more closely. Outside birds sang and the breeze smelled of honeysuckle and orange blossoms. She suddenly jumped up and down in glee, rubbing her hands together. She felt great! No pain, no difficulty breathing, no aches! She had never felt so physically free in all her life! She got out the acrylic paints and a blank canvass and proceeded to paint something beautiful for her wonderful Lord. She soon lost herself in her work and painted with gusto. After what seemed hours she paused and stepped back to see what her hands had wrought and frowned. This is not what she had been trying to paint! The colors were all different than what she had used and the painting made absolutely no sense. It looked an angry child had taken a bunch of finger paints and used every color there was until it all blended into one large blackish/greenish mess. She just couldn't figure out what had happened! She set the canvass aside and covered it with a muslin tarp; there was no way she was going to give that as her gift to her Savior! It had turned out hideous!

Perhaps a different medium? She went to the cabinet and found stamping supplies, a heat gun, glitter, ink pens and embossing powders. She would do an elaborate Valentine card to Jesus to tell Him how much she loved Him!

She sat down at a different table and worked meticulously. She didn't want to overdo it and make it look messy and cluttered and she wanted it to express her heart of gratitude for this respite away from her sickbed in the hospital. Hours later, when she felt it was perfect, she looked upon it and cried aloud in pain and disappointment. It was hideous!! *What was wrong with her? Nothing she put her hands to do to make for Him was turning out right!* Donna felt like crying with frustration. This surely wasn't heaven! Heaven was not supposed to be a place of frustration! She looked around the room again. She would try one last time to make something lovely and meaningful for Him. She found a potter's wheel and a lump of clay on it. She had never worked with clay before but since nothing had turned out right in the mediums she was good at, perhaps this time would be the charm.

She put on an apron, sat on the stool before the gently spinning wheel and began to experiment. First she tried a bowl but it came out lopsided. Then she tried a vase but her hand bumped the clay just as she had it almost the way she wanted and the entire thing collapsed into a misshapen mess. Donna was frustrated beyond belief and so disappointed with herself. Somehow she knew the time was quickly approaching when Jesus would return and she had achieved nothing but making a mess of everything she had tried to make Him. Her head hung low with shame and she began to sob hot angry tears of frustration and grief.

"Do not weep, my beloved," said a gentle voice behind her. Donna half-jumped out of her skin in surprise but was instantly calmed as His arms encircled about her and lifted the lumpy misshapen object from the Potter's wheel to admire it.

"I'm so sorry, Lord!" she said, trying not to sound like a whiny baby. "I tried so hard to make you something beautiful because I love You so much and nothing came out right!"

"I do not know what you mean!" Jesus replied, his eyes looking at her with a knowing smile. "It's absolutely lovely!" Donna looked from His face to the clay back to His then did a double take. In His hands the clay had become an exquisite long-necked urn with swan-neck handle from which to pour water from. Donna's mouth hung open…not sure what to say. Jesus turned and went to where her painting sat on the easel, covered with a cloth to hide its ugliness. He threw back the cover and admired it with a great big smile. It was a lovely pastoral scene of sheep grazing peacefully in a flower bedecked field under a cloudless sky. "Beautiful!" He said, turning about to smile upon her. He then crossed to the drafting table and lifted the large Valentine card she had made for him. He read her words in silence, closed His eyes in sheer delight and then gave her such a grateful smile it took her breath away.

Donna did not understand what was happening at all! Jesus again reached out His hand to hers and she walked forward into His warm embrace.

Suddenly they were back in her hospital room and He was again sitting on her bed.

Lord, she thought in her head since she couldn't speak with the ventilator over her mouth, *this was a lesson of some kind for me, wasn't it?*

Yes, He nodded, holding both of her hands in His. *Even though you think what you created as a gift for Me was a mess, because it was made with love, it was exquisite in My eyes. Now let us take your life...do you think your life is a mess?*

Donna hung her head, nodding, feeling deeply again the depression and hopelessness that had been her companion for so many years.

In My eyes you are perfect! Gorgeous. Exquisite! He said, his silent words piercing her dark heart like a beam of sunlight. *You are the clay in My hands and though the way I fashion you may seen harsh and ugly, it is beautiful in My sight. I am making of you a heavenly vessel. You may think you have become useless and decrepit but I see you as gold in the refining fire of my love. It isn't pleasant and it doesn't feel fair but when you come out on the other end, you will be My treasure. Can you now see what measure of trust I have placed in you to allow you to endure so much for Me?*

For you, Lord? Donna responded. *But I thought that this was all just bad luck and living in a sick sinful world. I could do so much more for You if only I weren't sick all the time!*

But you already do as much for Me as I would ever want! responded the Savior, cupping her cheek in His hand. *Despite all the pain and all the suffering, you still demonstrate child like trust in Me. How could I want anything more than that?*

Donna had no come back for that. Suddenly a nurse entered the room to check on her. She took no notice of the Savior sitting on the bed but before leaving, Jesus whispered something only she seemed to hear and she tucked the covers around Donna's perpetually cold feet and legs and then paused to bow her head and offer a silent prayer before leaving the room again.

Did you give her the idea to do that, Lord?

Yes, of course! Came His gentle response. *Every act of kindness, every thoughtful gesture, every visitor who comes to see You to offer their love and encouragement is my personal emissary so that you will know that I am acutely aware of you at every moment of every day. I will send them to you now and then as a gentle reminder of My eternal love and care for you. While I may allow you to have suffering in this life, it cannot be compared to the glory that awaits you in the next. Continue to trust in Me, beloved. I will never fail thee nor forsake thee and when this brief life on earth is over, that art studio you visited today will be waiting for you.*

With those words of encouragement branding themselves upon her soul, Donna fell into a peaceful sleep, feeling as though her Savior's arms were wrapped about her like a warm blanket with His warm cheek next to hers.

NOTE: Days before submitting this manuscript, I received the following news from Donna's friend, Marian: *"Donna died at the end of August (2010). She never got out of the nursing home other than to go to the hospital. She suffered a lot and still trusted the Lord. She is at peace now."*

CHAPTER TEN
"Courtney's Adventure"

A friend in Courtney's Youth Group requested this story. He told me about the entire group and then about Courtney specifically. It was very difficult to nail down what the wish would be when all he could tell me was that she was bonkers over a Christian group called Reliant K (who I, as a middle-aged uncool person knew nothing about). I was given very sparse information but apparently I hit the nail on the proverbial head!

"Courtney's Adventure"

Courtney nervously steered the car down the highway, casting worried glances at her mom who was riding shotgun, her hands balled into nervous fists of extreme tension. Courtney really hated driving with her mom because she was such a nervous wreck when her daughter was at the wheel. She much preferred her dad who was much calmer when she made mistakes. Even if her mom didn't say anything aloud, she could still hear her in her head: *"Courtney! You're going too fast! Courtney! You didn't come to a complete stop! Courtney! Courtney! Courtney!"* It was enough to make her not want to drive at all but today she'd had no choice because her mom had just had a minor medical procedure with a sedative and wasn't allowed to drive herself home and no one else had been available.

"Courtney!" shrieked her mom, stomping on a brake pedal that wasn't on the passenger side in her panic. "Don't you see that bus off on the shoulder!"

"Mooooooooooooooooom!" Courtney wailed. "How am I supposed to concentrate on my driving when you keep nagging me all the time…" her eyes widened in disbelief as she took in the site of the bus and she stomped on the brake herself. The car skidded loudly to a stop. Fortunately, no one had been behind them.

"COURTNEY!" yelled her mom in protest although she had been trying to do the very same thing herself. Courtney couldn't answer; she was in total shock as she looked at the words painted onto the side of the large tour bus: **RELIANT K.**

It was too good to be true! She blinked and rubbed her eyes unable to believe her good fortune. There standing in front of the broken down tour bus with downcast looks on their faces were the band members: the two Matthew's, Jon, and Ethan. They all looked up when Courtney's van screeched to a halt alongside of them.

"Could you use some help?" she found herself volunteering while her mother vainly tried to signal to her that she shouldn't be talking to strangers.

"Sure could!" piped up Matt, the lead singer. "Are you a bus mechanic?" The other band members guffawed at the joke but looked hopeful.

"No but I could take you to where you need to go to get one." Courtney replied, unable to believe she was behaving so calmly in front of her favorite band in the entire world. "There's no cell phone service in this area for a few miles; it's a total dead zone."

"Yeah, we figured that out real quick!" replied Ethan. "We have a concert 50 miles from here in about 2 hours. Even if we had a mechanic magically appear now it wouldn't help."

"Could you give us a lift to the venue?" piped up Jon sizing up her van mentally to calculate if they and their essential gear could fit. Fortunately, they had just had the van detailed that week and all the usual junk that was in it was gone, leaving room for 4 more passengers, and their guitars.

"What about the drum set?" Ethan said. "Where are we going to put that?"

"Courtney!" hissed her mom, poking her in the ribs. "Who are these people? Let's go! We can't possibly help them!"

"Mom! Please do this one favor for me!" pleaded Courtney, tears welling in her eyes. "I'll never ask you for another thing for as long as I live. SWEAR."

Courtney's mom looked at the naked pleading in her daughter's eyes and couldn't find the heart to deny her. She sighed. *Teenagers and their obsessions!* "Of course you will," she relented, "but you just remember this the next time you try to tell me how mean I am!"

"Promise!" breathed Courtney, unable to believe her mom was backing down. It was a miracle! Her mom got out of her side of the van and pointed at Ethan.

"You!" she said in a motherly voice. I've got a cargo net in the back, we can put your drums on the rack on top. The rest of you pile in with just the essentials you need. As soon as we get to a live cell I'll phone in your bus to our local mechanic and have it towed to his garage. Now let's get to work!"

Courtney couldn't believe her ears (or eyes for that matter). *Was this her mother?*

Her mom's only reply was to wink at her. The two Matt's, Jon and Ethan needed no more urging. They hauled out their guitars, cords and amps from the bus in record time and stuffed them into the van and all of them carefully helped to load the drum set on top. Within 20 minutes they were back on the road and speeding towards their destination.

"Gee, thanks for doing this!" Jon said, suddenly realizing that he did not know the names of their rescuers. "Ummm, I'm Jon, this is Ethan and-"

"I know who you all are!" piped up Courtney, bouncing up and down in her seat with glee. "You are my FAVORITE BAND IN THE ENTIRE WORLD."

"Our fan!" exclaimed Matt, elbowing the other Matt in the ribs. "What a lucky break you came along." We've been stuck in that spot since the early morning. You were the only car to stop and help us."

"I'm so sorry!" Courtney said, ashamed on behalf of her county. Courtney's mom twisted around in her seat to look at the men crammed into the back of the van, their instruments filling all the spare space that was left.

"Have you boy's had anything to eat since this morning?" she demanded, her motherly instinct coming out. All four shook their heads "no" as their respective stomachs all growled in confirmation.

"Courtney, take the next exit and let's stop to get them a pizza and some drinks. Can't go onstage and sing when your bellies are agrowling!"

Courtney looked at her mom, her eyes wide in sudden mock horror. "Okay," she hissed under her breath. "Who are you and what have you done with my mom?"

Her mom just shrugged and grinned at her. "I was a big Journey fan when I was your age. If I had seen their bus break down like these guys, you bet I would have moved heaven and earth to help them!"

They pulled up to a local Pizza parlor and while they were selecting their pizza (two pepperoni and two all sausage with onion) plus sodas, Courtney's mom was able to use the public phone to call a mechanic who promised to take care of the bus for them. (Apparently he was a Reliant K fan as well).

Back on the road, eating pizza and sipping sodas, the mood became more sociable.

"So, do you play an instrument of any kind, ma'am?" questioned Matt T., trying to unsuccessfully bite in two the long rope of cheese that kept stretching from the back seat to the front with his teeth.

"Not now, but my daughter, Courtney here, plays Ukulele like there is no tomorrow!" responded her mom.

"Mooooooooom! Sssh!" Courtney said, embarrassed beyond all belief.

"Really?" said Ethan leaning forward. "We just wrote a new song that is just screaming for a Ukulele but we haven't been able to find anyone to play it on the road with us and Matt is still learning. Would you like to learn the song?"

"Me?" bleated Courtney, her eyes growing as big as saucers as she looked in the rear-view mirror. "Are you kidding me?"

"I never kid," replied Ethan with a very serious look on his face.

"He never kids," affirmed Matt, Matt and Jon solemnly.

"But you'll have to trade places with your mom and let her drive so you can learn the song. How fast can you pick up a song without sheet music?" continued Ethan.

Courtney slammed on the brakes. All the guys held onto the car straps for dear life as they were flung forward. Fortunately they didn't lose their pizza and drinks. Her and her mom performed a quick "Chinese Fire Drill" and traded spots. At the same time Matt and Jon got out their acoustic guitars so they could help Courtney learn the song. Her mom put the car into gear and crossed herself. *Medical procedure be dammed this was show business!*

Courtney spent the remainder of the trip turned around backwards, strumming along on her Ukulele learning the yet unperformed Reliant K's song "On the Right Track". She was concentrating so hard on getting it right she forgot to be nervous. An hour flew by and the next thing they knew they had reached the venue and were driving around to the performer's entrance in the back where a security guard tried to stop them.

"No one allowed in but-"

"WE ARE THE BAND!" Matthew said in a commanding tone of voice, flashing his ID. "We're late, let us through!"

The guard was about to argue but then saw the drum set on top with the name RELIANT K screen printed on the kick drum. He waved them through. Courtney's mom swiftly pulled up to the backdoor of the concert hall and the band members piled out.

"You sure learned that song fast!" Jon enthused, unloading the gear. "If you'd like to come onstage and play with us on just that one cover it'd be great but no pressure. It's just that we were hoping to introduce it tonight."

"Are you serious?" Courtney said, clutching her Ukulele. "You really want me to play that song with you?"

"Well…." drawled Matt T., rubbing his head. "We will have to make you an honorary member of the band, just for tonight. Are you game?"

Courtney couldn't believe her luck. The day had started out so lousy and now here she was with Matt, Matt, Jon and Ethan of Reliant K and she was going to play in front of their fans with them on her Ukulele. *How cool was that?!*

"Game on!" Courtney grinned at them. "Lead the way!"

CHAPTER ELEVEN
"Captivated"

This was a request from a teenager who was very specific about what she wanted. She is a very outdoorsy kind of girl and trains horses so she wasn't about to take any guff from anyone and that was the kind of story she got. She wanted to be the heroine in a slave-ship story set in ancient Ireland.

"Captivated"

Gwyn watched in mounting frustration as her brothers August and John took turns practicing against each other with their mock swords. They had been "training" for the better part of the morning and still had not gotten around to working in the fields as their father had commanded them. They hated field work and longed to be off serving as squires-at-arms to the local Duke. Their father had sent Gwyn to "deal" with them.

"Get off with you lazy lads! To the fields with ye!" she chided them in her lilting brogue. The brothers stopped and regarded her with annoyance.

"Lazy?" repeated August, making a great show of sheathing his practice sword. A dulled ugly thing in comparison to the ones he had lusted after at the blacksmith's shop a fortnight ago when last in the village. She could barely haul him away, so consumed with lust at the gleaming blades and bejeweled hilts. "Have ye not regarded with what gusto we have trained these past few hours?"

"Aye! Lazy me arse." John guffawed.

"You'll not be addressing me so cheeky!" Gwyn said, stepping forward, a menacing look on her face. The faces of both brothers instantly quelled and went white as a banshee's. Their eyes round with horror. Gwyn hesitated…*surely she didn't look that fearsome!* She only wanted them to get to work in the fields; not terrify them!

"Gwyn!" squeaked John, looking past her; his body trembling. Gwyn turned and looked about just as she felt arms of iron wrap about her body and physically haul her up onto a horse. The next thing she knew she had been slung stomach down over the back of a horse like a trussed sow. With sudden terror, she looked behind and saw her brothers experience the same fate. Marauding English slavers had entered their land by stealth and taken many captives. She saw a long line of her fellow villagers tied to one another by a common rope, their wrists bound and their faces gagged so they couldn't cry out a warning.

"Let me down off this flea infested nag or I'll cut off your ear's as soon as soon as I draw breath!" she managed to growl to her smelly captor.

"Shut yer pie hole, wench!" he growled right back at her, taking a stave and smacking her smartly on the rump. "If you don't mind yer manners I'll sell ye to a cathouse instead of a serving woman to a fine manor house!"

Gwyn was ready with a smart retort but thought better of it. She was in no position to indulge her vast vocabulary of bawdy insults on a knave who held her and her brother's fate in his grimy hands. She pressed her lips together in a firm line and concentrated on drawing breath in the most uncomfortable position she had ever assumed on a horse. If only she hadn't worn her corset that day; the combination of both was making her light-headed for lack of breath.

The slavers didn't even pause to rest for the night, knowing the hot-tempered Celts would be on their heels like hounds to recover their loved ones. They paused only long enough to tie Gwyn and her brothers up to the rest of their unhappy countrymen and made to march triple time until they reached the sea. It was almost nightfall and the slave ship was almost invisible beyond the surf line. A waiting coracle; large enough to seat 20 (if crammed in like sardines) waited upon the sand for the slaver's "catch". As they herded their captives into the freezing cold surf to get into the boat, Gwyn, August, and John finally got a brief moment together again.

"You alright, lassie?" August asked her with concern. Gwyn nodded, putting on a brave smile.

"You?" she asked both brothers. They nodded; unable to hide the naked fear in their eyes. They were all being taken from their homeland and would probably be split up; never to see each other again once upon the other shore or know of each other's fate. It made Gwyn's blood boil with fury. *What right did these vermin think they had to kidnap and enslave freeborn Irish to work in their slaughter houses and brothels! What gave them the right?*

At that moment, the chief slaver caught hold of her arm to pull her into the coracle. Gwyn shook his arm off with a scowl and spat in his face. A hush descended upon all; except for her brothers who perked up and bellowed with laughter at the insult she had dealt him.

Their laughter was silenced with a brutal blow to their heads and they were unceremoniously thrown into the boat. Gwyn stood her ground, arms akimbo, legs spread wide, prepared to do battle without so much as a dirk. She had grown up with two rough and tumble brothers and knew well how to handle herself. The slaver regarded her with wary eyes; trying to assess just how much damage she might be capable of doing to him. He crouched low as if he were about to spring and nodded. Gwyn realized her stupidity too late. It had been a ruse. She was grabbed from behind by a smelly bear of a man while another grabbed her by the ankles and lifted her bodily off the sand and dumped her on top of her brothers and the other captives in the boat.

She screamed and struggled with a fury like a she-cat as they hog-tied her, bruising both herself, her brothers and the other captives by her struggles.

"Easy Gwynnie!" August protested, grunting with pain as her knee connected with his ribs. "It's us you be hurting not them!"

"Aye!" grumped John, rubbing his now black and blue side with the side of his arm. The next thing they all knew the coracle was being pushed into the arms of the waiting sea and rowed to the slave ship. There they were all pushed and herded down into the bottom-most parts of the ship and chained together with leg irons. If the ship went down in a storm they would all certainly drown. The only small blessing was that Gwyn and her brothers were shackled together. They huddled in cramped misery in the bitter cold, trying to keep other's spirits up and their bodies warm in the sickening plunge and yaw of the ship as it slowly made its' way to Britain. It was a miserable trip. Just about everyone ended up sick and vomiting, causing even those without seasickness just to retch from the stench. The smell was overwhelming, the trip unending and no sleep was to be had. They were all cold, hungry, and miserable and covered with filth by the time they reached shore two days later.

Several of them had gotten sick and were now shaking with chills and fever. Gwyn and her brothers were a little worse for the wear but otherwise unscathed (except for their clothing which had become so rank it was only fit for the dung heap). They had neither eaten, drunk nor slept since the moment of their capture but instead of defeating their morale it only made them more furious. Gwyn was chafing for an opportune moment and then heaven help the poor sot when she was done with her tongue lashing!

The next day, after a brief rest where they cleaned themselves up as best they could in a nearby stream, given stale mead and hard bread; they were then forced to frog march again where one by one they were sold off to various farmers, merchants and tradesmen as slaves. The slavers pocketed less than they would have liked and were saving Gwyn and her brothers for last, hoping their strong bodies and fine looks would bring a better price from the Baron to whom they hoped to sell them as a threesome. Gwyn as a maidservant/serving wench and the boys for whatever menial labor the master could think of.

It was late afternoon after two more days of trudging when they finally reached a large estate. The seneschal had been expecting them and was waiting impatiently by the gate with a disdainful scowl. He gave August and John a sneering once over, wrinkling his nose in distaste at their "ripe" fragrance which only served to make the hackles rise on the back of Gwyn's neck in protective indignation.

To be sure you wouldn't be smelling as sweet as a rose either if you had been captured, shoved into a stinking ship's hole and made to sit in your own reek for days with naught but a dirty stream to wash in! She fumed.

As if he had heard her thoughts, the seneschal turned about and glared at her. "You!" he said with a sneer. "Come hither!"

Gwyn may have had shackles on her wrists and ankles but she was no man's slave to be commanded! She crossed her arms and stood with her feet firmly planted a shoulder length apart in absolute defiance. August and John shared a knowing look. *There was no messing with Gwyn when she got her head up…*

The seneschal scowled at her, obviously unused to be defied. He slowly walked up to her, swung his arm back and backhanded her. The blow sent her reeling backwards, tripping over her shackles and sprawling onto her backside into a mud puddle. Mud spattered everywhere. August and John were incensed and lunged forward but were restrained by their slavers who had been expecting a reaction.

"Gordon!" snapped a voice that left no doubt it came from a much higher authority. The seneschal immediately bowed and remained bowed as a large man in rich clothing brushed past him to where Gwyn still lay flat in the mud puddle, fighting back her tears of anger and humiliation.

"Give me your hand," he ordered, extending his to her. August and John sucked in their breath, wondering what their sister would do next. They hadn't long to wait. As the master bent lower to grasp her hand, Gwyn clasped hold with both of hers and yanked down as hard as she could, catching him totally off guard. He wound up sprawling in the mud beside her, completely ruining his costly tunic and velvet cloak. All stared in hushed silence except for August and John who were practically bursting with the need to laugh out loud. *Gwyn had shown them all who was boss!*

The master regained his composure, sat back on his haunches and regarded Gwyn with nonplussed look on his face. The seneschal grinned, anticipating that a good whipping would now be in store for the impertinent little strumpet!

A bellow of laughter punctured that hope and deflated it instantly. The master bent forward at the waist and continued to laugh with abandon, completely surprising and disarming Gwyn, his laugh taking all the fight out of her. He stood to his feet, still offering his hand to help her up, which she accepted with deep chagrin.

He pulled with all his might, hauling her up and then lifted her, slinging her over his shoulder like a sack of meal. Turnabout, after all, was fair play. Gwyn took to this new humiliation with renewed rage and flailed and kicked at him while he marched her past the seneschal, her brothers, the slavers and remaining few captives all the way into the main house. He strode through several richly appointed rooms which she got only a passing glance at (and upside down at that) and finally out into a courtyard where he unceremoniously dumped her into a large fountain.

She plunged amongst the lily pads with an enormous plop that sent a backsplash flying up which in turn drenched the Master who stood there with his mouth hanging open in mid guffaw.

“Hah!” Gwyn shrieked at him in triumph, crossing her arms.

“Hmph,” was the only response she got. He left her sitting there dripping and shivering and returned a short time later with a large blanket. He lifted her out of the fountain (since it was impossible for her to climb out with shackled ankles) and set her on her feet, wrapping it around her. If her teeth hadn’t been chattering so hard she would have shoved him away but all she could manage was a sneeze. He began to lead her back into the main house but the shackles made progress agonizingly slow. With a sigh of exasperation he stopped and scooped her up, carrying her into the house, up the stairs and into a room where a surprised chambermaid stood with her mouth hanging open in shock.

He stood Gwyn back on her feet. "Prudence, get this chit cleaned up, into a fresh pair of clothes and bring her back before me when she's more presentable." He instructed, with a cocked eyebrow in her direction.

"Yes, milord," curtseyed the maid, eyeing Gwyn in fear. Gwyn realized at that moment that her fate had been sealed. She was his property now…*well, she wasn't going down without a fight!*

She picked up the nearest thing at hand and flung it at his head. It missed by bare inches and instead crashed against the doorframe at the precise moment the door closed behind him.

"I'll be dammed if I ever bow to the likes of a fusspot like you!" she shrieked at the top of her lungs. The door reopened and Gwyn found herself ducking as an urn came flying at her head.

"I believe you just did, milady!" replied the Baron with a devilish grin.

CHAPTER TWELVE
"Emerelda"

Tessa is a high school aged girl who is home-schooled and this is her wish: *"I think it would be amazing to be able to be one of one of my own characters in one of my favorite books. I would love to be an elven dragon rider named Loriena (Lor-ee-na) with a dragon named Emerelda."*

"Emerelda"

Loriena scowled at the old milk cow in front of her. Benna was being unusually obstinate and uncooperative that morning and Loriena was out of patience. The stupid animal had kicked the milk bucket over for the third time in what seemed like an intentional act of ruining her already miserable existence while her impoverished family tried to eke out a living on the tiny farm. Benna mooed loudly, shifting from one hoof to the other; her udders aching with the need to be milked but agitated by some unseen pest.

"Benna, so help me, if you don't stop your bawling and fussing, I'm just going to let your udders explode!" growled Loriena, setting down the milking stool for the tenth time. Benna finally settled down long enough for Loriena to fill the pail with the milk. Relieved, she stood up, shoved away the milk stool and bent to lift the pail when Benna mooed loudly again and kicked it over, dumping all the milk onto the barn floor.

"ARGH!!" Loriena shrieked, frustrated beyond belief. Her father was going to be sore-vexed with her for this. She reached down through the straw to fling the first rock she could find at the stupid cow and raised her arm to let fly but the rock in her hand suddenly went white hot. She dropped it with scream and jumped back. It fell onto the mud-packed floor and rolled a few feet away but the green glow coming from it was unmistakable in the early morning light.

Was she seeing things? She crept forward; daring to breath, not caring that she was dragging her skirts through the spilt milk and mud. She crouched down to study the rock closer. The glow was starting to fade now. She touched it tentatively; afraid of burning herself again. The rock was now simply warm but still pulsing with a beautiful green light. She cradled it in her palms, studying it; a strange feeling building in the pit of her stomach. Suddenly a tiny crack appeared, then another, then another until it began to resemble an exotic egg that had broken. A tiny puff of smoke issued from the biggest crack and Loriena gasped in mixed terror and delight.

"Loriena!" snapped the voice of foster father, Jarrod. "What goes on here? Where's the milk?" He got his answer when saw the large puddle spreading slowly across the barn floor. "Ye gods, girl, what has gotten into you?" he demanded, striding up to her to yank her up by the arm. Instead his attention was diverted to the green glowing oval rock which Loriena was also staring at in astonishment. The cracks had grown so large that now she could see the creature wriggling inside; fighting to free itself. Jarrod froze in his tracks.

He had been warned long ago when he had first agreed to foster Loriena that this day might come, he just had never really truly believed it would! He watched in horrified fascination as the creature finally freed itself from its egg casing and looked straight into the eyes of Loriena, imprinting itself upon her. Loriena stared right back, transfixed as if in a spell.

"Loriena," said, Jarrod, his voice hoarse with the realization of what was about to happen. "We must get thee away, quickly! Today! Before you are discovered and word spreads about your beastie there." He grasped her arm and carefully put the tiny dragon into a leather satchel where it squeaked in protest.

"Huh, What?" she replied, too mesmerized to respond. Unable to think of anything else except the sight of the beautiful, tiny green dragon that had looked right into her soul. She half-ran, half-stumbled along as Jarrod hauled her back into their farmhouse, talking out loud to himself the entire time.

"…she'll need at least a month's supply of food and water and a safe place to hide until it's full grown. The caves should serve well and there is a spring nearby…" he muttered, flinging supplies onto the shaky wooden table.

"What are you doing? Where are we going?" Loriena pleaded, suddenly coming out of her stupor. Jarrod was making plans for her life without so much as her say-so!

"You must remain in hiding until it's full grown and it can protect you!" he repeated, his eyes round with fear. "The enemy has kept watch on this place for years. If they find out you have a hatchling, they will come after all of us!"

"Hatchling? Enemy?" repeated Loriena, nonplussed. "What are you talking about and what is that creature you put in your satchel?"

"No time to explain!" hissed Jarrod, stuffing cured meats, dried fruits, and wayfarer's bread into a leather satchel at frantic speed. He added to this a warm woolen cloak, a flint rock and some kindling all the while muttering a constant stream of oaths. When he had everything packed, he pushed her out the door again and led her behind the farmhouse and into the thick woods which bordered the property. The pace he set was almost impossible for Loriena to keep up with; some unspeakable terror was driving him and she had no choice but to go where he led her. They marched the rest of day and took no rest until late afternoon when they reached the mouth of a large cave that was half-hidden by heavy forest and brush.

"Here you must stay, Loriena." Jarrod commanded her, flinging the leather satchel and what looked like a strange saddle into the mouth of the cave.

"You're abandoning me *here*?" Loriena began to cry, her eyes filling tears. "What have I done wrong? I'm sorry about the milk!"

Her tears seemed to bring Jarrod back to the present. He regarded her with pity and cupped her cheek in his hand. "Have you never wondered why you didn't look like either of us?" he asked, gazing at the beautiful child he had fostered for the past

14 years. Loriena shook her head. She had never seen what she looked like, except in a wavering reflection of a brook or pool of water. "You were brought to us as an infant, for safe-keeping." He said, trying to explain as best he could in a short space of time. It was getting dark and he did not want to be caught in the forest at night. "We have taken care of you as if you were our own, Loriena, but you are elf-kind!" He took her hand and placed her fingers at the top of her ears which were elegantly curved into points. She gasped, having never paid attention to them before. She stared back at Jarrod whose brown eyes were now filling with tears. "It is no longer safe for you to be on our farm with that hatchling. Word will get out and they'll come looking for you. I will come back as soon as I can and bring you fresh supplies but you must stay hidden here until it is full grown."

"*Until what is full grown?!*" Loriena demanded with a scream, bringing him up short. The whole day had started off like a nightmare. First the cow and the spilt milk, then the rock that had burned her hand, then the tiny green glowing creature and now Jarrod prattling on like a crazed lunatic with every intention of dumping her in this god-forsaken cave.

"*YOUR DRAGON.*" He growled, pointing to the creature wriggling out of the satchel. Loriena eyes followed to where he pointed and found the creature staring up at her with an intensity she found both compelling and frightening. She was utterly transfixed, unable to tear her eyes away from it. Its' skin was a sparkly emerald green and it's pale green eyes piercing.

Loriena! Said a tiny voice in her head. She gasped and the tiny dragon blinked at her.

"I must go now!" Jarrod said, backing away. "I'll come back in a week to see how you're getting on. Stay hidden and learn well!"

Loriena barely noticed him leave, still caught in the spell of the little creature. She squatted down and held out her cupped hands. It crawled forward and with a flick of its tiny tongue, settled itself into her hands. She straightened and carried it into the cave.

*Fire, s*aid the voice inside her head. Obediently she knelt down, arranged the kindling Jarrod had carried with them and set it ablaze with the flint rocks.

Hungry, came the next thought after the fire was crackling merrily away. Loriena searched inside one of the satchels and found a strip of cured meat. She tore it up into tiny pieces and put it before the tiny dragon which snatched it up and gulped it down without chewing.

The days and nights passed swiftly, so intent was Loriena on bonding with the dragon that was growing at an exponential rate. When the day came that Jarrod returned with fresh supplies, he was obviously taken aback at how swiftly it had grown and was terrified at its sheer size.

"Father, come closer, Emerelda won't hurt you," Loriena said, patting the neck of the dragon which now towered a full man's height above them. It was a magnificent beast and only a third full grown. It was going to be a nightmare when it reached full maturity! Jarrod balked at the idea of coming any closer but the dragon merely stared at him with benign eyes. He laid down the satchel of fresh supplies and rubbed his beard, suddenly realizing that he had not brought enough food. The beastie alone could eat every morsel and still not be sated; leaving Loriena with nothing.

"Emerelda, eh?" he said with a grin in Loriena's direction. "It suits her well." He looked at the meager supplies he had brought. "I don't think there's enough for the two of you…"

Saddle! Hunt! came the words into Loriena's head. She went into the cave and came back out carrying the odd saddle Jarrod had left a week ago. "Is this for my dragon?" she asked, laying it at Jarrod's feet.

He nodded, looking over the fine leather and stitching. "It will protect you from the scales." He answered, hefting it up. He put it into her arms. "She will allow only you to put it on her." He said, backing away. As if on cue, Emerelda went onto her belly and allowed Loriena to lay it upon her. Speaking mind-to-mind, the dragon instructed her on how to fasten it securely then lay down again so Loriena could mount.

Hunt now! No sooner had the words appeared in her mind that the dragon took off for the first time, flapping its' great wings like a giant bird of prey. Loriena held on for dear life, barely able to open her eyes because of the streaming wind. The landscape of the forest suddenly lay far below them and clouds swiftly passed underneath as they sped through the air. It was freezing up so high but the dragon's warmth enveloped her and kept her comfortable as they glided. Loriena could suddenly see from Emerelda's viewpoint and with her eagle-like eyes, she spotted a large buck grazing in a meadow.

Suddenly a shadow covered them, blotting out the light of the son. A mighty roar issued from what only could have been another dragon. The noise was deafening.

With streaming eyes, Loriena watched in amazement as a blue dragon swooped down to the same level as she and Emerelda. On its' proud back was another rider just like her, only it was a young man with a large sword and his dragon was wearing armor!

Boy and Blue Dragon want us to land in glade below, said the voice of Emerelda in her head. Without further hesitation, the two dragons folded their wings and wheeled down in spirals until they both reached the meadow. The young man leapt off the saddle of his dragon and strode over to her.

"My dragon heard the heartbeat of your dragon a week ago; we have been watching and waiting for you." He said, removing his helmet.

"Why would you be waiting for me?" asked Loriena, her head spinning with the sudden cataclysmic changes in her world. She had gone from lowly farm-girl to looked-for elf and dragon-rider in the space of a single week.

"You have been kept in hiding until the day you could join us in the war against our enemy."

"War?" squeaked Loriena. At the mention of the word, both dragons lifted their long necks high into the sky and roared, sending twin plumes of fire rising high…

The door to Tessa's room flew open with a bang causing her to suddenly sit up in bed in alarm.
"Tessa, time to get up!" her mother's voice rang out as she marched down the hall. Tessa looked around her room, temporarily bewildered. The meadow, dragons and the boy were gone. Reality hit hard and it was a huge disappointment. *It felt too real to have been just a dream!* She had often day-dreamed about being in such a story after reading her favorite book but she had never had a dream of such detail before. With a resigned sigh, she swung her feet out of bed and attempted to stand up but instead fell as she tripped on a small round object.
She looked down and felt her heart nearly stop. With shaking hands she squatted down and picked up the large, round egg-like rock which began glowing and glittering in her hands as if it were lit from within with green fire.

"Uh oh!" she said.

CHAPTER THIRTEEN
"A Little Bayern Goes a Long Way…"

This Hannah loves fantasy and some sci-fi, and wishes she could live in the land of her favorite novelist. One should be careful what one wishes for…

"A Little Bayern Goes A Long Way…"

Hannah stared at the computer screen before her, chewing on her finger while she thought about the graphic image she was trying to create. She knew what she was trying to achieve but just couldn't seem to make her mind and fingers work together in harmony. She turned her head to look outside her bedroom window, hoping for some inspiration. The weather outside was dark and stormy; she could hear the distant rumble of thunder approaching. Suddenly she jumped out of her seat with a scream as a bolt of lightning hit right outside her room. It sounded like a bomb going off. The lights went out and all went dark. Then suddenly the light of a fire kindled before her very eyes.

Hannah blinked a few times and looked up to see a young woman staring right back at her with the same look of shock and surprise as she.

"Who are you?!" demanded the girl, raising her hands in a threatening way. In her upraised open palms were twin balls of fire which were rotating ominously. Instantly Hannah realized where she was.

"Enna!" she shrieked; launching herself forward to embrace her with wild abandon. The young woman was so startled that the fire in her hands was immediately extinguished and she found herself standing awkwardly as Hannah continued hugging. After a moment Hannah stepped back, feeling a bit sheepish.

"Who are you?" demanded Enna, straightening her forest gown. Hannah stifled a giggle. She found it rather amusing that a fictional character was demanding an explanation from her; a real person!

"My name is Hannah Nicole," she replied.

"How do you know my name?" Enna continued, her brow furrowed together in suspicion. "Did Sileph send you?"

"Nooooooo," replied Hannah looking about to indicate her bedroom, computer, bed, printer, etc., only to freeze when she realized she was no longer in her room but in a forest. No wonder she was freezing!

Enna looked her up and down and the suspicious look was replaced with a look of compassion as Hannah wrapped her arms about herself, teeth starting to chatter. She removed her heavy cloak and wrapped it about Hannah and took her by the arm.

"Come with me," she ordered. Hannah nodded obediently; she was in Bayern; she could tell and though she was familiar with the realm because of reading the books; being transported into the mythical forest in the dead of night was rather unnerving; no matter how much she had always wanted to be there.

They reached the cottage a short time later and Enna pushed her inside. It was pitch black inside but in a moment Enna had a bright fire crackling in the hearth using her powers. Hannah looked about her in barely contained glee. She was inside one of her favorite stories with one of her favorite characters! She looked up and found Enna glaring at her in a suspicious way which took her aback. She didn't expect one of her favorite heroines to be so hostile.

"Are you a People, Animal or Nature Speaker?" Enna demanded. Hannah was at a loss. She looked around the rather shabby cottage and noticed some things.

"I'm a beauty-maker!" she said with a big grin. Before Enna could protest, Hannah began gathering up things she found around the cottage and to arrange them in a pleasing way. Enna watched in suspicious yet fascinated silence as Hannah busied herself transforming her hovel into something very homey and lovely. But Hannah wasn't done yet. She went outside with a large empty pitcher, filled it in a nearby stream and began cutting and arranging wildflowers in it. By the time she was done she had a gorgeous bouquet which she set onto the table; beaming at Enna with pride.

Tears filled Enna's eyes. This girl was a total stranger to whom she had been particularly unkind and here she had done this selfless act of beautifying her homely cottage with just what she found. She covered her face with her hands to hide the tears that began to slide down her cheeks. Her shoulders began to heave. No one had been this nice to her in a very long time.

Compassion filled Hannah's heart and she went forward and embraced Enna to comfort her. "I'm sorry about what happened to Sileph," she said. That opened the floodgates. Enna wept terrible deep heaving sobs and all Hannah could do was to pat her back and making soothing sounds. After ten minutes of heavy-duty sobbing Enna looked around, wiping her nose with the back of her sleeve.

"Thank you!" she said, meaning every word. She looked at Hannah's strange clothes (she was wearing blue jeans and a cute purple paisley smock top) with great curiosity. "These are strange garments," she observed, rubbing the rayon/cotton blend in her hands. "But these!" she said indicating the blue jeans. "Most unladylike!"

Hannah looked down at her jeans with the carefully created bare patches in the knees. It would do no good to explain and Senna wouldn't understand anyway.

"Ummmmm sorry." She said. An awkward silence ensued then a sudden thought froze Hannah's heart. She was inside her favorite book but how was she going to get back home? The thought of living in Bayern had always appealed to her but now that she was really here she felt totally out of place. Then another feeling made her begin to panic. "I need to use the ladies room." She said to Senna; hoping she would take the hint and direct her to the nearest bathroom. Senna stared at her for a moment with a perplexed look on her face.

She threw out her arms to indicate the small hovel around them. "This is a lady's room." She explained slowly as if Hannah were mentally retarded. Hannah shook her head.

"No, you don't understand…uhh, I need to uh…well you know…*relieve myself!"*

Enlightenment came over Senna's face and she nodded. She turned about, bent over and picked up what looked to be a pail. She held it out to Hannah with a grim smile. "You'll need to do this behind the cottage," she instructed.

Hannah was aghast. She had to do it *in a pail? What was she supposed to do with it afterwards?*

Senna picked up a slender twig and spoke a word over it so it would glow. "You may use this to light your way," she said, handing it to Hannah then gently pushed her towards the door. The cottage door opened as if by magic all by itself and the next thing Hannah knew, she was standing in her own bathroom holding a bucket and a twig that still glowed. She dropped both with a shriek which brought her mother running up the stairs.

"Are you okay?" her mom asked, not even noticing the foreign pail or now smoldering twig. Hannah looked up and nodded, relieved to be back in her own world.

"I saw a spider." She fibbed. Her mom nodded, picked up the pail as if it had belonged in the family for years and without a second glance went back to her chores.

Hannah slowly turned about her room to reassure herself that she was once again in the "real" world but for a split second, she thought she caught of glimpse of Senna's forlorn face staring back at her in her bedroom mirror…

CHAPTER FOURTEEN
"Heart of Darkness/Heart of Light"

(This is a true story - the names have been changed to maintain anonymity): *John's story is a heartbreaking one. When he was very young, his mother began selling his body to a couple of men in order to pay the rent. This went on for several years. His mother is an alcoholic, and she either gave him alcohol or at least didn't keep it away from him, and now he is an alcoholic, too. He had been doing fairly well at staying away from it--he's been through rehab--but all of a sudden, he started back in and some other things started happening in his life--things that really point to demonic activity. His wife and my daughter (who has been more of a mother to him than his own mother by far), tried to get him to go for counseling (and maybe deliverance) with her church pastor and his team.*

On Wednesday, John went as far as the door to the church with Jane, and she said it was as though someone grabbed him and threw him against the wall of the church. He lay there unconscious for awhile, then jumped up and ran out to the middle of the street and threw himself down in the street (this is in a city). They got him up from there and called for help. Some officers came, supposedly to take him to a mental health clinic to put him under a suicide watch, but instead, they took him to a regular hospital. Then they either released him or he walked out on his own and went home. My daughter picked up Jane and picked up the kids from school and went back over to their apartment, where John proceeded to threaten Jane (that he would kill her). My daughter took Jane and the kids to her own home. John called several times with more threats then yesterday morning called and told her that since she didn't love him anymore he was going to move in with his mother (who lives in a nearby city) and from there he was going to go to another state where he will live with a man there. Jane wants him to come back if he will: (1) go to church with her and (2) stay away from alcohol. Keep in mind here--John is normally a loving and gentle soul, quiet and happiest when he can stay in the background. These past few days' activities sound so totally unlike him that it's hard to believe it is the same person. I think if he has a wish to be fulfilled (at least when he is himself), he would wish to be free or maybe even to be able to start his whole life over. **NOTE: John has since returned to his family and while he still struggles, things seem to be getting a little better. I'm told he keeps a copy of this story on the wall of his home and that when he finally got to read it, it sent shivers down his spine.**

"Heart Of Darkness / Heart Of Light"

John sat upon the park bench staring at nothing in particular. His heart was in shreds and filled with a darkness he could not escape. He was oblivious to the beauty around him; the soft breeze that caressed his face, the warm sunshine, the butterflies that flitted here and there amongst the flowers and the sound of birdsong. He was trapped in a vise of despair and silent desperation that closed ever tighter about him like a boa constrictor; crushing the life from him.

The steady sound of weeping slowly brought him to the surface for a moment and he looked in the direction of the sandlot where a little boy was cowering before two larger boys who were obviously bullies. They kicked him, slapped him and shouted vile things at him. John's heart filled with rage at the plight of the little boy and before he knew it he was striding towards the bullies who were preparing to do even worse damage from the look of their curled fists.

John caught the first bully's arm as he swung back to land a crushing blow; his rage at the mistreatment of the smaller boy filling him with a righteous anger. He threw the bully down onto the sand and then turned to deal with the next one. What he saw made him recoil in horror. It was not a boy but a monster disguised as a boy. Its yellow eyes were filled with hatred for both him and the small boy crouching before him in a fetal position, shielding his head from the oncoming blow. John quickly recovered. He would not let this *thing* hurt the young boy; not anymore! He flung himself upon it and grappled it onto the ground. It shrieked with an ear-splitting scream but despite its' size it was no match for John's fury and after a few minutes struggle he quickly subdued it. It ran off along with other one, disappearing from sight.

Breathing hard and shaking with the adrenaline coursing through his veins John turned his attention to the small boy. He put a gentle hand upon the lad's shoulder that looked up at him gratefully with a tear-streaked face. John stepped back a few paces in bewildered shock and fear. The boy looked strangely familiar and it frightened him. The boy reached up both arms to him desiring to be picked up and comforted after his fright. Despite his unwillingness to do so, John could not find it in his heart to refuse. He picked up the lad in his arms and held him close to his breast. Together they wept; mourning the loss of innocence and the years of childhood stolen and stained by evil. John wept great heaving sobs and the harder he cried, the softer the boy cried then suddenly the boy was gone and it was John who was the little boy and he was being held in the arms of a man that blazed with a light so great he couldn't open his eyes. His tears became a cleansing flood that washed away the grime and guilt of years past; his shoulders shaking. All the while, the man who held him whispered words of indescribable love and forgiveness into his ear. He felt his spirit healed, his wounds soothed. John's sobs gradually abated and when he finally looked up he was staring into the eyes of eternity and in them he found complete acceptance and forgiveness.

"Who are you?" he asked in a coarse whisper although he already knew the answer.

"I am the One who loves you," came the soft reply, "and I am waiting for you to welcome me into your heart so I can restore the years that have been stolen from you. If you will trust Me and give all of yourself to Me; the years before you will be truly blessed."

John stared at him; he was at a crossroads. Which way would he choose…The way of life and restoration or the path of destruction? He straightened up and placed his shaking hand into that of the Savior's and was greeted with a brilliant smile that filled his broken heart with joy.

CHAPTER FIFTEEN
"Sword of the Spirit"

"I am a native Michigander; have lived in Michigan all of my life. I grew up in a home headed by my mother and grandmother. My parents were divorced before I was born, and I did not have a father figure of any kind. I accepted Jesus as my Savior in 1987; subsequently turned my back and went back into the world. I returned to Him in 2001 and will not be going back. Returning to the Lord reminded me of the joy I had been missing. This time, I felt like Peter, who said, when Jesus asked His Twelve Disciples in John 6:67 "You do not want to leave too, do you?" Simon Peter answered him, "Lord, to whom we shall go? You have the words of eternal life. We believe and know that you are the Holy One of God." I am married to the most gentle and wonderful man in the world, Fred, and am the 'mother' of two amazing English Cocker Spaniels, Toby (born in 1995) and Shelby (born in 2004, a year before our wedding date!). I enjoy reading, movies, music, marathons, traveling, serving on the Video Tech Team and as a Women's Ministry Life Group Leader at church and blogging. My wish is to be able to put the past behind me and live the rest of my life for His glory."

"Sword of the Spirit"

Andrea was dreaming...or so she assumed…for suddenly she found herself standing, in of all places, a blacksmith's shop and an ancient one at that. She stood and watched in fascination as he worked and slowly became aware that she was not standing there alone. She looked to her side and then up…up…up to find a ten foot tall, incredibly gorgeous angel standing next to her. He didn't exactly look like an angel…he had no wings and no flowing white robes but someone she knew…he was definitely an angel. *Her angel. Her guardian angel.* He looked down upon her with eyes full of love and affection and then silently directed her attention back to the smithy.

The large burly man was sweating profusely and hammering away with his hammer and tongs upon a long metal object. Andrea could feel the heat from the furnace but when the Blacksmith plunged the metal shaft into the heart of it, she felt as though it was she. Tears sprung to her eyes and she found herself unable to breath until once again he withdrew the metal and began pounding away on it again, flipping it over and over, tempering it relentlessly. Now she could feel each stroke of the hammer, it didn't exactly hurt but every time the hammer fell, she sensed it. She began to panic when she saw him readying to plunge the metal again into the white hot fire and the angel put his arm about her. This time she felt only warmth. Slowly she began to comprehend…she was the metal!

At that instant, the blacksmith looked up and straight at her. While his exterior was large, burly and muscular (with rivulets of sweat pouring down him) there was no mistaking his eyes! A tingle rushed up her spine.

Several more hours passed as he worked the metal, alternating between holding it to the fire, beating it down, plunging into the water and repeating the process over and over again. Finally it was done and when he had finished it was a thing of beauty. He had affixed a magnificent hilt bestudded with gemstones and gilded with gold to and upon the flat of the blade he had etched a glorious design. Then he carefully wrapped it in a cloth, picked up another shaft of metal about the same size and walked out of the smithy. Andrea and her angel followed along afterwards, walking just behind him as he wove his way up a winding road to a magnificent castle upon a hill. No one seemed to take notice of any of them and he continued walking, crossing through the main entrance and finally into a glorious throne room that no words could describe. Andrea felt herself begin to tremble. Even the touch of her angel's hand upon her shoulder couldn't quell her tremors. Except for the King who sat upon the throne and two knights upon either side, the throne room was empty. The blacksmith knelt upon one knee before him and presented both the tempered sword and the unworked shaft of steel to the King.

He lifted both in his hands then handed one to each of the knights upon either side of him. With a quick bow, they took up the sword and steel rod and began to circle each other, moving away from the throne, Andrea and her angel. It was over in seconds. The very first blow shattered the untempered steel into shards which flew in all directions. The pieces passed right through Andrea and her angel as if they weren't even there.

The knight returned the gorgeous sword to the King with a bow, who held it aloft in his hands and admired its' beauty. As he turned it this way and that, his smile broadened and with a nod to the worthy blacksmith, he laid it upon his knees.

"The workmanship is exquisite!" said the King to the blacksmith approvingly.

"But what of the other sword, your majesty?" asked the Blacksmith, acting as though the shards were not scattered about his feet.

"Useless," replied the King. "Did you not see how it could not bear up under pressure, how it shattered at the least insult? It was not tempered in the fire nor by the forge, therefore it is useless."

Upon uttering these words the King looked directly at Andrea and beckoned her forward. With her knees knocking, she stepped slowly forward, irresistibly drawn to Him despite her fear. She stood only inches before him and felt his arms go about her in a fatherly embrace.

"You resent and wish to forget the years of your tempering, do you not my daughter?" He said, his eyes kind and understanding. Andrea nodded, her emotions welling up. Her chin fell upon her chest and her shoulders began to heave. Pent up years of hurt, embarrassment and pain welled up inside of her and bubbled over like a gushing fountain. The King's other arm went about her and he held her close as she sobbed and wailed until she felt cleansed inside and out. His hands then went up to cup her cheeks and his wonderful, penetrating eyes searched her own deeply.

"I know every pain," He whispered softly. "I have experienced every sorrow right beside you," Andrea looked at him and suddenly it was the King and it wasn't. It was the blacksmith and the King and upon his body were the bruises that he had shared with her and also taken for her.

"Only the finely tempered steel is worthy to serve in the army of the King." He whispered, bending forward and placing a tender kiss between her eyebrows. "Go in peace, my daughter, and never resent nor regret the tempering of thy spirit."

With those words Andrea suddenly found herself sitting up in her bed staring at the nightstand clock which read 3:00am. *Had it really all been only a dream?* Suddenly she got the distinct impression someone was grinning at her. She turned her head and practically screamed aloud; almost waking Fred up. Next to her bedside stood her angel and this time he had his wings on and his glowing white robes.

He started dissolving like so much sugar in a cup of hot tea.

"Wait!" hissed Andrea, reaching for him. "At least tell me your name!"

"Rupert!" he responded, solidifying just a bit. "And, yes, I have always been by your side, since the moment you were born."

"*Always?*" breathed Andrea feeling both blessed and disappointed at the same time. "Then…why…?" The unspoken insinuation hung in the air, despite everything she had just experienced. Rupert bent down and cupped her cheek in his hand, reminding her again of the King/Blacksmith.

"There are many things I did protect you from, my little one," he whispered, his eyes full of love and compassion for her, "but you will never know of them and that is as it should be. Let it be sufficient to know that all you have gone through has made you the child of God you are today, a finely tempered sword in the hand of the eternal King!"

Finally it sunk in and Andrea bowed her head in submission. Before he faded away from her eyesight she felt his kiss upon her bowed head.

"We are with you always," came his faint voice like a sigh upon the wind and with that, Andrea sunk back into a peaceful sleep; her heart much more at peace than it had been in many years.

CHAPTER SIXTEEN
"Illuminated Miguel"

Miguel is a young man who lives in a very bad part of town. To say that his family is dysfunctional would be in an understatement. The world he lives in is full of violence, substance abuse, and despair. One of the few positive things in his life is a ministry called RYTMO ***((Reaching Youth Through Music Opportunities)*** *which is a Music Technology and Artist Development After-School Program for Youth in Orange County (website:* **www.rytmo.org***). I visited the recording studio and met Miguel who is a gifted graphic artist. I wanted to write a wish fulfillment story for one of the students but none of them were interested in sharing their personal "wishes" with a virtual stranger so I came up with one of my own. If I were Miguel – what would be my wish?*

"Illuminated Miguel"

Miguel walked into the back of the RYTMO house with an internal sigh of relief. This place had become a second home for him. It was a place of peace and refuge, of learning and feeling wanted and appreciated.

"Hey, Miguel!" called out Joey with a broad smile in his direction. "I got some good news for you!"

Miguel walked up closer where he could see Joey beaming at him like a proud father. He held up his hand and in it was an official looking letter. Joey was practically jumping up and down with glee. He thrust the letter into Miguel's hand.

Trying not to let his hand tremble, Miguel lifted the letter and his eyes fell upon the Art Institute logo. Miguel read the letter in silence while Joey rocked with glee up and down on his heels.

"It's a full ride scholarship to study graphic arts, Miguel!" he said, pounding him on the back. "I sent them some of your stuff and a letter and the graphic arts director called me a week ago.

After I told him about you and your brother, and how hard you have both worked and turned your lives around, they wanted to give you a full scholarship! Isn't that cool, mijo?!"

Miguel didn't know what to say. Nothing could have prepared him for this enormous gift. He fought back the tears but did allow Joey to hug him and pound him again on the back.

"Let's get you something to eat and then we can discuss it if you want." Joey practically skipped away muttering out loud to himself over and over "*Miguel is going to The Art Institute! Holy Mackerel!!*"

Miguel stood before the gleaming glass building both excited and terrified. It was his first day of class at the prestigious college with a brand new backpack and laptop that had been donated to him when news had reached the supporters of RYTMO that one of their own had earned a full-ride scholarship to The Art Institute based purely upon the calligraphy and graphics he had created both on computer and by hand. He tried to look calm and casual but inside he was trembling with mingled terror and joy.

"Are you just going to stare at it or ya going to come in?" said a cheerful voice behind him. He turned around and found a pair of bright blue eyes staring back at him and a bemused smile.

"I'm Jessica!" said the pretty blond, sticking out her hand to shake his. "You must be new here!"

"Uh…yes, I am," said Miguel, shaking her hand briefly. Her smile widened and Jessica hooked her arm through his.

"C'mon!" she said, propelling him into the building. "I don't have my first class for another hour. I'll show you around!"

For the next hour Jessica gave Miguel the grand tour of The Art Institute, showing him the registrar's office, classrooms for the culinary institute, fashion design, and last of all, the media arts (Miguel's career choice). Last of all she took him to the cafeteria (located next to the culinary institute's kitchens). Incredible smells were emanating throughout the room and Miguel's stomach grumbled so loudly it made Jessica giggle.

"Let's get you something to eat or your stomach will be interrupting your instructor's first class!" she said. She shoved a tray into his hand and led him to the food counter. "Don't eat anything that has the name Debbie next to it!" she hissed, nodding at a rather disgusting looking side dish made up of what he didn't know what! "She likes to experiment with really weird stuff. I can't believe she hasn't gotten kicked out of the school for food poisoning yet!"

Jessica chattered on happily while piling more food on his plate than Miguel would ever be able to eat. It all looked and smelled incredible and his stomach rumbled loudly again. They took their trays to a table and while he ate, Jessica plied him with questions he couldn't answer because his mouth was too full.

"Hey, Jess!" a voice called out. Jessica and Miguel looked around to see a red-headed girl come towards them with a big smile.

"Are you new?" Beth asked, sticking out her hand to shake his. Miguel nodded his mouth too full to answer.

"I was just showing him around but I have to get to my next class." Jessica said, standing up. "Since you're on break – could you help Miguel find his first class? You guys are both in media arts."

"Coooooooooooool!" responded Beth, giving Miguel a huge dimpled smile. "If you're done eating, get your gear and come with me!"

Miguel was reluctant to leave all the great smelling food but he managed to tuck an apple and muffin into his coat pocket before shouldering his backpack and laptop. He followed Beth down the hall and stepped into a classroom filled with students hunched over their laptops, talking animatedly and admiring each other's work before the instructor walked in.

Beth showed Miguel to an empty seat at a table, helped him log into his new account on the Institute's website and got him set up for his first class before returning to her own seat.

The instructor entered the classroom with his own laptop. Once he got online, he motioned for attention and waited while the students quieted.

"Good day, class!" said Mr. Bledsoe, smiling at all of them. "Before we begin, let's all welcome our newest student, Miguel!"

"Hey Miguel!" the class chorused. Some waved others gave him a "thumbs up".

Not sure what he should do, Miguel nodded in acknowledgement and waved back, smiling shyly. The formalities having been dispensed with, the class began and Miguel, feeling welcomed as never before by a bunch of strangers, felt a warm feeling come over him and an emotion that had come late to him in life: *hope*. His life lay before him and it was filled with hope and promise…and it had all started in a little house in Anaheim that was known as RYTMO where he had been given a second chance and loved just for himself. He would make good on their investment of trust and he would succeed and excel in his chosen field. And perhaps in the near future, he could go back to RYTMO and help some of the new kids there know that there was a different kind of world out there than the ugly, dark and hopeless one they were used to. A world where anything was possible…

CHAPTER SEVENTEEN
"Two Peas in a Pod"

Sandra has become a good friend. She is a middle-school teacher in Florida and lost her sister a couple of years ago whom she misses terribly. Here is her bio: *My sister was born Gloria Jean. For some reason I grew up calling her Jeannie. From a young age she took care of me and kept me under her wing. I don't have a lot of memories of when we were younger because she was seven years older than me. When we were young she could not pronounce my name so she called me Jacquh. As we grew older she learned many things that she passed on to me. She would sit and read to me. She and I were so much alike. Where my younger sisters were very outgoing and noisy, Jeannie and I were the quiet ones. We preferred quiet activities. She learned to knit and of course I had to know how. I made and sold knitted headbands at school that year. She and my grandmother taught me to do hand embroidery and she was the one who first taught me how to make a quilt. When she would learn a new craft I would get a package in the mail. The package always contained a sample of the new craft for me to try. If I liked it then she would send me more. She sewed all of her clothes, including her wedding dress and my dress for the wedding. She would always buy extra fabric so that she could send it to me. I made doll clothes out of them. I loved spending hours just sitting and talking with her whenever we were together. Because she lived 1200 miles away she would call me at least once a month. She called me because she worked double shifts as a nurse.*

I always knew I wanted to be a teacher and when everyone else told me there was no money in it and that I shouldn't pursue it she was there to encourage me. When I would stray from God she was not judgmental, she would talk with me and give me her view on the situation and then drop it. There was no preaching at me. I knew she loved me. Our birthdays were only 10 days apart. I always called her on her birthday; however she was terrible at writing or emailing because she was so busy, but she was never too busy for a call. When her pulmonary fibrosis began to get bad she would still take time to call. When she could barely breathe she would make sure I knew she was there for me but just couldn't talk. Jeannie died in October of 2008 and I still miss those times. She was the only one in my family I could talk to like that. Even today when I am down or not sure what to do I find myself thinking about what she would tell me. I look forward to the day when I meet her in Heaven and embrace her and can talk with her for eternity - Sandra.

"Two Peas in a Pod"

It had been one of "those" days. Sandra's students had been exceptionally rude, uncooperative and snotty all week and she was *done.* It had taken every ounce of strength she possessed to keep her cool and deal with them according to the current parameters. How she longed for the days when principals and teachers could paddle their young charges into better behavior but now the inmates were running the asylums!

It was Friday afternoon and she had a short weekend in which she must cram grading of papers, reading challenges, dealing with family, cleaning house, etc., before it all started over again. *Something had to give.* She felt like a rat on a treadmill! She was burned out and needed some kind of retreat. She lugged her papers, books and laptop to the car and drove home, going over in her head all the things she needed to take care of before she could go to bed. She was exhausted just thinking about it.

When she got home, she checked the mail and found nothing but a brightly colored envelope in her mailbox. No junk mail, no circulars, nothing else. She looked at it closely. Her heart practically stopped when she recognized the handwriting of her sister, Gloria, on the envelope:
"Special surprise inside for my little sister, Sandra"

All the other items in her arms slid out and fell unnoticed onto the pavement as she began to shake. *If this was Brad's idea of a joke, it wasn't funny!* She began to fume. She ripped open the envelope and suddenly the world around her began to spin faster and faster. It felt like she was caught in a tornado but instead of dust, rooted up bushes, and farm animals swirling around her, the wind was glittering like fairy dust. When the whirlwind finally stopped she struggled to catch her breath. Her heart was pounding and she felt dizzy. She looked around and sucked in her breath.

"Toto, I don't think we're in Florida anymore ..." she murmured to herself. She didn't know where she was! She looked around and saw beautiful, undulating meadows as far as the eye could see, weeping willows scattered here and there and in the midst of it all, a lone white clapboard cottage with a wrap-around porch, a white picket fence, geraniums growing in the black window boxes and lacy white curtains blowing in and out of the windows with each sigh of the wind. Under the eaves an orange canary was trilling a beautiful tune in its cage. With a surge of nervous anticipation, Sandra walked up to the front door and raised her hand to knock. Before her fist could meet the door it flew open and she found herself enveloped in a giant bear hug, her vision obscured by a cloud of curly, golden brown hair.

"Sandra! Sandra! Sandra!" cooed the familiar and beloved voice rocking her in strong arms. Tears burst out of Sandra's eyes and she pushed herself back enough to take in the view. Standing there, alive, healthy and beaming was her dearly departing sister Gloria! "*Welcome*!" Gloria bellowed, her grin spreading from ear to ear.

"What, who, when, how-" screamed Sandra looking her up and down over and over again, sounding like a journalist pursuing a story.

"God decided you deserved a weekend retreat quilting, crafting, talking and eating!" Gloria announced, her face beaming. "I have all the supplies we need, all our favorite foods but no television, no phones, and no surly students. Just the two of us! Two peas in a pod!"

"How is this possible?" Sandra demanded, allowing Gloria to pull her into the house by the hand.

"With God all things are possible!" Gloria responded with a mysterious wink, making it quite clear Sandra was going to get no further explanation. She entered the cottage and sucked in her breath at its' cozy charm. White painted floorboards, white wainscoting, and cheerful yellow walls with red accessories here and there, a large quilter's table with two chairs with a quilt already started stretched across it. There was a smaller crafter's table with supplies spread all over it, a cheery fire in the fireplace, and a sideboard loaded with all the comfort food one could want and in the background soothing Christian worship music was playing.

"The Master thought of everything!" beamed Gloria, rubbing her hands with glee. "I've have been longing for this day for over a year!"

At these words, sobs bubbled up outside of Sandra and she covered her face with her hands, remembering the sorrow and grief at losing her sister and best friend in the whole world and the day of the funeral when she had had to say "goodbye".

"Gloria," she choked, unable to express what she was feeling. Gloria's smile didn't fade but her eyes became tender and understanding.

"I know it hurt to lose me, Sandra…" she said, enfolding her sister in her arms again to comfort her. "But I really am in a better place. Heaven is more lovely than I could ever express and doesn't it make it seem that much more real to you now that you know someone you love is there waiting for you?"

Sandra nodded feebly, unable to speak.

"We won't be parted much longer," Gloria said, rubbing her back tenderly, "and you will always have this time together again to look back on and find joy and hope when you need it. Now, dry your tears sit down and let's start! What do you want to do first?!"

With that the sister's sat down and spent what seemed like an entire week talking, laughing, quilting, eating and just enjoying one another's company. Sandra never saw her sister cook anything but every day and at every mealtime there was new and wonderful food all prepared, piping hot and then mysteriously cleaned up so that they could spend their time just having fun.

It all came to end too soon for Sandra and the day arrived when there was no more food prepared and all the craft projects had been completed, much to the sister's satisfaction. It was the best time Sandra could ever remember having, completely free of responsibility, deadlines and interruptions. Just "Sandra and Gloria" time. She was sad to have it end.

"There is one more thing…well, several more things, surprises really, we have for you before you return." Gloria said, sitting her down in a large, overstuffed cotton chintz floral chair.

"What?" asked Sandra, wondering what on earth could possibly be better than the week she had just spent with her sister. Her soul felt thoroughly refreshed but she was still apprehensive at having to leave and face the real world again. The pressure, the deadlines and the students who acted as if they were serving a prison sentence instead of being given the privilege of getting an education that was supposed to help prepare them for life…

"Just wait and see!" Gloria grinned, sitting down in a chair next to her, clutching Sandra's hand to her heart with excitement. At that moment the doorbell rang, practically making Sandra jump out of her chair in fright. For an entire week there had been no noise but the sound of their chatter, laughter, and music and eating. It was so abrupt it really startled her. With a grin and a wink, Gloria went to the door, and flung it open to reveal a tall, distinguished looking executive.

He was dressed in a gorgeous pin-striped business suit, was clean-shaven and had a suitcase in his hand. He walked right up to Sandra's chair, got down on one knee, took her hand in his and in a wavering voice said just two words: "*Thank you!*"

Sandra was speechless and didn't know how to respond. After him came another man, this time it was a professor of literature, then a woman in a nurse's uniform; on and on it went until the room was filled with professionals from all walks of life of varying ages, all standing there and looking down at her with eyes brimming with tears and smiles of gratitude.

"Gloria…" Sandra said, rising to her feet, her voice shaking. "Who are all these people?"

"We have all been students of yours at one time or another or are yet to be," explained the nurse, gesturing to all those around her.

"I don't understand…" Sandra said, although she was beginning to get an inkling of what was happening.

"At one time, during the course of our lives as your students, *(both past and yet future)* you gave each one of us either an encouraging word, a helping hand, or maybe just an understanding smile that made all the difference in the course of our lives," said the first man. "We were on a road that was leading us nowhere but the fact that you gave of yourself to us as a teacher and mentor changed everything. We have all asked for special permission to come here and tell you *thank you* so that you will know that your labor has not been and is not in vain."

"Thank you, teacher!" they all chorused, gathering around her.

Sandra turned and looked at Gloria who was crying and laughing at the same time, beaming at her little sister.

"Never forget, little sister, just how very proud I am of you!" Gloria said and held her close for one last long embrace.

In that moment, Sandra knew that everything was going to be better no matter what the circumstances of life might bring. She closed her eyes…ready to finally part again if only for a little while.

Gloria wasn't really gone, she was just on the other side of the veil, waiting on the day when Sandra too would join her and their reunion would be permanent. For now, it was sufficient to realize that all she did day in and day out at school, in her church and at home had a meaning and purpose much greater than she would ever be able to know this side of eternity and for now…that was enough.

CHAPTER EIGHTEEN
"Mary's Wish"

Mary and I have become good friends...sisters actually as a result of the Life and Faith Concert in Richmond, VA where she arranged for me to meet Amy Grant, the Christian artist whose song, "Fairytale" inspired the idea for my book, The Victor. Mary lost all of her immediately family at a very young age. Her mom and dad both succumbed to cancer when she was only in her teens and then the only relative she had after that was her Aunt Mary Anne and her older sister, who died tragically in a head-on collision when Mary was only 18. Mary is now waging her own battle with kidney cancer and an assortment of other serious medical problems but you would never know it from talking to her. She loves the Lord and trusts Him like a child despite all the physical and financial trials she is going through right now. This is her Wish Story and I hope it blesses your heart as much as it did hers. She is a wonderful woman and needs your daily prayers.

"Mary's Wish"

Mary cuddled her Yorkshire terrier, Luke, close to her cheek. He seemed her only comfort lately. Things had gone so badly; their finances were a wreck, her health was awful and it was a daily struggle to get up and soldier on; keeping her faith intact and trusting in her precious Lord regardless of the circumstances. Sensitive to her every mood, Luke planted doggie kisses all over her face in his attempt to comfort her. *Dogs are truly furry angels sent by God*, she thought to herself.

She got up from the couch, restless at heart and wishing she knew what to do about all the trials that were confronting her. She opened the front door to go outside and stood blinking in bewilderment. Instead of looking out her front door at her front yard, she was looking into the family room of place that had been very near and dear to her heart.

"Is that you, Mary?" called an achingly familiar voice. A head poked around the corner of the wall and Mary felt her heart clench with joy and shock.

"Auntie Mary Anne?" she whispered; unable to believe her eyes. Her aunt's full body came into view with arms outstretched to embrace her. Mary didn't question the how or why; she just flew into the arms of the woman that had meant so much to her over the years and allowed her tears to flow freely. Her Aunt just held her close, rubbed her back and cooed softly into her ear endearments that she had not heard in years.

"Come and sit down, honey," her aunt finally said, leading her to an overstuffed couch. With tears streaming down her cheeks, Mary allowed herself to be settled down, little Luke jumping up into her lap panting and smiling. "Tell your auntie what's on your heart."

It was all Mary needed to hear for the floodgates to open. She had been holding in her emotions so much for so long; trying to be strong but now the "dam had burst". Her tears came out in a torrent as she unburdened her heart and her beloved Aunt sat quietly, her arms about her, letting her vent. When it was over, Mary felt cleansed and lighter inside than she had been in a long time. Her aunt wiped the tears from her cheeks with a gentle smile.

"I can't promise that things will get better while on this side of heaven, sweetheart," she said. "But the Master has heard your heart's cry and knows all of your burdens and wants you to give them over to Him. In the meantime, He has arranged a little present for you as a sign of His infinite love."

She swept her arm out and there stood before her the faces of those she had long missed; her sister, her mom, Linda, and her dad who had all been gone for so many years.

They all came forward to embrace her and she found herself weeping and laughing with joy. They all looked young and healthy and had the light of heaven in their faces. Together with Mary and her aunt they all sat down at a dinner table piled high with all their favorite foods and told Mary what they could of the wonders and delights of heaven and how they looked forward to their next and permanent reunion there in the presence of their Redeemer.

"He truly does wipe away all tears from our eyes," said her aunt, cupping Mary's cheek in her hand. "Just trust Him, child. That's all He desires from you; is your child-like trust and in that you have been most faithful."

"Can't you all stay here with me?" Mary pleaded, holding her aunt's hands in hers. "I feel so alone most of the time."

"My darling daughter," her mom Linda said, coming over and putting her arms around her. "We have never left you really. We are all with you in our hearts and talk to the Master daily about the trials and tribulations that confront you. You may not see us; but we see you and we love you. One day soon we will all be reunited in our Master's kingdom and there will be no more sorrow, pain or suffering."

At that moment, another person entered the room and Mary turned around to find her daughter Linda with a good looking young gentleman. She seemed older and beamed with an inner beauty that bespoke peace and contentment. Mary glanced down and saw a wedding ring on her finger and knew suddenly that this was her baby, Linda, in the future; married and content in heart at last with the man God had chosen for her.

Her aunt stood and slipped an arm about her waist, greeting her daughter and her husband.

"My goodness, child, how you have grown!" Mary Anne exclaimed with a laugh throwing her arms out wide. Linda fell into them then introduced her husband to all in the room as if nothing was unusual at all; beaming at her mom with delight and pride. The couple joined them at the table and they talked long into the night, eating and enjoying one another's company.

Finally it was time for the reunion to end. Her mom, dad and Aunt Mary Anne walked her back to the couch, each of them kissing her face in turn and whispering prayers of blessing over her.

"Remember, Mary…we are with you but even more

importantly; the Master is watching over you and He loves you infinitely more than we!" With those words of endearment in her ears Mary closed her eyes and when she next opened them she found little Luke sitting on the couch and looking up at a tall stranger, his little tail wagging fiercely.

Mary looked up and for the briefest of moments saw the face of her beloved Redeemer, Jesus, smiling down upon her.

"I am with you always, my dearest one," spoke His gentle voice, filling her soul with His peace. "Even unto world's ending. Have no fear."

CHAPTER NINETEEN
"Wistful Wedding"

Veronica is the youngest child and only daughter of Jim and Jan, who live in a small town in Indiana. Veronica was born to them later in life and quickly became the center of their lives. She was raised in a Christian home and gave her life to Christ at a young age. She stated that she wanted to tell EVERYONE about Jesus.

As the years passed, Veronica grew into a very beautiful and intelligent young lady. She was skipped a grade in school because she was so bright. She won recognition and awards for her prowess as an oboe player. Life was beautiful in their home and they were very happy. Life wasn't always easy. Jan lost both of her parents at very young ages to illness. Jim suffered from cancer and was forced to endure several surgeries and numerous courses of treatment and he emerged victorious by the hand of God.

Veronica was a very serious student and developed a desire to go to university in France since the schools there were known to be among the best in the world for what she wanted to study. She had a talent for learning foreign languages and had determined to become a translator. Jim and Jan gave their blessing on her plan and all seemed well until the fateful day when Veronica took time over spring break from her classes at Indiana University to visit the university in Paris, France.

Who knew that while there she would meet and fall in love with a handsome young Frenchman? Shortly thereafter, she flew to France against her parent's wishes to be with her new beau and got married. Jan was devastated. Not only had the daughter she was so close to run off without prior warning but in getting married in France, had denied Jan the joy she had hoped to experience in being part of her daughter's wedding.

"Wistful Wedding"

It was a late Sunday afternoon. Jan sat at her desk finishing up on the papers she still had left to grade and preparing for the next week's lesson. It was still early fall and the leaves had started to change color. A hot, humid summer had given way to cool crisp temperatures but most of the beauty of the fall foliage was lost on her; her heart was still too heavy with regret and grief.

Her beautiful daughter, Veronica had done the unthinkable over the summer. She had "flown the coup" in the most deceitful way possible by flying to France to be with her boyfriend who was a nonbeliever. Jan had been beside herself with hurt, anger, disappointment and feelings of betrayal. Veronica had been her crown jewel and until recently they had been as thick as thieves but all that had changed when Veronica had met *him*. Since the day she snuck off to the airport, Jan had heard almost nothing from her and was frantic. She had no way to get a hold of her and her daughter had cut off all communication. The *coups de grace* came when Veronica had finally contacted her through Facebook of all things to flaunt her wedding pictures in France. That was the moment that all of Jan's most cherished hopes and dreams for her daughter came crashing in. She was devastated. Since the day her baby girl was born she had dreamt of her wedding day only to see it go up in a puff of smoke. There would be no bridal showers to attend, no getting to accompany her daughter to try on wedding gowns, no conspiring together on all the many details that went into planning the wedding of her dreams. No, all that had been stolen away from her because of a civil ceremony several thousand miles away without so much as an invitation to attend. She found out after the fact and it was a crushing blow.

That had been several weeks ago and life had to go on. Jan forced her feelings of loss and rejection to the back burner to meet the demands of the new school year but it still felt like a knife was buried deep in her heart and that she had suffered irreparable loss.

The doorbell rang. "Jim, would you get that?" she called out, trying to finish up the last few papers. She heard Jim's feel shuffle to the front door, then the hinges squeal as it opened and then silence.

"Jan! You better get down here…quick!"

Who could it be at this hour? Jan rose with an effort and made her way to the door. She froze, not believing the site that met her eyes. Was she seeing a ghost?

"Mom!" cried the beautiful young lady, rushing to embrace her mother. All the stuffed down emotions from the past few months rose instantly to the surface. Jan began to blubber like a baby but she didn't care. She rocked her daughter in her arms as they two of them embraced and wept together. "I'm so sorry for all the pain I caused you," she continued, her voice slightly muffled.

"Why didn't you call and let me know, darling?" Jan wept, stroking her hair. "I would have gotten your room ready for you and made you something to eat." At that moment, Gilles, stepped into view. Jan was ready to go into battle but the expression on his face stopped her. He actually looked ashamed and embarrassed. Before Jan could give him a proper dressing down for stealing her daughter away (and all her dreams for her future), he got down on both knees, took her hands in his and kissed them.

"Please forgive us," he said, unable to meet her eyes. "We have done you both a grave injustice."

Jan's mouth opened and shut a few times in total confusion. *Say nothing…hear them out* came the still small voice into her head. She looked at her Jim to see if he had spoken but his gaze was still transfixed on his daughter; every bit as shocked as she was. Veronica joined Gilles on the floor and took her mother's and father's hands into her own; tears spilling down her cheeks.

"I know I hurt you deeply, mama…" whispered Veronica, her bottom lip trembling. "I wouldn't blame you for not forgiving us after the way we deceived you and cut you out of our lives." She looked up and in their blue depths Jan saw a light blazing. "But we are recently changed, mama...Gilles has given his life to the Lord and the moment he did, he felt convicted and told me that we had to return to make amends and ask your forgiveness."

Jan looked over at the handsome young Frenchman and in his eyes saw the same light.

He nodded in affirmation of her daughter's claim and gave her an apologetic smile. "There is no excuse for how we have dishonored you but we hope by returning here we might begin to make up for it a little."

Jan finally found her voice. "Wha-what do you mean?"

Veronica stood up and put her arms about her mother. "Mom," she said in the voice where Jan could deny her nothing. "Would you do me the honor of planning a small wedding and reception for our family and friends here in the states?"

Jan's leaden heart suddenly soared with eagles wings into the stratosphere. "Wedding?! You want me to give you a wedding?"

Veronica's smile was a million watts. She nodded. "Nothing too expensive…God also told me to tell you to give you free reign on all the details, so…have at it mom! Do your worst!" She grinned.

Jan couldn't believe her eyes (or her ears). She looked over at Jim who was now openly weeping. *He would get to walk his daughter down the aisle after all…*

The four of them embraced, laughing and crying and went into the kitchen where Jan and Jim whipped up an impromptu dinner of pasta and salad. Then they got busy on the computer and phone; emailing and calling up everyone they knew to "save the date".

The next few weeks were a flurry of activity. When Jan wasn't teaching class, grading papers or prepping, she was either out shopping with Veronica, on the phone coordinating all the wedding vendors, or making plans for the wedding. She was absolutely exhausted but giddy with joy. Veronica was back to her old self and more than making up for lost time. They had dinner together every night as a family (since they had effectively moved in with them), talking late into the night about their shared faith. Jan cherished every moment they spent together making plans, cooking meals and cleaning up as the two men chatted away in the other room about the Bible, what it was like in France and how he came to give his heart to the Lord. Now that she was a bride, Veronica was taking a special interest in cooking and wanted to learn all the favorite family recipes to make for Gilles. There was no talk of when they would return to France and Jan let the subject disappear; she was having too much fun at the moment to ruin it with thoughts of the two of them leaving her again.

As Jan had always dreamed, her daughter and Gilles agreed to have the ceremony performed in the church where Jan's father had been pastor, The Apostolic Pentecostal Church in Springfield, Ohio. The ceremony would take place just before Christmas and all the important check off items had been completed. They had the Pastor, Florist, Bakery and Photographer all booked and the reception would be held in the fellowship hall afterwards. The only thing that remained was making the hundreds of wedding favors (personalized M&M candies in pale blue and lavender in little organza bags). Gilles and his father-in-law spent many hours running around on wedding errands together without complaint; and were almost becoming inseparable. With each passing day Gilles endeared himself more and more to them as a son.

One night, a week before the wedding ceremony, Veronica came into her parent's room. It was almost 2:00 am and she had been unable to sleep. She crawled into her mother's side of the bed and snuggled close. Jan awoke, her heart instantly swelling with love for her daughter.

"What is it pumpkin?" she whispered, holding her close.

"Mom, I have a very special request I'd like to ask of you, but please don't feel obligated to say "yes" unless you really, really want to do it."

Jan couldn't even imagine what type of request would wake her daughter up in the middle of the night but curiosity brought her to full wakefulness.

"Ask, if I can do it, I will."

"Would you play a clarinet solo during the ceremony?" whispered Veronica. "I know you miss playing and I would really like you to."

Jan's breath caught in her throat which was already constricting with unshed tears. "What song would you like, honey?"

"Jesu - Joy of Man's Desiring."

"I'd love to," Jan whispered, drawing her daughter close into her arms.

Practically everyone in the church had already RSVP'd that they would be in attendance. Most of Veronica's closest friends had been available even with the short notice and had already found matching dresses off the rack in a lovely shade of lavender. Friends and family carpooled to the venue or stayed at local hotels so they could rest up before the festivities.

The day of the ceremony finally dawned and everyone was exhausted as well as a jumble of nerves. The day was sunny and crisp. Jan, her daughter and the bridesmaids sat around the kitchen table as the hairdressers worked their magic and then they all slipped into their wedding day finery. Not long after that, the limousine showed up to bring them all to the church where Jim, Gilles and a few groomsmen waited, pacing nervously in their tuxedos. The guests filed in the pews, murmuring amongst themselves. Jan hadn't slept all night. She was a nervous wreck at the thought of playing the solo during the ceremony. She had practiced religiously since the day Veronica had asked her but she could have used another few weeks. She just hoped she wouldn't cry while she was playing! Just thinking about it gave her a frog in her throat.

Finally it was time. Jan was escorted down the aisle by her sons, Derek and Alexander but instead of sitting down she took her place upon a chair off to the side of the dais and picked up her clarinet.

Please God…don't let me mess this up. She watched in mounting anxiety as the bridesmaids came down the aisle to the Canon in D and then the back doors shut momentarily while the bride and her father got ready for her entrance.

Jim looked down upon his daughter, barely able to keep the tears from sliding down his cheeks. She looked luminous in her white gown. Veronica looked up at him and saw the tears swimming in his eyes.

"Don't cry, daddy," she whispered, standing up on tiptoe to kiss his cheek. That did it. After that, Jim was an emotional wreck. All he could do was nod and tuck her arm into his. The doors opened upon the church Nave which was lit up with candlelight and flowers in lavender and robin's egg blue.

That was Jan's signal. With shaking hands she put the clarinet to her lips and began to play *Jesu Joy of Man's Desiring*. As she played an overwhelming sense of peace enveloped her like a soft blanket. She watched her husband and daughter walk down the aisle arm-in-arm, the notes filling the sanctuary with their magic. Jim gave his daughter to Gilles and the rest of the service was a hazy blur. Jan had gone to sit with her husband and as the couple recited their vows they wept like babies as they witnessed them partake of their first communion together as husband and wife. After the photos were taken the entire church and wedding party went to the reception. After the feasting, photos, cake cutting and garter throwing, Veronica and Gilles approached the table were Jan and Jim were sitting and talking with relatives.

"Mom…dad – could we see you for a minute?" Veronica said, stretching out her hands to her mom. Jan stood and together she and Jim joined her daughter and young son in law in a quieter corner of the reception hall. Veronica and her new husband looked like they were ready to burst with joy.

"What is it sweetheart?" Jan asked, taking her hands in hers. "Is something wrong?"

"No – nothing is wrong. Everything is wonderful! Gilles and I just wanted to thank you for all you've done for us and to tell you that we won't be going back to France for the foreseeable future."

"Oh?" Jan said. This was welcome news. Now that they were all reconciled she would like to see a lot more of her daughter and new son in law.

"We also have a special wedding present for you both." Gilles said, smiling conspiratorially at his new bride. Jan and Jim looked at each other. *What could possibly be better than all this?*

"I'll be returning to college to finish my degree and Gilles has taken an interest to learn daddy's business…there's just one thing…"

"Yes?" responded Jim and Jan in unison.

"Could we live with you until I finish college? That way Gilles can save up enough money so we buy our own place near you."

This time Jan's eyes did flood with tears. She choked, nodded her assent and gathered them both into her arms; it was all she could have asked for and then some!

CHAPTER TWENTY
"A Basket Full of Wishes"

I have two children, Chris and Aimee, and 8 grandbabies (four for each of them). I wish that they all lived close to me so that I could enjoy my babies. My biggest wish is that they be saved and that Chris will find the job that he needs. I would like for my children's dad to open his eyes and believe that there is a God and to be saved. I would love to have a major breakthrough for my book and for it to become a best seller. I would love to find my soul mate. We could go fishing, hiking in the woods, ride four wheelers and motorcycle riding, boating and all the things that make life enjoyable.

I have a secret wish that is hard for anybody to understand but I would love to have such an anointing on my life that people could see it all over me and that God would give me the gift of singing in the holy language of the Angels (singing in tongues) and that people would be saved thru this. Also, the gift of healing so I could lay hands on sick people and have them be healed, especially Mary.

"A Basket Full of Wishes"

Mable sat at her kitchen table eating a bowl of cold cereal for dinner. There was little point in cooking anymore when she was the only one in the house (other than her pets). She was tired from her long day at work and enjoyed the peace and quiet of her home, but it sure got lonely a lot. All of her children and grandbabies lived too far away for her to visit whenever she had the whim (which was always). She stared out the kitchen window at the fading light of day and was surprised to see someone coming up the walk carrying a big box.

Suddenly the doorbell rang. Mable popped up and had it open in a jiffy but the delivery person was nowhere to be seen. She stepped outside and looked all the way around but could see no one nor any sign of a truck. *Well, that was strange!*

She bent over to pick up the enormous box wondering how she was going to lift it much less get it through the doorway but it was very light; almost as if it were completely empty. She managed to get it through the doorframe and plopped it onto the kitchen table so she could get a better look at the return address. She guffawed instantly; this had to be someone's idea of a joke. All it said was "GOD". The ship to address wasn't much better: "MABLE"

She went out the front door again and this time circled her property. No one was lurking about to watch their little practical joke play out. No cars were loitering on the street.

"Harrumph!" Mable snorted. She went back into the house, got a scissors and sliced the duct tape that sealed the box shut. *I bet it's a bunch of shredded newspaper with fake doggie pooh!* She had the flaps open in seconds. No foul odors greeted her nostrils. *So far so good...*She reached in and pulled out a large wicker basket. *"Oohhhhhhhhhhhhh!"* she couldn't help cooing. It was beautiful. The handle was festooned with raffia and real sunflowers, hyacinth, and snapdragons. The obligatory red plaid tablecloth edges peeked out from under the lid. On the handle was a note with handwriting on it.

"ONE AT A TIME" it read. Mable's brow furrowed. *What in heaven's name did that mean?* She opened the lid, reached in and found a single scrap of paper.

"Open the front door." It read. Mable put her hands on her hips in disbelief. Now the basket was giving her orders! She reached in to see what the next note would read, hoping it would be something more interesting…like the winning lotto numbers and the winning ticket…She pulled out the second note and read: "OPEN THE DOOR!!!" This time in all capital letters.

"Well okay!" griped Mable loudly. *Great...now she was talking to a picnic basket!* Might as well play along…she went to the front door and flung it open.

Mable screamed and jumped back. There on the stoop were her kids, Chris and Aimee with their families and all eight of her grandbabies!!

"MOM! GRANDMA!!" They all tumbled in; taking turns kissing and hugging her. Mable was too overjoyed to question them and ushered them all inside.

"I wish I'd a known y'all were coming – I would have fixed y'all something to eat! She exclaimed. The moment she turned around she found them all seated around the table that held the basket. The oldest kids began to pull things out one by one. First it was a large Tupperware filled with hot fried chicken. Next came biscuits, then corn on the cob, then a green salad and finally a plate of Angel Fluff brownies. The house became filled with the aroma of food.

"Where did-" she began to ask then decided not to. Better to play along and see what happened next. She sat down next to Chris who planted a kiss upon her cheek.

"Mom – I have some good news!" he said in-between mouthfuls of chicken and biscuits.

"What is it, baby?" she said, smiling at him in anticipation.

"I just got a great job and you'll never guess where the company headquarters is!"

"Here?"

"That's right! How'd ya know?" Chris replied, his eyes wide.

Mable glanced at the basket. "Uh…a little bird told me." She fibbed.

"They're paying for the relocation and everything! Not only that, but they hired Aimee's husband too so we'll ALL be moving back…and just in time for CHRISTMAS!"

A strange feeling began to come over Mable. She felt this overwhelming desire to cry and laugh at the same time. She glanced at the basket again; somehow it managed to look like it was grinning at her. She enjoyed her family's company for the rest of the evening, talking and laughing until late into the night. Soon they all piled out of the door with several sleepy grandbabies draped over the shoulders of their parents as they called out their goodnights and promises to be all together soon.

Mable closed the door, prepared to do a sink full of dishes only to find that all had already been cleared up.

She craned her neck back and looked up at the ceiling, cupping her hand to her mouth. "Okay, Lord…what next?" she shouted. She jumped almost three feet off the floor and screamed when a telephone began to loudly ring from *inside the basket!* With every jingle the entire thing vibrated violently and began to move towards the edge. Mable dived and caught the basket just as it tipped over; the phone inside still ringing madly. She was almost afraid to answer it.

"Hello?" she ventured, wondering whose voice would be on the other end. *Jesus? Moses? The Tooth Fairy…?*

"Mable?" bawled the voice on the other end in-between sobs. "Is that you?"

"Junior?" she responded, pulling the receiver away to look at it as though his face would pop out of the ear piece.

"Make it stop! Make it stop!"

"Make what stop, Junior?"

"Those black things flying around my house all afternoon shrieking like the devil!" *Get away from me!* She could hear him scream to the things in his house. "Mable, it's like the pit of hell opened up into my living room! There's now here I can hide! The shrieking is terrible and they won't stop pinching me! They keep telling me I'm going to die tonight and go to hell unless you intercede on my behalf!!"

Mable stared at the phone again. "Junior – is this your idea of a sick joke?"

His bloodcurdling scream was the only response she got. She heard the phone on the other end fall to the floor and the voice of her ex-husband pleading. Her heart suddenly became very fearful for him. A warm sensation began to build in her throat, rising higher and higher until it filled her mouth. She opened her arms and mouth wide, closed her eyes and gave in to the song that filled the house and rocked it on its foundations. A joyous song filled with overwhelming power. It was so magnificent she couldn't believe it was issuing from her own vocal chords! The music went into the phone and despite the fact she was no longer holding the receiver to her ear, she could hear her ex-husband quiet plainly regain his courage and order the "things" from his home in the name of Jesus. "Keep singing, Mable!" she heard him yell. "Don't stop! Don't stop – they're shrieking in pain and disappearing! Keep singing!"

Books, vases, dishes, cups and glasses rattled inside the cupboards as Mable's song grew more and more anointed. Junior kept screaming encouragements until finally, after what seemed an eternity, all evil had been put to flight. He returned to the phone, sobbing like a baby. "Mable?"

"Junior?" Mable clutched the phone, shaking, exhausted and exhilarated all at the same time. "Are you okay? What just happened?"

"You drove them out," panted Junior, his voice all atremble. "I don't know where they came from or why but your singing drove them out." He began to sob. "I'm so afraid, Mable. What if they come back? What am I going to do?" He was absolutely terrified.

"Junior – do you truly want them to never come back? What are you willing to do to make sure they don't?"

"Anything!" he screamed. "I'll die of a heart attack and go to hell if they come back! Please, please – tell me what to do!" This is what Mable had been waiting to hear all of her adult life.

"If you pray with me and repeat everything I say and mean it with all your heart, they will never come back again," she promised. She could hear that Junior was convulsed with sobs but also that he was listening very closely. After several moments of silence he answered.

"Okay," he said in a small voice. "I'll pray." Mable then slowly and deliberately led him in a prayer of repentance; unable to resist having him list and name all the things he had done wrong by her and his family. Junior was in no shape to argue or be prideful anymore. He was convinced that if he did not pray at that moment and receive God's forgiveness that all the demons would return and this time they would take him down to hell with them! When it was over Mable was completely drained and Junior was exuberant. “I don’t know why in tarnation it took me this long to come to my senses!” he crowed, jumping up and down.

“Because you are a prideful fool who needed the hell scared out of him!” Mable retorted with a smile. “Junior…it’s been a day. You’re safe now and I need to get to sleep. I’m done in and I have to get up early for my first book signing at Wal-Mart.”

“Okay! Okay!” he said, giggling like a little girl. “I’m going to find my old Bible and start reading, right after I dump out all the booze in the house!”

“You do that!” Mable grinned and hung up. She watched as the basket lid slowly floated down and closed and waited some more. When nothing further happened she shrugged and went to get ready for bed. She slept like a baby that night and rose before the alarm, anxious to see what the basket would do next. She opened the lid but all she found was a bunch of black felt pens, several bottles of water and some snack foods.

She quickly got ready, a bit nervous. She had never done a book signing before. Her local Wal-Mart had agreed to let her bring a small box of her books to sell but had done nothing to promote or advertise the event. Mable had invited everyone she could through email and Facebook but no one had RSVP'd they would come. Well, she’d give it the old college try for an hour, then pack it up and do some shopping. She drove in the early morning sunshine towards the superstore and was peeved to run into a traffic snarl from two blocks away. She made a quick u-turn and found the less known way back to the Wal-Mart but still was perplexed as to the line of cars snaking in to find a parking space. The lot was completely filled. *Must be having some sort of super giveaway* she thought to herself, parking in the employee lot where she had a space set aside for her. She walked into the employee entrance with her box of books, pens, water and snacks, entered the main store just inside the book department and froze. About a thousand pairs of eyes all instantly riveted onto her face and the crowd broke into a simultaneous roar of welcome. Hundreds of camera flashes went off; blinding her.

Everything in Mable's arms crashed onto the floor while her mouth gaped open like a cavern. There was a line of people snaking in and out among the display racks as far as the eye could see. Posters of her book were everywhere with the words screaming out: "MABLE DOTSON – TODAY ONLY SIGNING COPIES OF HER BESTSELLER!" Some of the Wal-Mart employees rushed to gather up her dropped items.

"Good thing you brought a lot of pens!" a young girl smiled at her, placing them back upon the table. "You're going to need them!"

Mable allowed herself to be lead to the signing table. The young girl even had to put the first pen in her hand before she could utter a coherent word. "I didn't bring enough books." She finally managed to observe out loud. The salesgirl smiled at her and gestured to several dozen cartons.

"We've got plenty, believe you me!" she grinned. For the next four hours, Mable did nothing but murmur hello's and autograph her name onto copies of her book. She vaguely remembered taking dozens of pictures with "fans" who bought a copy but she couldn't remember a single thing anyone had said to her. By the time the last book was autographed; she was completely exhausted. The store manager came up to her and helped her from the chair that her butt had been glued to for the past half a day.

"Mable Dotson, I'm a big fan!" he grinned, clutching one of her books to his chest. "I managed to hide one for myself. Would you mind?" Mable looked up to find a good looking middle aged man with salt and pepper hair grinning at her.

"How would you like it autographed?" she asked, unable to tear her eyes away from his baby blues. She glanced down at his left hand…no ring.

"To Thomas," he said as she scribbled upon the page. "…and don't forget your phone # so I can ask you out for a date! Do you like to do out-doorsy stuff?"

Mable looked up at him in shock and then bellowed with laughter. He was so forward but in such a flirtatiously delicious way that she didn't mind. She grinned at him and wrote her phone number down in very large print. Thomas picked up the book, took her hand in his and kissed her palm.

"I'll be picking you up on my Harley!" he said then left to supervise the cleanup of her book signing.

Despite her fatigue, Mable felt exhilarated. She walked on air all the way back to her car and drove home, anxious to open the basket again and see what would happen next. When she walked in the door, instead of the basket all she saw was her well used and beloved Bible sitting open on the kitchen table. A scripture verse seemed to be glowing but before she could look at it the phone rang.

"Mable? Whatcha been doing?" came the beloved voice of her close friend Mary. "Darling – you will just not believe what happened to me today!"

"What?" replied Mable, getting her reading glasses onto her nose so she could read the glowing print better.

"I got a message today to call you and ask you for prayer because tonight was the night God is going to totally heal me of all my infirmities and He wants to use you to do it!"

A thrill went down Mable's spine and she knew the words that Mary spoke were true.

"Well then, let's pray right now!" she said. When she was done they were both praising the Lord and giving Him glory. Mary had felt as though liquid honey had been poured all over her from the moment Mable had begun to pray. She could feel her kidneys renewed, her stomach come back to healthy life, her esophagus healed and the gout in her leg recede. Her entire body was tingling with new life and they both knew that at long last, after years of suffering, God had finally healed her friend.

Mable opened her eyes and was finally able to read the scripture from her Bible: *"Therefore I tell you, whatever you ask for in prayer,* ***believe*** *that you have* ***received*** *it, and it* ***will*** *be yours."* *Mark 11:23-25*

"So who gave you the message to call me today?" Mable asked, rubbing her eyes with fatigue.

"It was a note that came inside this crazy picnic basket that some mysterious person delivered to my house today!" replied Mary.

CHAPTER TWENTY-ONE
"Waterfall Blessings"

My favorite TV program is "Extreme Makeover, Home Edition"!!! My husband and I watch it almost every Sunday night, and most of the time we are in tears by of the program!!

I told my husband, Ron (who is also the Pastor of Living Waters), that I really wish that our church had the resources and finances to do similar things for people in need (primarily from our Living Waters Church family) who live in the Raleigh/Durham/Chapel Hill area!! We have so many families in our church who are in need, and I think it would be wonderful if we could do things like this for them!

We have, in the past, helped members of our church pay light bills and waters bills to keep their power and water from getting cut off. One Christmas, we paid off one family's entire mortgage (it was only a few thousand dollars), and we paid another single mother's mortgage payment for one whole month!!!! My husband has such a giving heart, but recently our church offerings have really fallen down! And we had several missions' trips this year that just took a toll on our finances!

Our first priority as a church is to save souls and preach the gospel, but I really do wish we could help those in need on a grander scale!!!!! – ***Gail & Ron Watts, Pastor and Wife of Living Waters Community Church in Raleigh, NC.***

"Waterfall Blessings"

Gail and Ron sat in their living room before the fireplace with the stack of prayer request cards in their hands. Every week the pile seemed to grow larger as more and more in their body fell upon hard times. One by one they prayed for each need, their hearts heavy; aching with the desire to provide tangible help but unable to do so with continually shrinking resources. So many hurting people in their church family; so many needs…it became almost unbearable sometimes. They finished their prayers together and left the cards on the desk. They would be taken back to church where others would also lay hands upon them and pray for them throughout the coming week as well.

"Honey – it's almost time!" her husband reminded her, sitting down before the television to watch their favorite television show: *Extreme Makeover: Home Edition*. It never failed to touch their hearts as they watched families in desperate circumstances suddenly find their fortunes change when Ty's team of designers and volunteer construction workers showed up on their doorsteps. Gail sat down next to her husband and snuggled up in anticipation of another feel-good episode.

"Oh how I wish they could come to our community and help some of our people!" Gail sighed as the opening credits began. As usual, Ty and his team were on the bus and he was ready to prep them for this week's worthy family.

"Well team!" he said, standing with the remote in his hands. "Today we have a very unusual project that we are going to work on…"

"Hey….isn't that our grocery store they just drove past?" commented Ron, pointing at the television.

"Sssh!" Gail said, holding her finger over her lips. "I don't want to miss anything!"

Ty continued. "Today we're in North Carolina but we're not here to help a single family; we're here to help out quite a few! Since this is our season finale, I thought we'd do things a little differently! Watch this!" Ty flipped on the television and video recorder and instead of a family doing the usual intro of themselves and why they needed help, all they saw was a reflection of themselves in the television screen with the proverbial "deer in the headlights" expression on their faces.

Gail turned to Ron. "What's wrong with the television?" A few seconds later she heard herself say it again but this time it was coming from the television screen in front of her. Ron and Gail looked at each other, then back to the television to find themselves staring back at themselves and then back at one another again.

"How are they doing that? Are you playing some kind of joke on me?" she grinned. Ron shook his head "no" very slowly and deliberately. They looked back at the television and found Ty Pennington grinning back at them with the bullhorn to his mouth. He was standing on very familiar ground…

"Is that our…?" began Ron.

"Yes it is! Oh my goodness!" cried Gail just as Ty's voice came blasting both out of the television as well as their front yard.

"GOOOOOOOD EVENING PASTOR RON AND GAIL WATTS!!" he screamed, the design team behind him jumping up and down with glee.

"It can't be!" stammered Gail. "All these episodes are prerecorded-"

"COME OUT! COME OUT WHEREVER YOU ARE!" screamed Ty again. They could hear the sound of front doors slamming open up and down their street as curious neighbors came out to see what the ruckus was. Gail and Ron began to visibly tremble. They grabbed one another's hands and timidly went out their front door to find the large Extreme Makeover: Home Edition bus parked in front of their house. Gail's knees nearly buckled beneath her. Ty stood grinning at them with not one design team but ALL of the designers. They looked up and down their street and found hundreds and hundreds of people in blue Extreme Makeover t-shirts approaching on foot wearing hardhats. The cameras trained on Ron and Gail to catch their reactions. Their mouths hung open so wide bugs could have flown in and out freely.

Ty walked up to them grinning like a Cheshire cat. "Surprise!" he said, giving each of them a hug.

"But we don't need a house…we're fine!" said Ron, struggling to understand.

"I know!" Ty said. "We got a letter from an anonymous person in Southern California telling us about your wish and how much you love our show. The entire design team and I decided that instead of building just one extreme house for one family that we would create an entire neighborhood for those in your church who need homes!"

At this point, tears began to flood Gail and Ron's eyes and spill down their cheeks. Ty turned around and directed his bull horn to the bus.

"Bus Driver – open that bus!" he yelled. The doors opened and out came at least a dozen families from their church all of which had been in dire straits. They poured out sobbing and laughing, all taking turns hugging their Pastor and his wife. Ty turned back to Gail and Ron. "I understand that each service you pray over every single request." He said.

Ron and Gail nodded, wondering where he was going with this. "May I see them?" he asked, gesturing to their home. Again they nodded and together the three of them went into their family room along with the camera crew. They sat down on the couch and Ron handed Ty the prayer request cards. Ty held them up and looked the Pastor and his wife deeply and seriously in their eyes.

"If it lay within our power to grant any of these requests," he said, his voice soft but earnest. "You can consider them answered. Whether it be getting specialized medical attention from experts, to a new car, home…jobs…I've been given carte blanche by the producers (who are fellow Christians) to do it all. Are you with me?"

Gail and Ron nodded enthusiastically, unable to speak for the frog in their throats. They felt like they had walked into a dream and that an enormous weight had been lifted off their shoulders. Ty put his arm around them. "We want to come to your next church service and make the announcement after the service, if it's okay with you." He emphasized. Ron and Gail looked at one another; their hearts in agreement.

"Okay," Ron gave Ty a hug. "Thank you!"

"Don't thank us, thank the Lord!" Ty grinned.

By the following Wednesday word had spread like wildfire throughout the community. Everyone came to the church service and when it was over Ty stood at the podium with Gail and Ron on either side. "We know times are hard," he said to the congregation. "…and we wanted to help. So if you will all form into lines outside, we'll take down your information and begin working on how to resolve some of the problems, beginning with those who are in desperate need of homes."

To Ty's surprise (and that of his entire design team, everyone who came forward seemed reluctant to accept help for themselves. Instead of listing their own needs (which were many and severe) they told of family and friends who needed help more. Before long Ty and the entire crew were crying; so touched were they at the selflessness of Ron's flock. He and the producers met with Ron and Gail afterwards.

"We've never seen anything like it," Ty said, shaking his head. "Almost to every last man, woman and child…no one wanted to talk about their own needs; just the needs of others who they knew were in worse shape than themselves. So here's what we're going to do. We have the prayer request cards and information about the needs of others given to us by your congregants. We know of at least six families who are about to be homeless so we've made arrangements with the home developer of Briar Creek to donate several of the houses that haven't sold because of the poor market. We're going to take those undeveloped pads and build custom homes for those families starting with…."he flipped through the cards, "Mary and Ronnie Jackson. I hear she also has kidney cancer and some other serious problems as well?"

"Yes," said Gail. "Mary is always the first one volunteering to help and will never take anything in return. She is the most selfless person I've ever met."

"Okay – we'll feature them and the house we build them on the episode while we still build homes for all the others. That way it will personalize the episode more. I don't think she was on the bus with us."

"She's probably all the way out in Middlesex by herself," Gail explained. "Her husband and daughter have to work and take the car with them so she gets left all by herself without television, phone or internet service. She's completely isolated out there."

"Not anymore!" grinned Ty. "Let's go pick her up and surprise her!" Gail and Ron followed him to the bus and jumped onboard.

"I've ALWAYS wanted to do this!" she giggled, admiring the gorgeous vehicle. They drove the hour and a half out to Middlesex as Gail told Ty more about Mary and her plight. They arrived to find the singlewide mobile home in a green pasture. They could hear the sound of two little dogs barking inside in response to the sound of their bus pulling up. Ty jumped out and handed the bullhorn to Gail with a grin.

"Go for it!" he encouraged.

"May I?" beamed Gail, unable to believe he was letting her do the honors. She held it up to her lips.

"Gooooooooood afternoon, Mary Fields Jackson! Come out! Come out! Come out!"

Not more than 20 seconds later the door opened up and two tiny Yorkshire Terriers bolted out and ran to greet Ty, Gail, Ron and the film crew, barking hysterically. Mary came down the steps with a look of stunned joy on her face followed by her husband Ronnie.

"Gail, Ron, is that you?" she cried, holding out her arms. Gail dropped the bull horn and took Mary into her arms. "All your troubles are over, Mary!" she said, holding her close. "God has provided in a most mysterious way! He sent the Extreme Makeover Team as Ministering Angels!"

"Nooooooooooo!" chortled Mary, looking from Ty to Gail to Ron and back to Ty again. "I'm fine! Go help someone in more need!"

Gail turned to Ty. "See? Didn't I tell you?"

Ty came forward, a warm smile on his face and put his arm around Mary's shoulders. "Don't worry about all the others," he reassured her. "Their needs will all be met but you are going to get the featured custom house! Orders from headquarters!"

"Orders from what headquarters?" Mary demanded. She didn't want all the attention when there were others who were in need.

"A-B-C." Ty replied. "Show me the house!" he gestured to the single wide.

"I'm not taking you in there," said Mary. "It's a mess and I haven't mopped the floors!"

Ty grabbed her by the hand and pulled her to the single wide. "C'mon let me see it!" he grinned. His smile was irresistible. Mary gathered up the dogs and led the way in. Ty's tall 6'2" frame came up almost to the top of the ceiling. He had to bow his head to fit inside. He took a look around at the tiny shelter and shook his head at the sad condition of the place.

"Is that mildew and mold I'm smelling?" he said, his eyes beginning to water. Mary nodded. "I poured an entire gallon of bleach into the A/C unit to clear it up but nothing I do works and I just don't have the money to fix this place up. This is all I'll have after the bank kicks us out of our home." She explained.

Ty looked like he was going to break down in tears. "Tell me, Mary, what are your dreams and deepest wishes?"

For the next half hour Mary and Ronnie spoke with Gail and Ron by their side, and just like all the other people in their church, they spoke of other's needs instead of her own. Ty nodded and when Mary was done he unfolded a letter. "The anonymous "tipster" told us that you might not tell us about your own wishes and so they provided a wish list for you," he explained.

Mary leaned forward to peer at the letter but Ty wouldn't let her see it. "So I guess it won't just be one room that is my secret project…" he teased. "It'll just have to be THE WHOLE HOUSE!!! Now pack up your clothes and whatever else you need because while we're building your house we're going to send you on a little vacation. Would you like to know where you're both going?"

Mary and Ronnie nodded, her heart beginning to pound with excitement. Ty grinned at them; he just loved this part.

"Since we're doing multiple homes, we're sending you on a TWO week vacation to…" he paused a very long time; driving them all crazy with anticipation.

"If you don't spill the beans soon I'm gonna have to smack you!" Mary cried, jumping up and down in impatient agony. Ty threw back his head and laughed. He raised his hands in surrender.

"Okay! Okay!" he guffawed, trying to hold it together for the camera. "We're sending you on a two week vacation to Southern California to visit your friend in Orange County!"

Mary screamed with joy and threw her arms around Ty's neck. "Thank you! Thank you! Thank you!" she said over and over again, jumping up and down. Then she began to cry with happiness. Gail began to choke up too and hugged Mary.

Gail then followed Ty into Mary's trailer home and together she, Mary and Ty packed up what few belongings Mary needed for her trip. Then Gail escorted Mary out to the waiting limousine with her little dog, Luke nestled in her arms. Gail and Ty waved goodbye as the limousine sped away to the airport then looked at each other.

"Let's get to work and do some DEMOLITION!" Ty screamed.

Gail clapped her hands with glee, jumping up and down. "Can I have the first swing?"

"Absolutely!" he grinned.

For the next two weeks the Extreme Makeover Construction Crew worked day and night to make the dreams of Gail and Ron's flock come true. Instead of their usual catering service, Ron volunteered his skills as chef and enlisted the help of many in the church and prepared wonderful meals for all the workers and volunteers. The cast, crew and volunteers absolutely loved everything he cooked and thanked him over and over again but he just waved them off with a grin saying it was the least he could do to say "thank you" for all they were doing for his people. Large grocery chains, department stores, pharmaceutical companies, banks and various other businesses from all over the country were contacted and told of the dire needs in the church body. A list was made of those who were sick, without insurance and unable to afford doctor visits or medications, those who had lost their jobs and/or homes as well as all of the other needs. Every single company gave generously and every single need was met in some way or another. By of the two weeks, a new row of homes stood in the Briar Creek neighborhood and the crown jewel was the house that had been custom-designed for Mary. Gail and Ron had been kept away from the job site because Ty and the other designers wanted to surprise them as much as those who would live in them.

The final touches were made to the landscaping by Eduardo Xol and the crew of General Lawn Care and then the signal was given to bring everyone in for the "big reveal". Limousines were dispatched and picked up all the families who needed homes who had been away on Extreme Makeover vacations and last to be picked up from the airport was Mary and Ronnie.

"Gail, hurry! The limo is here!" cried Ron.

"I know, I know but Travis is on the phone! Christen's just gone into labor!" Gail protested, trying to juggle her cell phone, purse and camera as she made her way to the limo.

"Okay, we'll leave for the hospital just as soon as we do the reveal!" Ron said, helping her out the door with her things.

"We'll be there in a couple of hours, Travis!" Gail cried, clambering into the limo. "Mercy heavens, of all days to go into labor!" She fanned herself with her hand. "I wish I could be in two places at once!" She declared to the other passengers. The limo sped off and soon they were parked in front of not one, not two but six other Extreme Makeover buses so their view of the homes could be completely blocked. Barriers had been set up on the street to keep the crowds manageable. Gail got out of the limo and could not believe the amount of people that had shown up to witness the big event. It looked like the entire communities of Raleigh, Durham and Chapel Hill had all come!

Mary clambered out of the last limousine holding the hand of her friend, Marlayne, who had flown back with her from Southern California to witness the reveal.

Ty was working the crowd and getting them revved up to a fever pitch. While he was doing that, Gail was going up and down the line of needy families, hugging each one. Ron stood off to one side speaking quietly to the contractors, who had given of their time, goods and wealth to provide homes for the families, his heart bursting with joy. Finally it was time. Ty gathered everyone in front of the buses to lead the now well known cheer: "BUS DRIVERS! MOVE THOSE BUSES!"

The engines roared to life and one by one they pulled away.

The recipients clutched each other's hands and held their collective breath.

Then they all screamed at once; Gail the loudest of all.

There were six new homes, each as different and unique as the people for whom they were built and every single one of them breathtaking.

"Gail, look! Look!" cried her husband Ron, pointing. He began to sob.

At the entrance to the neighborhood was an enormous water feature complete with lush landscaping done voluntarily by General Lawn Care and designed by the owner, Donnie. It was a waterfall surrounded by enormous boulders and each one had the name of a recipient family carved into it (Hayes, Allen, Winders, Core, Garcia, Ramirez, Gaura, etc.,) but the biggest one had the name of their church: LIVING WATERS.

Gail's arms shot into the air as she collapsed onto her knees in praise. "Thank you, Lord!" she cried, tears streaming down her face. "Thank you, Jesus! Thank you, Lord!"

All of the families followed suit. They all got down on their knees, held each other's hands and lifted them high and simultaneously broke into songs of thanksgiving.

The television crew grew silent, looked at each other then turned off their cameras, got down on their knees, bowed their heads and began to pray. Soon all the volunteers, contractors, tradesmen and onlookers up and down the street as far as the eye could see followed suit. The street became absolutely hushed except for the sound of praise songs that filled the air. The presence of God descended, blessing all. When the singing finally stopped and everyone had risen back up onto their feet they turned the cameras back on. Everyone squirmed in nervous anticipation as one by one each family was led into their new home and told of the provision that had been made for them: free medication and physician assistance for those with chronic afflictions who had lost their health insurance, college tuitions for their children, new cars, debts paid in full, and every single home had been stocked full of food for each family. One by one they were given the grand tour of their homes by each design team that had worked on it. Every detail was perfect for the family for whom it was designed, down to the colors and accessories. Last to go was Mary who was practically apoplectic with anxiety and nervous anticipation.

Ty smiled down on her as the cameras rolled. "We've saved the best for last," he grinned. "We've all been made aware of the physical challenges you have been facing, the loss of your home, no insurance and isolation and I want you to know that we've done everything possible to make things easier for you, starting with your house. Would you like to see it?"

"Ty – if you don't show me that house right this minute I'm going to burst!" Mary bawled at him, jumping up and down.

"Go look at your new house!" Ty yelled and Mary was off and running, dragging Marlayne behind her. Ty followed behind, grinning from ear to ear.

"It's got a wraparound porch!" Mary shrieked, jumping up and down with glee. The large white veranda was covered in white wainscoting (both the floor and the ceiling) and ceiling fans were spaced every five feet. On the porch was a porch swing, rocking chairs and tables and chairs all set with gorgeous china as if they were waiting for a tea party. She opened the large front door with leaded glass and shrieked as soon as she beheld the interior.

"It's my own private bookstore!" The entire front room was a bookstore with cherry wood shelving holding dozens and dozens of books and at the back end was a small counter with a cash register. The sign above the counter said: "Mary's Books & Bakery". Scattered around the generous bookstore were tables and chairs where patrons could read and eat. A large gleaming copper Espresso machine stood in one corner and next to it was a pastry case already filled with baked goods.

Mary jumped up and down screaming and crying at the same time while Ronnie stood by shaking his head in disbelief. Ty grinned but he was also wiping tears from his eyes as Mary cooed and admired all the lovely little details he had put into the bookstore/pastry shop.

"Now you can work from home doing what you love the most!" he said.

"How did you…?" Mary demanded then looked over at her friend, Marlayne, who was grinning sheepishly.

"Guilty!" Marlayne volunteered, raising her hand. Mary hugged her and planted a big kiss on her cheek. "I've got to see the kitchen!" she said and marched off with Ronnie close behind. When she went through the swinging door with the round glass "portal" window she froze and covered her mouth with her hands. It was the most gorgeous kitchen she had ever seen in her life! Paula Dean would have been pea green with envy!! The cabinets were all white bead board and there was not one but two each professional Wolf ovens and two dishwashers. The décor was Country French in blue and yellow with beautiful window treatments to match. It was almost as big as an ice-rink and had a center island that was large enough to seat a family of ten as well as a charming breakfast nook. The cameras recorded every reaction as Mary went from one beautiful room after another, only to discover that not only was the home a bookstore with a bakery, it was also a genuine Bed & Breakfast Inn! Every room was decorated in a different color: sage green, black and white toile with red accents, lavender, Cape Cod blue, beige and white, pink and green and each had a special design scheme. Last of all came her Master bedroom which was all dark cherry wood with beautiful Amish quilts, rugs and a giant fireplace and soaking bath.

"We had to pull some strings to get it re-zoned for you," Ty explained as tears streamed down Mary's face. "Now you can be self-sufficient and always have guests so you won't be alone and lonely." His own eyes were filled with tears as Mary held out her arms and gave him a grateful hug.

"Thank you so much," she wept, her shoulders heaving. "I'll never be able to repay all this kindness! Not in a million years!"

"Also, we've made arrangements for you to see the world's leading Kidney Cancer specialist and a few others so you can receive the best care and the pharmaceutical companies will also be providing you with a lifetime supply of whatever medications you need. In addition, we've paid off the debts so you, your home and your cars are all yours now." Mary nodded then went to hug Gail, who had been standing by the entire time weeping with joy. She embraced Mary and patted her back, bursting with happiness.

Ty then turned to Gail and Ron. "Now it's your turn!" he said. "Time to get back into the limo!" Gail and Ron looked each other, wondering what on earth the surprise was. The limo drove for about fifteen minutes and parked in front of another bus that was hiding the "surprise".

They all piled out and stood in front of the bus that was blocking their view. Ty turned to them.

"Every single one of your church members came up to us and told us of how giving you are and how much you care for them on a personal level and we wanted to do something nice for you. This is the first of two surprises…are you ready?"

Ron and Gail clasped hands, lumps in their throat and nodded.

"Say it with me!" Ty grinned. The cameras trained on their faces.

"BUSDRIVER – MOVE THAT BUS!" They all cried. The bus moved away to reveal their own home.

Gail screamed and collapsed against her husband. "They did our house!" she wailed. They were standing in front of their home which had been completely remodeled and updated. Ty took them inside and let them look around. Every single room had been updated with new window coverings, flooring, carpet, paint and the kitchen completely renovated with professional appliances. Gail ran from one room to the next, sobbing and clutching her heart at the generosity shown to her and her husband. She never in all her wildest dreams expected to receive blessings for herself personally. It was enough that their flock got what they so desperately needed. Ty led them to a new door that led from the kitchen to some mysterious new room that hadn't been there before they left.

"This was one of my special projects," Ty explained. "Everyone told me of how you are always cooking for others and handing out food to those in need so we wanted to do something to help you out with your work. Go and take a look!" He opened the door.

Ron and Gail stepped through and their mouths hung open in shock. It was an enormous food pantry with shelf upon shelf stacked ceiling high with food. On one side was a large meat locker and at was a locking roll up door which made loading and unloading easier. One wall was painted to function as a large black chalkboard where lists could be made but on it were signatures and personal messages from all the people in their church thanking them for all the assistance they had given to them. Ron's head dropped and his shoulders began to heave with quiet sobs.

"Thank you so much," was all he could manage to say.

"We've talked to several large food companies and they have promised to keep this food pantry filled as long as you have needs in your community." Ty added. "Now…we have one last surprise…are you ready?"

"I don't know how much more my heart can take!" Gail declared, fanning her face which was still streaming tears. "But lead on!"

Ty got them all back into the limo and it sped in the direction of their church. There was no bus blocking their view for the surprise lay within. Ron and Gail exchanged glances, wondering what could be up. They clambered out and followed him to the front doors of the church.

"Ready?"

Ron and Gail nodded. Ty opened the doors to the foyer and that was when they saw it. A gorgeous natural waterfall had been built into the foyer of their church with the name LIVING WATERS carved into it. Gail collapsed upon her husband, bawling.

"A waterfall in our church! It's just what I always wanted!"

At that moment her cell phone rang…it was Travis again.

She put it up to her ear, worried that something had gone wrong.

"Mom?" came her son-in-law's voice.

The cameras swung around and trained on Gail who was trying desperately to collect herself.

"Is everything all right, Travis? How's my baby girl doing?"

"Everything is great mom! Christen just gave birth! It's a girl and we named her Abigail!!!"

Gail dropped the cell phone, covered her face with her hands and wailed with happiness.

It was *the* most watched episode of Extreme Makeover Home Edition in its' ten year history.

CHAPTER TWENTY-TWO
"Appointment with Destiny"

Ronnie is the fiancé of someone I hold very dear. Years ago he went through an ugly divorce in which his wife cut off all contact between him and his beloved son when the alimony was cut down by the courts. To make matters worse she bad-mouthed him to the point where his son, Taylor, wanted nothing to do with him at all; a tragic but all too often common occurrence among divorced couples. Ronnie and his son have not seen each other in years and he wishes with all his heart that even if he never see's his son again that Taylor will at least find Jesus as his Savior so they can be together again in heaven.

"Appointment with Destiny"

Taylor sipped from his coffee cup in his local coffee shop, waiting for friends. It was a cold and rainy day in Virginia and he decided to treat himself to something hot. He looked up as the door opened, hoping to see his friends but instead it was a middle-aged man with white hair and what looked like his son. They were talking animatedly and had their arms around each other's shoulders. A knifing pain went through Taylor's heart; a horrible aching longing. He had not seen his own father for many years and while he didn't think about it most of the time for some reason this image of a father and son had dredged up all the pain and resentment he had stuffed down inside him. He didn't want to watch but he couldn't seem to tear his eyes away from the father (who looked so much like his own) and son as they continued to chat and smile at each other and then he had to admit it: he was jealous.

"Why are you jealous?" asked a gentle voice. Taylor looked up in surprise to find a stranger sitting down at his table with him.

"Do I know you?" Taylor asked, a bit taken aback that a total stranger would sit down and invade his personal space so flagrantly.

The man smiled at him. "I hope you will someday," he replied, sipping from his own cup. His brown eyes were warm and friendly but for some reason it made Taylor very uncomfortable. He decided to give him a subtle hint and checked his watch.

"Oh they've been delayed." The stranger informed him.

Taylor's eyes narrowed with suspicion. "Who?" It was almost a challenge.

"Your friends from nursing school," came the calm response.

Taylor nearly dropped his cup. "Now how do you know that?!" he demanded, hackles beginning to rise on the back of his neck.

The stranger grinned at him, unnerving him even more. "I know *a lot* of things," he replied.

Taylor was totally creeped out by this time and decided he had had enough. He picked up his jacket, car keys and cup but when he tried to stand up he couldn't. It was like his butt had been super glued to the chair.

The stranger just smiled benignly at him. "Please stay, Taylor, I mean you no harm."

Taylor still tried to stand up but the chair just rose with him; still attached to his butt. The other patrons were now beginning to stare at him. He sat back down, glaring at the stranger.

"What do you want from me?" he asked. It was obvious he was never going to be let "free" until he had done whatever the man wanted. He just hoped it wasn't something illegal or immoral.

"Your father," the man began, glancing over at the father and son who had just left through the exit. "Do you miss him?"

Taylor's spine stiffened. This was a very sore subject for him. "Did he send you?" he demanded and tried to stand up again, forgetting that the chair was still fastened on. He sat back down with an angry thud. The other patrons glared at him and snickered.

"I sent Me."

Taylor relaxed a little.

"You still haven't answered my question," the stranger gently reminded him.

Taylor crossed his arms, squinting his eyes. "And you haven't told me your name!" he replied.

The stranger smiled at him, it was dazzling. "Can't you guess?" He brought his hands up to take another sip and that's when Taylor saw the wounds in his wrists. He lurched backwards violently and the chair tipped over, spilling him onto the floor with a crash. The manager and several patrons got up to help him, tipping him back upright. His coffee had spilled all over his shirt.

"Could you get him a replacement drink?" said the stranger. "I'll buy, one Venti Carmel Macchiato, if you please."

"Of course," said the manager, eyeing Taylor with a look that said he really needed to have a lot more caffeine in his system.

"Why me?" hissed Taylor, aggravated. "I mean, it's not like I've had anything to do with You all these years…or my father!"

"Because he has been praying earnestly for you, Taylor, *that's* why I'm here," replied the man, "and I *ALWAYS* hear the cries of a sincere and contrite heart. Time is very short; I'll be returning soon and I thought you might like to get your life in order before I do so."

The words struck terror into Taylor's heart. "Returning? For real? How soon?" he whispered.

Jesus leaned forward, taking his hands into his own, His eyes intense. "*Very, very soon.*"

Taylor gulped and even though he was beginning to tremble uncontrollably, the hands which held his own were comforting somehow.

"I love you, Taylor." Jesus said, looking at him affectionately. "I know you have been in a lot of pain over the divorce and have grown to hate your father, but that is really your mother's doing isn't it?"

Taylor nodded, finally admitting to himself the truth of the matter. Deep down inside, he had always known that his mother's actions and bitter words had been the poison that had killed the relationship he had had with his dad; he hadn't seen or spoken to him in years.

"I can feel the ache in your heart," Jesus said, his eyes swimming with tears. "It's the same ache I have over missing you. Let me into your heart; I alone can heal your wounds and reconcile you both to each other as well as My Father."

Taylor's eyes filled with tears, his heart convulsing with emotion. "*You* miss *me*?" he whispered. "The God of the Universe misses me? Why?"

"I created you to have fellowship with Me. How could I not long to be reconciled to you? I died for the privilege!"

Taylor stared at him, finally comprehending. "Wha-what if I choose not to?" he asked, his eyes wide with fear.

A look of abject horror passed over Jesus' face and for a brief instant Taylor could see the eternity that awaited him should he reject the Savior's gift. "It's not a punishment," Jesus explained. "It's just the only other alternative if you want nothing to do with Me. I would much rather have you with Me, Taylor..." He added softly.

Taylor could tell that he really meant it. His heart began to soften. "Okay!" he said abruptly, making his decision. "What do I need to do?"

The smile that Jesus gave him lit up the room. "All you have to do is ask Me. I don't come in uninvited."

Taylor squirmed, then shook off the inner voices that were arguing with him to think it over, delay and refuse. He looked the Savior squarely in the eyes. "Jesus, please come into my heart. Heal me and reconcile me to You and my father."

Jesus grinned at him. "I thought you'd never ask!" he exclaimed. To Taylor's utter amazement and shock, the winsome man before him shrunk down to 3" height onto the table. He walked straight up to Taylor's chest. Taylor looked down and gaped when he saw a little door propped open. Jesus waved up at him and stepped into the door leading to his heart, closing it after him. A sensation of warm liquid honey began to spread outwards from his chest into the rest of his body. The black cloud and heaviness that had lain upon him for years fled away and in its' place was overwhelming joy and peace. Taylor stood to his feet, threw back his head and crowed. Everyone in the coffee shop stopped their conversations and stared at him. He didn't care. He dug into his pants and pulled out his cell phone; looking for a number he had not dialed in a very long time. His hands were shaking as he listened to the phone ring.

"Hello?" came the voice on the other end of the phone. "Who's this?"

"Dad? It's me, Taylor…dad…please don't cry. Listen, you're never going to believe this…"

CHAPTER TWENTY-THREE
"A Full Quiver"

I am Carrie, 37 married to Scott, 39 (he is an adolescent Hodgkin's cancer survivor). We have been married 16 years this month and met on what would have been my high school graduation day in June of 1991. He had just finished his treatments about 3 month prior. I had always dreamed of a house full of kids when I was a teen but that was not in the cards for me as I married my best friend who is sterile from his cancer treatments. Scott loves children but has kept himself guarded over the years. We just completed a cycle of fertility (IVF) treatments this spring that ended in a miscarriage in week two. We learned my body cannot handle the meds and have decided to donate our 3 frozen embryos to another couple. Instead we have moved forward with foster to adopt. I am still believing that God will heal my husband and I will bare for him his heart's desire: his own flesh and blood child some day.

This gift of life will be more than a gift to just Scott and myself, his family was very excited about the possibilities and just as disappointed as we were this Spring as his brother Darryl, his daughter Emily and son Alan all wanted a chance to name the baby.

I have been a "Hannah" for several years- thanking God for what I know He is going to do, God's timing is perfect and I will wait on Him.

"A Full Quiver"

Carrie and Scott walked hand in hand through the local mall, discussing the Foster/Adopt orientation they had just attended. It had been an emotionally draining experience, discussing the real life situations of most of the children that were available for adoption. Drug babies, children either abused, neglected or both to varying degrees. The questions on the type of children they were willing to take were equally if not more disturbing. As they walked past the display of the Pottery Barn Kids store, she turned her head. It was getting harder and harder to see children's bedding, children's clothes, families with young children and even worse, pregnant mothers strolling past them; the ache in her heart growing to a sharp pain…but baby showers were the worst. She felt like Hannah from the Bible despite knowing that the conditions which had led to their infertility were the result of her husband's battle during his adolescence with Hodgkin's cancer. The treatments had left him infertile and despite all their efforts to conceive using modern medical techniques, they had run into a wall. Short of a miracle, they would have to go the foster/adopt route and that was fraught with an entirely new set of challenges.

"Want to get some dinner here?" Scott asked, beckoning to their favorite eatery.

"Sure" Carrie shrugged, not really hungry but knowing her husband was. She peeked at his face under her lashes and could see the depression and resentment lurking there. He tried his best to cover it up and make the best of things, but Scott knew how much their infertility situation was hurting his wife and it made him feel guilty and resentful despite himself. *Why them? Why this?* He thought of all the people in the world who had no business getting pregnant and having babies and it just seemed so unfair. They would be great, loving and responsible parents…*why of all things was this denied them?*

He suddenly looked up to see a little child staring at him. She couldn't have been more than 4 or 5 with curly brown ringlets, inquisitive deep green eyes and freckles.

"Hi!" she said, smiling shyly at him.

"Uh, hi." Scott replied, not knowing what else to do. He looked around the restaurant to see if he could find the parents of the child. It wasn't safe to let kids wander by themselves anymore…

"Where's your mommy and daddy, honey?" Carrie asked her.

The little girl giggled. “You’re funny!” she said. Without warning, she climbed up onto Scott’s lap, took her chubby little hands, and pressed them to his cheeks. They stared intently at one another for a moment. “Don’t be sad,” she cajoled him.

Her words struck a place deep inside Scott’s heart and almost on cue; the tears began to pour down his cheeks. A strange feeling began to come over Carrie; not alarm, not fear, but a thrill.

The little girl wrapped her arms about Scott’s neck and snuggled into him. “Don’t be sad, Daddy,” she repeated.

“What did you call me?” Scott whispered his eyes large with alarm.

“Daddy!” she said, smiling coquettishly at him.

Carrie looked around the restaurant but instead of tables, chairs, waiters and diners, she found herself transported to a lovely park-like setting. All around them as far as the eye could see was a beautiful landscape filled with trees, flowers, butterflies and children playing with abandon.

“Scott,” Carrie nudged him to look up for he had been unable to tear his eyes away from the little girl who continued to stare at him. “I don’t think we’re in Kansas anymore!” she whispered hoarsely.

Scott suddenly noticed the change in venue. “Where are we?” he wondered.

The little girl jumped up and down, clapping her hands with joy. “Heaven! Heaven! Heaven!” Then she grabbed both of their hands and ran to what appeared to be a real grizzly bear.

“Teddy!”She squealed, launching herself before Scott or Carrie could stop her. They watched first in horror and then disbelief as the large bear rolled over onto its’ back to receive a belly rub from the little girl.

Scott and Carrie couldn’t believe their eyes. *Were they having a joint hallucination? Had they died in a car accident on the way to the mall? What in heaven’s name was going on?*

The little girl ran back to fetch them and pulled them towards the bear which still lay prone on its’ back like a pet dog.

"Rub him!" she instructed them. When neither responded, she took Carrie's hand and put it on the bear's belly. Instead of coarse smelly fur full of bugs it was warm and soft like a real-life stuffed Teddy Bear.

"What do you think you're doing?" Scott hissed at her. Carrie grinned at him despite herself.

"Try it!" was all she could say.

"Try it, daddy!" encouraged the little girl. She placed his hand on the bear's belly. He jerked it away, startling the bear. Its face screwed up and it almost looked like it was going to cry.

"You hurt his feelings," the little girl accused. She patted the bear. "It's okay, Teddy, don't be sad. He's just scared of you is all…"

As if understanding every word, the bear looked from her to Scott and back again, then put on his large cold snout into Scott's hand and gave it a gentle nudge.

"Pet him! It's okay!" the little girl said. Scott finally did as he was asked. Satisfied at last, "Teddy" lumbered off in search of others distractions.

"Want to see where I live?" the little girl asked them, pulling them forward.

Scott squatted down and Carrie followed suit. He looked the little girl deeply in the eyes.

"Please tell me the truth, now," he said, in his gentlest voice. "Who are you and where are we?"

"I already did! Why don't you believe me?" she replied, her blue eyes round and serious.

Scott tried another tack. "What is your name?"

"Sarah," replied a gentle male voice behind them. "Sarah Hannah Hancock."

Chills went down both their spines as they turned around to see who the voice belonged to.

"Jesus!" squealed Sarah and threw herself upon Him. He cuddled her close for a moment then turned to regard Scott and Carrie with a gentle smile.

A million questions sprang to their throats but died upon their lips as Jesus continued to look at them. His eyes were profoundly deep and filled with love for them.

"I know thy heart's deepest longings and regrets," He said, taking their hands into his own. They looked down and began to tremble when the saw the nail prints. Jesus continued. "This will indeed be a fiery trial and one that shall purify thy souls as nothing else but know that all I do for you, as my children, I do solely for thy sakes." He glanced down for a brief moment at little Sarah cuddled in His arms. "More than all else on earth, including thy devotion and service, I desire that you trust Me as a child, just like your little Sarah here."

"How…where…" stammered Scott, staring at the little girl who looked back at him with a shy little smile.

"She's the baby I miscarried!" Carrie exclaimed suddenly, kneeling down beside the Savior. "Aren't you?"

Sarah nodded and wrapped her arms about Carrie's neck so she could embrace her. She did so, her heart nearly breaking.

"I gave you a child but her dwelling was always destined to be here with Me; safe from the world, sin and all harm." Jesus told them, rising and setting Sarah on her feet. His put his arms about them and drew them close. "I have much invested in both of you," he smiled. "Because of your great desire to be parents and your unselfish love, I have appointed both of you as rescuers for my little ones that have been born into a world of fear, darkness, abuse and neglect. It will not be an easy road and fraught with many of its own unique heartaches." He cupped Carrie's cheek in his hand. "Do not expect to receive rewards in this lifetime, my child, but know that because you cared for My little ones and taught them of Me that My blessings will be ever upon you. *Whosoever gives even a cup of cold water to one of these little ones because he is my disciple, I tell you the truth, he will certainly not lose his reward." (Matthew 10:42)*

He looked at Scott. "I know thou art angry and resentful," He put his hand on Scott's shoulder which began to tremble. "Never try to hide your feelings from Me, my son," he said. "It separates us from one another and that I cannot bear. Come to Me with all your anger, sorrows and regret and you will find restoration."

Scott's head hung and his shoulders began to heave with all the pent up sobs and sorrow he had stuffed down inside for so many years. The tears were cleansing and left his heart feeling lighter. He looked down to find little Sarah reaching up for him. He lifted her into his arms and cuddled her close.

"All better now, daddy?" she asked.

Scott nodded and gave her a little smile. "Much better," he said, meaning every word. He put her down and looked back upon their Savior.

"Remember the commission I have entrusted to you," He said, beginning to fade from their view along with their little daughter. "Feed my little lambs, clothe them… love them…for in so doing, you do it unto Me."

CHAPTER TWENTY-FOUR
"Cabin Fever"

Hi, My name is Deana, my husband is Donnie, we stated dating as teenagers and got married when we were both nineteen years old. We are both in our late 40's now. We have 3 daughters, Brook, Alex and Lindsey. Brook has a three year old son, Noah Lee.

My wish is that we would all be very close and I want Brook, Alex and Lindsey to have a heart for Jesus, to love him and serve him. At this point in their lives they go to church some, but they are still not as interested in Godly things as much as I wish they were. I pray that the Lord will lead godly friends and young men into their lives. I want them to marry men that love the Lord, and give me more grandchildren, and never move too far from home. Noah calls me Nanny, but I called one of my grandmas Maw-Maw, I spent a lot of time with her growing up and she showed me so much unconditional love that if I am half the grandma she was I'll be a good one.

"Cabin Fever"

Deana and her husband Donnie watched with great anticipation their daughters open up their Christmas presents before their brick fireplace. Besides all the usual books, movies, games, small electronics and clothing, this year, they had decided to do something extra special.

"Can we open them now, mom?" Lindsey the youngest groaned, her delicate hands prepped to rip open the package, the last to be opened. Her sisters, Alex and Brook had exact copies and they too were chafing at the bit.

Little Noah smacked the package up and down with his little arms as he sat upon his mom, Brook's lap. "Open! Open!" he said.

Donnie grinned at his large brood. "Okay, on your marks, get set….let her rip!"

The girls ripped open the packages and took out the various items one by one with bewildered looks on their faces. Out came mittens, woolen neck scarves, and packets of instant hot cocoa. Donnie and Deana grinned and nudged one another, enjoying their daughter's momentary confusion. They looked at one another, their noses and brows wrinkling.

"Keep digging, girls!" Deana encouraged, knowing that the Pièce de résistance still lay within the package.

"There's nothing else in here except a folded piece of paper!" Lindsey complained, pulling it out. She unfolded it and her eyes went wide...then she screamed.

Brook and Alex followed suit, unfolding their own papers and reading quickly.

"We're really going to have our next Christmas in a log cabin up in Ashville?" Alex exclaimed, jumping up and running over to hug her mom and dad. "WE'RE GOING TO HAVE A WHITE CHRISTMAS!!!" The significance of the gifts finally clicked in and then all three girls were screaming and jumping up and down with glee then taking turns to hug their grinning parents.

"Are we there yet?" Lindsey groaned, straining her neck to drink in the fresh air from the open car window. Motion sickness had overwhelmed her and the winding mountain road was making her stomach do flip flops.

"It's freezing in here!" Brook sneezed, adjusting little Noah's blanket over him. "You're going to make us all sick!"

"Well if I need to barf would you rather I do it out the window or in the car?" Lindsey retorted.

"We're almost there, girls! Just hang in there for ten more minutes!" Donnie said over his shoulder. This was met with another series of groans.

"Not off to a great start, are we?" commented Deana in an aside to her husband. Donnie grinned at her.

"Just wait until they get a look at the cabin!" he replied.

The words were barely out of his mouth when there came a chorus of "ohhhhh's and awwww's" from the back seat. The SUV crested the hill and sitting at the top like a wooden castle stood a magnificent three story log cabin. The interior of the car fell completely silent as the passengers gaped in open-mouthed awe. Even little Noah was quiet. Donnie pulled the car to a stop inside the three-car garage and everyone piled out to ogle the magnificent cabin.

The logs which formed the structure were enormous and fit together like Lincoln logs. Their color was a deep honey gold and the roof was green aluminum with heating elements that would keep the snow from building up. Large windows were on all sides with hunter green decorative shutters and window boxes filled with holly and poinsettias'. The large front door was a cheery Christmas red and already had a garland wreath upon it.

Deana shivered. "The temperature is dropping fast!" she muttered to her husband. "We better get our stuff inside soon before the sun sets!" As if to punctuate her comment, a few stray snowflakes drifted down from the cloudy sky. "You didn't happen to listen to the weather forecast for Christmas week by any chance did you?"

Donnie shook his head. "Too busy with last minute things at work and church!"

"Girls, get Noah into the house and start helping me unload the car!"

When they all walked into the cabin for the first time their mouths all got a second airing when their collective jaws dropped in unison. The entryway brought them into the great room. Their eyes traveled up the three stories, following the large hand hewn beams that arched high over their heads.

"Mom…look!" pointed Alex. Deana followed her finger to the large stone hearth already crackling with a welcoming fire. Upon the heavy timber mantel lay Christmas garland festooned with cinnamon twigs, scented pine cones, dried orange slices as well as Christmas stockings. Brook carried Noah up closer to get a better look and squealed with delight.

“They have our names on them already!”

Everyone run forward to admire the beautiful stockings fashioned in deep maroon, chocolate brown and hunter green suede and embroidered with gold thread.

“Look!” pointed Donnie, seeing the 12’ Christmas tree in an alcove designed just for that purpose. It was all lit up with tiny white lights but the owners of the property had left the decorating to their house guests. Boxes were piled up around the base filled with gorgeous, rustic ornaments and of course a gorgeous star topper.

“Can we decorate it tonight?” Alex asked.

“Sure just as soon as we get settled,” smiled Deana.

The family formed a “bucket brigade” line from the car to the front door and swiftly emptied the SUV out of luggage and wrapped Christmas presents. The snowfall grew heavier as it grew darker so it didn’t take much cajoling to get things inside as quickly as possible.

They then all took turns lugging their respective luggage upstairs to the bedrooms. With each new discovery there were renewed exclamations of awe for the gorgeous rooms. Each one had a different theme and color scheme. The master bedroom was Wedgewood blue and white and decorated like an icy fairyland. The furniture was all white with crystal knobs; the large white sleigh bed was covered with a white flannel duvet with crystal snowflake embellishments. The hardwood floor had a large white fur area rug and on one end of the enormous room was a white mantled fireplace with logs already stacked up and ready to be fired. One entire wall was taken up with a large picture window that looked out onto a balcony and beyond it the Blue Ridge Mountains. Donnie and Deana stood gaping in childlike wonder at the sheer beauty of the room. There was a white flocked Christmas tree already decorated with chandelier crystals, opal bead strings and tiny Venetian style mirror ornaments.

"Wonder what the bathroom looks like?" commented Donnie. Deana needed no further urging. She dropped her suitcase and ran into the bathroom.

"Oh myyyyyyyyyyyy…" she cooed. The bathroom was in blue and chocolate brown with white marble counters, gleaming white wood cabinets and an enormous Jacuzzi soaking tub big enough for two. It was already partially filled with water and had pink rose petals floating in it.

"They thought of everything!" Donnie commented, shaking his head. Suddenly squeals of delight came from the other rooms. "Let's go see!" he said, grabbing Deana's hand.

They found Brook in the doorway of the room she would share with Noah, also staring in wonder. Her room was a latte color with cream and gold accents and also had a large picture window but no balcony. There was another fireplace and a private bathroom as well. Noah was, however, oblivious to the décor, he only had eyes for the enormous brown Teddy Bear with the red ribbon sitting on the floor that was as big as he was and the miniature Christmas tree that had a LGB train circling around it.

Donnie and Deana made a quick tour of the other bedrooms, all just as enchanting and gorgeous as the next until they finally wound up in the huge kitchen. It had a large center island with barstools on one side and double sinks on the other with a large wrap around counter behind with. Although it was the biggest kitchen she had ever seen, it was still cozy, warm and inviting. She opened up the refrigerator to put away their groceries and found it already filled with all their favorite foodstuffs.

"How did they know what we like?" asked Alex, peering inside.

"I have no idea," Deana replied, equally amazed. She closed the frig and looked around and found a large Crockpot on the counter that had delicious smells coming out of it. She lifted the lid and sniffed…it was heavenly. "It's Beef Bourguignon."

They needed no further urging. The each grabbed a plate, piled it high with stew and homemade biscuits and sat down to eat together with soft Christmas music playing in the background. (Donnie had found the sound system and programmed all their favorite music). After cleaning up from dinner, they hurried into the great room to begin decorating the tree.

"Dad! Look at all the snow!" Lindsey pointed. Everyone turned to look out the large picture windows. It looked like a blizzard was going on outside. It was a bit intimidating to see how fast it was piling up outside the window.

"Well, we're definitely going to have a white Christmas!" he remarked, trying not to show the concern in his own voice. At the rate it was coming down, there would be no getting out of the cabin for a good number of days without outside help. For the time being they were warm, fed and content to decorate the tree. After the long drive, unpacking and great dinner they were all sleepy and decided to go to bed early.

Brook and Deana took little Noah up to the bathroom in their room and were delighted to find all kinds of tub toys waiting to be played with. Deana and Brook exchanged glances.

"Is this cabin magical or what?" Deana grinned. Noah jumped up and down, anxious to get into the tub and play with toys.

Once he was bathed, put into his jammies, read a story and tucked in, Brook took her own bath and joined him in the luxurious bed. Alex and Lindsey soon followed leaving Donnie and Deana alone to enjoy the crackling fire, twinkling tree and snowfall, cuddled into each other's arms on the brown leather sofa with cups of cocoa.

"It sure is coming down!" Deana remarked, trying to disguise the concern in her voice. The snow had piled up a third of the way up the huge picture windows with no signs of letting up.

"Yup," replied Donnie. He had no idea how they were going to dig their way out if they got snowed in. They snuggled closer in each other's arms, enjoying the peace and each other's company as well as the magic of the falling snow.

"Mom...dad...you better come look at this!"

Deana and Donnie bolted upright in bed; still groggy. They looked out their second story window but all they could see was white. They donned their robes, slippers and hurried down the stairs to find their children and grandson staring out the large picture window. It too was completely white.

"We're completely snowed in!" Lindsey exclaimed. It's up past my bedroom windows too!"

"Has anyone gone up to the third floor yet?" Deana asked. Everyone shook their heads "no". They turned around and ran up two flights of stairs to the top floor which held a pool table, pinball machines, large flat screen television, boxes and boxes of puzzles and board games. In another room was a sauna and exercise room. It also had a large picture window but no balcony, just a solid picture window. The snow came halfway up the window.

"O...M...G!" Brook, Alex and Lindsey said in unison. They could see the leaden gray sky and the snowflakes that were still coming down.

"We're going to be buried!" Deana said, her voice betraying her alarm.

"We're still in the Lord's care," Donnie said, hugging her. "We have heat, electricity, and food to last us for several days. We'll be fine! Think of it as an adventure!"

"I hungwee!" Little Noah piped up, tugging on his mom's robe.

"Well, let's get some breakfast going, girls!" Deana turned and went down three flights into the kitchen. She got the coffee started first and while Donnie set the table, she and her daughters made pancakes, bacon, eggs and fresh berries. After cleaning up, they all took turns straightening up their rooms, taking showers and getting dressed. Although her daughters had all stopped believing in Santa Clause years ago, the arrival of little Noah had brought all the "magic" back. Christmas this year promised to be especially wonderful and they were all determined to bring the legend of Santa Claus and the birth of Jesus alive for him.

The day was filled with baking and preparation for a very special Christmas Eve dinner of Turkey and all the fixings. It was rare when they got to spend hours of uninterrupted time with each other; usually everyone was running around and grabbing meals separately. It was Deana 's dream to have them all together under one roof for several days! Once all the baking and meal prep was out of the way, they gathered together on the third floor to check on the snowfall and to play some games.

They climbed the stairs with sense of dread, wondering how high the snowfall had gotten. It was halfway up the third story window. No one said anything and decided it would be a good distraction to play together. There was nothing they could do about it, after all. First it was a game of pool, then they moved on to the pinball machines and last of all they enjoyed a highly competitive game of Monopoly before it was time to actually get dinner on the table. Donnie tried to put on the stereo system to play Christmas music but for some reason it wouldn't work.

"We'll just have to sing our own carols!" he told his family with a shrug. Thus began a friendly competition amongst his girls to see who could out sing the other. The kitchen became filled with the sounds of their beautiful voices and laughter; and it was infinitely better than any recording he could have ever listened to.

When they all were ready to sit down to eat, the lights suddenly went out. Fortunately there were candles in hurricane vases on the table so instead of electrical light the table was gently illuminated by glowing candles. A hush came over his family and a profound sense of Jesus' presence filled the room. Even their daughters, who had somewhat fallen away seemed to sense it. Without his having to ask, they all bowed their heads so he could say grace. They ate their Christmas dinner in subdued silence while Donnie read from the Bible about the birth of Jesus in between mouthfuls of turkey, mashed potatoes, green bean casserole and mulled cider. His daughters listened intently as he described the conditions that Mary had to give birth in at the time, how there had probably been a lot of controversy over the circumstances surrounding her pregnancy and the Old Testament prophecies that foretold the birth of the Messiah in detail centuries before it happened. As if on cue when he was done, Noah yawned and rubbed his eyes.

"Time for bath and bed, little man! Santa Claus is coming tonight!"

"Santa! Santa!" he smiled. Brook picked him up and carried him to the bathtub while Deana, Donnie and the remaining girls helped to clean up, still singing Christmas Carols. A wonderful sense of holiday anticipation descended upon all of them in the candlelit kitchen as they sang, washed, rinsed and dried dishes by hand.

"It feels just like it did when we were little, doesn't it, Lexie?" Lindsey grinned.

Alex nodded, her eyes sparkling with anticipation. "I can't wait to wake up tomorrow morning and see what happens next!"

"What do you mean?" Deana asked, her curiosity piqued. The girls turned and looked at their mom.

"Can't you feel it, mom?" Lindsey said. At that moment Brook came downstairs after having tucked Noah into bed with threats of Santa Claus not coming unless he went to sleep pronto.

"The Christmas spirit!" Brook answered for her sisters. She hugged her arms about herself and practically skipped into the kitchen. "This cabin is filled with it! I think it's magical!"

The women finished cleaning up in the kitchen and now it was time to set out the cookies for Santa, enjoy some cocoa before the tree and wrap some last minute "Santa" presents they had kept hidden from Noah.

As the five of them worked to wrap the packages, the Christmas music suddenly came on.

"See, what did I tell you?" Brook said, with an arched eyebrow. "Magic!"

At that moment, the music changed from "Let it Snow, let it snow, let it snow" to "O Holy Night" in the middle of the song. They all fell silent.

"I think God would beg to differ with your conclusion!" Donnie smiled.

His daughter's exchanged glances with another; a little freaked out. From that moment on, the only Christmas music that would play was the blatantly religious kind as though God were determined to make Donnie's point. One by one the girls went upstairs to their respective bedrooms fully expecting to dream of sugarplums dancing in their heads. Donnie and Deanne stole some precious "Christmas Eve" time together, just the two of them in front of the glowing fire and the sparkling tree.

Deana laid her head upon Donnie's shoulder and sighed deeply. "I think this is going to be one of the most memorable Christmases we've ever had. I'm not sure what to expect next!"

"Me too," said Donnie. He turned to his wife and took her hands within his own. "I really think that whatever we prayed for tonight…it would happen."

Deana 's eyes filled with tears as she nodded. "Me too!" They grasped hands and bowed their heads. "Dearest Lord, we thank You for bringing us to this wonderful place that is filled with Your holy presence. Lord, You said that whatever we ask in Your Name in faith You would answer and tonight, Lord, as we honor the day of Your birth, we pray for our daughters and little Noah. We pray that You would draw them close to You and that they would recommit their lives to you fully. We also pray that You consecrate little Noah to Your service and that he would grow up as a man of God. In Jesus' precious name we pray…amen."

The music turned off. Donnie grinned at his wife. "I think God wants us to get into bed before Santa comes too!"

They ascended the stairs hand in hand, wondering how they were ever going to fall asleep with such an incredible feeling of anticipation in their hearts.

They all woke up at the same time. "Joy to the World" was blaring from the speakers below as if the stereo had set itself up as its own alarm.

Noah was out of bed like a shot. "Santee Kwaz! Santee Kwaz!" he shrieked, running downstairs.

Donnie and Deana stared at one another. "Do you smell coffee? She asked him. Donnie nodded. "Do you smell cinnamon rolls, bacon and eggs?" he asked her. Deana nodded. They threw off the covers and bounded downstairs, almost crashing into their daughters. The site that met their eyes froze them all upon the staircase (except for Noah who was already jumping up and down before an almost life-sized stuffed giraffe).

"Where did that come from?" Brook exclaimed, her eyes as big as saucers.

"Santee Kwaz!" Noah squealed, still bouncing like a Jack-in-the-box.

"How are we going to get that home?" Deana whispered in an aside to her husband.

"Sunroof," Donnie replied, his gaze sweeping over the great room. Candles were lit everywhere, Christmas music was playing, and the table had been set and already laid with a feast that looked like the Ghost of Christmas present had been very, very busy the night before.

"Wow…mom…how early did you get up to do all this?" Remarked Alex.

"Uh…I…uh…didn't." Deana replied, just as amazed as her daughters.

"Dad?"

"Don't look at me…I was sound asleep until five minutes ago."

"What about all the extra presents?" Brook whispered, looking at the pile that was wrapped in a plain white paper with beautiful bows and candy canes that she didn't recognize.

Deana shrugged then grinned. "Beats me!" she replied.

Alex, Brook and Lindsey knelt down, reading the tags on the mysterious packages. They looked up, Alex's eyes filled with tears, Lindsey's lip trembling and Brook's face was white.

"They all say they're from God!" Brook whispered. "Are you telling me that you guys didn't do this?"

Her father drew close and looked her deeply in the eyes. "You helped us pack the car and saw everything we put in there." He replied. "I can promise you…mom and I are every bit as surprised at all this as you are! It's not magic, Brook, it's the Lord!"

Brook stared back at him as did his other daughters; all of them on the verge of tears.

"Let's see what's inside," he said, kneeling upon the floor. He began handing out the white-wrapped presents, there was one each for everyone. They opened them one by one and with each reveal, the person to whom the gift was for broke down into sobs. Each gift contained a love letter wrapped in a gorgeous frame, accompanied by a sterling bracelet that had the initials of each girl. All was silent as each girl read their own letter, tears dripping down their faces. When they were done, they all went to their parents, and wrapped their arms about them.

"I want to pray right now!" Alex said, her blue eyes deadly serious. "I want to rededicate my life to Jesus!"

"Me too!" Lindsey said, tears still streaming.

Brook picked up Noah and kissed his warm cheek. "Would you pray with us, mom and dad?"

This time it was Donnie and Deana 's turn to weep with joy. "We thought you'd never ask!" he said. They all clasped arms, bowed their heads and prayed together with passion and fervor. When it was over the music came on again…it was Handel's Messiah and it was the Hallelujah chorus.

They all burst out laughing.

"Now let's eat breakfast before it all gets cold and open the rest later!" Deana suggested.

As they all sat down and bowed their heads for grace, she couldn't help thinking that she and Donnie had been given the best gift of all…their daughters' return to the God who loved them.

CHAPTER TWENTY-FIVE
"Romance to the Rescue"

Sheila is single and would really love to have a good Christian husband!!! She is 45 and feels like her time is running out. Also, her finances are not that great, but she would love to be in a position financially to help others less fortunate than herself! Her mother (who lived with her) passed away a couple of years ago and she is lonely a good part of the time. She has a sister, but doesn't see her all that often. She has a cute little house, but sometimes the mortgage is a challenge! She has a cute little dog named Lil Friskie which means the world to her who says that the dog is her baby!!!!

Sheila also wishes that she could be wealthy enough to have a village or a small town devoted to senior citizens where they could live without worrying about paying for their doctor bills or anything else and live there free of charge.

"Romance to the Rescue"

Sheila clocked out late at work and fumbled to find her keys as she hurried to her car in the parking lot. It was already getting dark and she needed to get to church and do some administrative work there before going home and making herself a lonely dinner. She got into the car; put the key in the ignition and…nothing. Not even a wheezing attempt to start. The battery was completely dead.

She pulled out her cell phone and called the church. "Gail? It's me…listen, I'm either going to be really late or not make it tonight at all. My car battery is dead. Okay…please do pray! I've got to hang up and call for a tow."

She hung up and after a moment's search found the number for a tow and dialed. The dispatcher took down her information and promised that help would be there within 30-45 minutes. Sheila hung up and decided that she might as well get herself something hot to drink while she waited. She walked back into a coffee shop and purchased a hot coffee then returned to her car to wait for the tow truck. It was completely dark by the time she saw the headlights pulling into the lot 20 minutes later. She got out of her car, stood up and waved to get the driver's attention.

The truck stopped and the driver stepped out. Sheila's mouth began a slow descent. He was tall, handsome and he was about her age. She couldn't resist the temptation to glance at his left hand. *No ring.* The driver removed his hat and nodded at her.

"Ma'm. Is this your car?" Sheila nodded, completely tongue tied after she got a good look at his ruggedly handsome face. The driver grinned at her, reading her reaction favorably. "Can you pop the hood for me?"

Again Sheila nodded and did as he asked. He lifted the hood and stuck his head inside. "Try turning the key again," he said. She turned the key as he fiddled with the cables. *Nothing but a click.* "It may not be your battery," he mumbled, reaching for the jumper cables. He hooked them up and gave her a nod to try again. Her car gasped, wheezed but still wouldn't turn over. He removed the cables, put the hood back down and gave her a grim smile. "Well you're definitely going to need a tow…do you have a mechanic you'd like me to take you to?"

Sheila's heart and expression both sank. Her budget was already stretched to the limit and now it looked like she was going to have an expensive car repair bill. The tow truck driver regarded her with sympathy as her eyes began to fill with tears. "Yes, but I don't think I can afford to get it fixed!" she replied. "What do you think the problem is….ummm…I'm sorry but I don't know what your name is?"

"Oh, sorry about that...name's Mike." He reached out his hand to shake hers. His grip was gentle but warm as was the look in his brown eyes. His rubbed his jaw on which he had a prominent, very masculine five o'clock shadow. "It could be your alternator…"

"Oh no…" Sheila responded. "That sounds like it's going to be incredibly expensive!"

"It's not cheap," Mike agreed. "Look, I'm an independent mechanic on the side. I don't have my own shop but I have a buddy, Murphy, who lets me tinker in his on my own car and it's the same make and model as yours. If you like, I can tow your car to his shop tonight and work on your car over the weekend."

Sheila couldn't believe her good fortune; Murphy was one of her closest friends. "That would be wonderful!" she smiled, her spirit's lifting a little. Her smile seemed to have a profound impact on Mike. He grinned at her. "All right then, let's get your car hooked up. I'll drive you home after I drop off your car."

In ten minutes her car was hooked up and she was sitting in the cab next to him. He drove about 15 minutes to Murphy's car repair shop and after he had it locked up safely inside, he got back into the cab and turned to Sheila.

"Where to?" he smiled. She gave him step by step directions to her home.

They arrived at her little cottage minutes later and before she could open up her door, Mike was already on her side of the car to open it up for her. For some reason she was really reluctant to get out of the cab. It was almost 8pm and she was starving.

"Have you had any dinner tonight?" she blurted out then instantly clapped her hand over her mouth. Mike chuckled.

"No, I haven't, ma'm," Mike responded, "and I sure am hungry. You were my last call tonight."

"Well, since you're helping me out so much the least I can do is to make you a home cooked meal." Sheila was amazed at her boldness but as long as Mike didn't seem to mind she plowed ahead. She gawked at him for a minute then stifled a giggle. She slid out of the tall truck and lost her balance as she dropped almost 8" to the ground. Mike caught her in his arms and helped her up. He smelled of grease, sweat and cologne; a very masculine scent.

"Careful, there!" he cautioned. Sheila's face burned crimson and she was glad it was dark so he couldn't see it as she fumbled for her house keys. She could already hear Lil Friskie Lee barking a welcome from the other side of the door. The nearness of Michael was a definite distraction.

"Does this help?" he shined a penlight onto the doorknob.

"Yes, thank you!" Sheila replied. She finally got the door open and Lil Friskie instantly began to growl at the stranger. "Ssh!" she chided her, picking the dog up. "Be nice! Mike here is my hero!" The words just slipped out before she could clamp her lips down on them. Lil Friskie began squirming to get closer to Mike who plucked him out of Sheila's hands.

"Hey there little girl!" he said, scratching the dog's ears. Lil Friskie began to lick him profusely, her little tail waving with pleasure.

"Make yourself at home, Mike," she said, gesturing to a chair. "Can I get you something to drink?"

"Ice water would be great!" Mike replied, still petting the dog. Sheila smiled at the two of them for a moment then went into the kitchen to see what she could rustle up on short notice. Within 15 minutes delicious smells began to waft out of the kitchen.

"That smells *wonderful*!" Mike called out. "It's been a long time since I've had a home-cooked meal!"

Sheila's heart skipped a little beat. "Oh…really?" She replied, trying to sound nonchalant. "How come?"

"Oh…my wife died several years ago and I can't cook so I eat out a lot; that's why I'm so chubby!"

His words were like music to Sheila's ears; she was getting more giddy by the moment. Soon she had the table set and platters of food set all around; meat, pasta, and mixed vegetables.

"Please have a seat," Sheila said, gesturing to a chair. Mike set down her dog and went to the kitchen to wash his hands first. Then he lumbered over to the table and held out Sheila's chair for her.

"Lady's first," he said. Sheila's heart did a little flip as she sat down. Once she was seated Mike sat down. Without her even having to ask him, he bowed his head for grace. He offered a simple prayer and then they began to dig in. Mike took a deep sniff of the food and nodded his head with a grin in her direction. "Nothing like home cooking!" he remarked then put a large forkful into his mouth. He closed his eyes and chewed with relish. Sheila stifled a giggle. She didn't remember anyone ever having that kind of reaction to her cooking before.

They spent a pleasant evening eating and getting to know each other and she was sorry when it came to an end. Mike helped to bring the dirty dishes into the kitchen and rinse them off.

"I have to get going home but listen, I got a proposition for you…I'll take you to work and then back home until I get your car fixed if you'll make me some more of those delicious dinners. Deal?"

"Deal!" smiled Sheila up at him. Their eyes locked for a moment and she could feel her face getting hot.

Mike took her hand in his and placed a kiss on the top. "See you tomorrow, Sheila!" he smiled. He walked to the door, picked up Lil Friskie Lee and let the dog slobber all over his face. "You too, squirt!"

Sheila closed the door and looked down at her dog who was smiling up at her. "Time to dust off the family cookbook, Lil Friskie Lee!"

For the next several days Mike showed up faithfully every morning to take her to work and always had a hot cocoa waiting for her in the cup holder. She found herself wishing that her car would never get fixed; she enjoyed his company so much. Every night after her shift at work he was waiting for her and took her home only to be rewarded with a delicious hot meal. He insisted on opening doors for her, pulling out her chair and always kissed her on the hand goodbye like a true gentlemen.

Finally the day she was dreading dawned. That night when he picked her up from work he had her car keys in his hand and he actually looked sad when he gave them to her. They drove in silence to Murphy's and she was really bummed when her car roared to life.

Mike shifted from one foot to the other, looking bluer by the moment. "I guess this means no more home-cooked meals," he mumbled. Sheila turned off the ignition and got out of her car.

"Mike, I would be happy to make you home-cooked meals for as long as you would like. It's been very nice to have your company every evening. I get lonely living alone."

Mike's head lifted, hope shining in his eyes. "Really?" he said, taking her hands in his.

Sheila nodded. "I just have one favor to ask," she said. "Would you be willing to go to church with me this Sunday?"

Mike gaped at her. "I was just about to ask you if you'd go to my church with me!"

"What church do you go to?" Sheila asked him.

"Living Waters," he replied.

Sheila's mouth dropped open. "That's *my church!*" she replied. "How come I've never seen you there?"

"Well I usually sit in the back row," he replied. "I hate the fact that I sit alone…"

"Not anymore!" Sheila smiled at him. "This Sunday you're sitting with me!"

The following Sunday morning she almost did not recognize him when he came to the door. Instead of his work overalls he showed up in a nice suit and tie all clean and sweet smelling. He looked so handsome! Sheila had dressed carefully that morning and changed dresses about 3 times until she was happy. When he offered her his arm her heart skipped a beat. They went to church together in her car and when they entered together a lot of heads turned in her direction. She was smiling so hard her face was actually starting to ache.

Gail, the Pastor's wife, was the first to greet them. "Well good morning, Sheila…Mike! How nice to see you both together!" She hugged them both then went to take her seat. Instead of letting Mike sit in the back row, she led him up to the second where she usually liked to sit and got even more curious stares from her friends.

Mike held her hand throughout the service and wouldn't let go even after she had stood up to leave. A lot of her friends gathered around, curious to know what was going on. Sheila wasn't quite sure what to tell everyone but Mike stepped up to the plate. He patted Sheila's hand. "We're becoming sweethearts!" he replied, eliciting gasps of delight. Then he steered Sheila out of church.

"Well, sweetheart," he grinned at her, making her heart do a huge flip flop. "How about some lunch and this time it's my treat!"

They drove a short distance to his favorite eatery, Bojangles, for lunch. As it happened, Bojangles sold lottery tickets in addition to their famous fried chicken. Sheila and he each bought a scratcher and scraped off the seal while they waited for their order. Mike's yielded nothing but when Sheila was done scratching she just sat there, staring at her scratcher in shock.

"Sheila, are you okay?" Mike asked, touching her hand. Sheila looked up at him, her eyes wide.

"I just won $30 million dollars!" she whispered, showing him her lottery card.

Mike took the card and examined it. "Holy smoke!" he whispered. "You did, you really did! What are you going to do with all that money?"

Sheila clutched the lottery ticket to her chest, tears beginning to roll down her cheeks. "I'm going to take care of a whole lot of grandma's and grandpa's!" she replied, "and then I'm going to buy you your own car repair shop!"

Mike took her hands in his and bent his head to give them a kiss. "Not unless you promise to make me home cooked meals for the rest of my life!" he whispered.

CHAPTER TWENTY-SIX
"Something New Under the Son"

Martha is a bank teller in North Carolina and has a very big heart. Her wish was to win a lot of money in the lottery so she could help her church, family and friends provide for the needs of the congregation, pay off debts, provide homes and even some much needed and overdue vacations in return for the years of care and nurturing provided to her family by others. I always pray before I write each story and ask God to give me the inspiration not to necessarily answer a "laundry list" of requests, but to deeply bless the heart and soul of the person who has asked for a story. I hope that the following Wish Fulfillment Story does all that.

"Something New Under the Son"

Martha woke up with a start. Instead of taking her lunch break with her friend at the bank or running errands, today she had decided to roll down the windows, eat then take a short little snooze in her car, setting her cell phone to wake her up ten minutes before she was to be back on "duty". She was incredibly groggy and did not immediately recognize her surroundings. She was still parked in the one shady spot in the employee lot, and her bank looked the same but there was a long line of people going in and then coming out with what appeared to be sacks of money. That woke her up fast! *Were they all robbing the bank?*

She bolted out of her car and was ready to dash inside, when a gentle hand restrained her. She fumbled in her purse for the bottle of mace; panic stricken.

"Peace unto you," said the calming voice of the tall stranger. Martha looked up, up up and felt her jaw going slack. The man next to her was at least 12' tall, gorgeous, was glowing softly and had two large wings spreading outwards from his back.

"Wha-wha-what are you?" Martha gaped.

"I'm your Guardian Angel, dearest," he replied, his blue eyes twin pools of pure love and adoration.

Martha clutched at her heart…*this was it! It was her time to die and God had sent her angel to come get her!*

Her angel put his arm about her and pulled her back up to an upright stand (as she had been sinking lower and lower). She could feel strength pouring into her body wherever he touched her.

"What is your name?" she asked, unable to tear her eyes away from his incredible face.

"Ooniemme," he smiled at her. "It is translated as 'gratitude' in Earthly terms."

Martha nodded and then her attention was diverted back to the line of people exiting her bank, carrying sacks of money. She dialed 9-1-1 but Ooniemme took her cell phone and waved his hand over it. It went dead.

"But they're stealing the bank's money!" she hissed in a panic. "I need to get the police here right away!"

"Take a better look," Ooniemme said, gesturing to the sign over the building. Martha looked up at the signage. Same navy blue graphics; same sunburst logo. She shrugged, feeling very dumb. "Closer," he encouraged her. She looked up and squinted her eyes…"SONTRUST BANK". *It was spelled wrong.*

She looked back at the 12' tall Angel; enlightenment beginning to dawn. She looked at her surroundings…no parking lot, no strip mall…just the bank and a line of people as far as the eye could see going in and going out. She started to feel dizzy.

"Let's go inside," Ooniemme suggested, taking her gently by the arm. She felt a thrill shoot through her entire body as she did so. They entered the bank but it looked nothing like the one she worked at. Instead of tellers behind a counter there were numbers of other guardian angels. Each of them had their hands upon the "customer's" heads in blessing as they knelt and poured out their hearts to God in intercessory prayer. She could hear the low murmur of their voices as they pleaded for loved ones to be blessed financially, physically and spiritually. When each one was done, their Angel handed them a sack; some small; some very large and almost bursting. Each left with a peaceful look upon their face that was indescribable.

Ooniemme touched one just as they were about to exit. The woman paused and looked up at him.

Martha gasped; it was her Aunt Laura! She looked exactly the same except for the expression of pure joy on her face.

"May we look into thy sack?" asked the Angel.

Laura nodded, opened it up and began to pull the contents out one by one. First was a ruby tiara which was inscribed with the word: *"Long Suffering"*, next was a diamond tiara that said: *"Perseverance"*. One by one she continued to pull more out; each more beautiful than the last and each with its' own name: *"Love"*, *"Hope"*, *"Joy"*, *"Peace"* until she came to the last one which was larger and more gorgeous than all the rest. It was magnificent beyond description and on it was the word: *"FAITH"*.

"This last would never be possible without all the others," smiled Laura. She carefully put them all back into her bulging sack and turned to leave.

"Where are you going, Aunt Laura?" Martha asked, her eyes filling with tears.

Her Aunt pointed off into the distance where stood a throne that blazed with all the glory of heaven. "To cast my crowns at His feet," she replied, her eyes welling with tears. She placed her trembling hand upon that of Martha's. "It was all worth it," she whispered, her gaze penetrating. "Every moment of it"

Her Aunt turned and left, her face a study in rapture. Martha turned back to find that her angel had stopped another person in line. Their sack wasn't quite as large.

"May we?" inquired Ooniemme. The stranger nodded and opened up the sack. In it was a small stack of money. He turned to go in the direction of the throne but the angel stopped him.

"Your money is no good there, my son." Ooniemme said gently. "But you may exchange it for a crown if you like."

"Okay!" agreed the man, turning to go back into the SonTrust bank.

"No, not there, down there," the angel pointed. Martha and the man looked down, down, down and saw the sphere of the earth turning below. "It is only possible to earn the crowns for the Savior down there," he explained.

The young man thought a moment. "But this money was to help all my friends, doesn't that count for something?"

The Angel replied. "Would you take away the opportunity for thy loved ones to cast their own crowns before the King?"

"No," he said, hanging his head. He offered his bag of money to Martha. She looked from the angel, to the sorrowful man to the golden throne in the distance and remembered her aunt's words... *"It was all worth it."*

Martha shook her head *no*. "I guess not," she said and smiled up at the angel. "I wouldn't want to deny my loved ones their opportunity to cast their crowns at the Savior's feet either!"

[5]And beside this, giving all diligence, add to your faith virtue; and to virtue knowledge; [6]And to knowledge temperance; and to temperance patience; and to patience godliness; [7]And to godliness brotherly kindness; and to brotherly kindness charity. [8]For if these things be in you, and abound, they make you that ye shall neither be barren nor unfruitful in the knowledge of our Lord Jesus Christ. ***2 Peter 1:5-8***

[2]My brethren, count it all joy when ye fall into divers temptations;[3]knowing this, that the trying of your faith worketh patience. ***James 1:2-3***

CHAPTER TWENTY-SEVEN
"Strength for the Journey"

Debra has a son name Hunter who is 19. Hunter has "Smith Magenis Syndrome". He has limited speech capability and is always swallowing things and almost choking to death which necessitates that she be by his side every minute of every day even when he takes showers or uses the bathroom. She even has to sleep with Hunter most of the night. She reads to him and waits until he goes to sleep. Debra's wish is that her son would be healed of the disease or at least not swallow things anymore. I prayed very hard about this story before writing it. I feel a great deal of responsibility to not make promises on behalf of God but rather to encourage, build faith, give perhaps a peek into what heaven might be like and let the subject of the story know that God is still in control and that He sees all our struggles and trials.

"Strength for the Journey"

Debra woke up from her deep sleep with the sense that something was not right. She sat up and looked at her son's side of the bed and felt panic rising in her heart. He wasn't there. Goodness only knew what could be happening to him at this very moment. He was constantly swallowing things and choking on them! Just as she flung off the covers a sight greeted her eyes that made her freeze in complete shock.

Hunter came into the bedroom carrying a beautiful breakfast tray with all her favorite foods, freshly squeezed orange juice and hot coffee. Despite the silver dome covering the plate, she could smell the delicious aroma of Eggs Benedict. There was even a slender vase holding a pink rose. She gaped at her son in complete amazement. There was something different in his eyes and in his bearing.

"Good morning, mom!" he said. He spoke clearly and his voice had a lovely masculine timbre to it. The sound of it made her own voice catch in her throat Tears instantly sprung into Debra's eyes.

"You can talk? You're healed?" she exclaimed, coming up onto her knees in the bed.

"Careful, mom…you'll spill the breakfast I made you!" Hunter warned with a smile. Debra drank in every word that came from his mouth as well as the sight of him. He stood taller, erect…and there was a self confidence there she had never seen before. Hunter set the tray down on her lap and laid a beautiful pale pink cloth napkin over her.

"Hunter…you made all this? Didn't daddy help you?" Debra still couldn't believe what she was hearing or seeing.

Hunter bent forward and kissed her on her cheek. "I made it all by myself, mom," he assured her. Debra thought she would weep at the sound of hearing him call her "mom" after so many years of frustrated silence. She took his face into her trembling hands and looked deeply into his eyes.

"Am I dreaming all this or has God miraculously healed you?" she whispered. Hunter placed his large warm hands over hers.

"This is a gift," he replied. "We have this one day together where I will be unfettered by my condition. You have devoted every moment of your waking life to me, mom, and I asked God last night to allow me to give you this gift. He answered my prayers and now I intend to spend the rest of the day giving back to you! I have it all planned out."

Debra was trembling uncontrollably; still staring at her son as if she were seeing a ghost. "I just can't believe this!"

Hunter gave her an understanding smile. "I know it's difficult, but we only have this one day together so let's make the most of it. If you like, I'll sit here beside you and we can eat together!"

"I would love that!" replied Debra, carefully scooting over. Hunter left and returned with his own plate of food and together they ate as she continued to marvel at the miraculous changes in him. He no longer seemed like a large boy but a full grown man, gentle and masculine. He told her all the things that had been closed up in his heart year after year because of his inability to speak. He told her how much he loved her and appreciated all the unending sacrifices she had made for him over the years and how all she did had been seen and blessed by God and how it was working towards an eternal weight of glory for her.

Debra did her best to eat but it was difficult to do because she couldn't stop sobbing. She finally gave up and handed the tray back to her son. "I'm too choked up to eat!" she gulped, "but I'm ready to start our day. Do I have time to take a shower first? Let me call Angel-"

Hunter placed a calming hand on his mom's arm. "You won't need Angel to watch me today," he reassured her. "I wouldn't do anything to ruin this day together, mom. If you want, I'll sit on the toilet while you shower and read a book so you can relax, okay?"

Debra nodded and went into the bathroom, unable to take her eyes off Hunter. He averted his eyes as she disrobed and slipped into the shower stall, then true to his word, picked up the Bible and began to read aloud from Mark 7:37 as she stepped under the hot stream.

Despite his assurances that everything today would be fine, Debra rushed through her shower as quickly as she could. Hunter was still reading the Bible aloud; his voice music to her ears as she toweled off, fixed her hair, put on her make-up and got dressed. She felt as nervous as though she were about to go on her first date.

Hunter gave her a smile and little wolf-whistle. "You sure are beautiful, mom!" he said, kissing her cheek.

"Thank you, Hunter," she said, fighting not to cry. Hunter extended his arm like a gentlemen and walked her down the stairs and out the door. There was a beautiful white limousine waiting for them.

"I asked the Lord to let me drive but He didn't think you could handle it!" he joked, opening the limo door for her.

"Where are we going?" she asked, ducking inside.

"You'll see!" he smiled mysteriously.

Despite herself, Debra found herself checking out the limo for any small, choking items.

"Mom, today you can relax – I won't be swallowing anything besides food and beverages!" he assured her.

"Habits are hard to break, son," she smiled at him sheepishly. The limo wound through the streets and came to one that looked familiar. It pulled up in front of Angel's house. Angel was already waiting outside, jumping up and down with excitement. As soon as the limo door opened she tumbled inside and caught her younger brother in a fierce hug.

"Hunter, I love you! I just wanted you to know that!" she said.

"I know that, sis…I love you too. Thanks for always being there to help mom out and give her a little respite now and then!"

"Whoo hoo….listen to those fancy words you're using!" Angel remarked.

Hunter pointed to his head with a grin. "Just because I can't talk doesn't mean I can't hear!" he chuckled. He banged on the dividing window. "Okay, Limo driver…let's go!"

The limo took off and within about an hour, they found themselves at Brier Creek Commons Shopping Mall. "Surprise!!" yelled Hunter opening the car door. All three of them stepped out and into the bright sunshine. "Follow me!" he called and began to march off at a brisk pace. Debra and Angel followed him as quickly as they could until they stood before the Skin Sense Day Spa.

"Today you get the works, mom and sis! Manicure, pedicure, facial and Swedish massage!"

Debra clapped both hands over her mouth, the tears already beginning to flow. "Where are you going to be?" She still couldn't bring herself to totally relax.

"I'll be in the Barnes & Noble shopping for some books!" he said. He kissed his mom on her forehead. "Today you can relax and enjoy yourself, mom. Remember, this is a gift from the Lord!"

Debra nodded. "Okay, I'll try but you promise to be here waiting for me as soon as we're done?"

"I promise!" he said earnestly, crossing his heart.

Debra and Angel allowed the estheticians to lead them into the back. Soon they were given plush robes, glasses of sparkling cider and shown to a gorgeous and tranquil waiting room. Soon they were taken back to small but elegant client rooms with lit candles, orchids and peaceful music playing. If Debra had planned on fretting and worrying over her son during the duration of her treatments she had another thing coming. First they started with the Swedish massage. The magical fingers of the masseuse working their magic and Debra was soon in a deep sleep as her tense muscles were worked on. She barely even woke up when she was helped to turn over for the facial. She finally awakened when cool cucumber slices were gently placed on her eyelids and a cool washcloth wiped down her wrists and feet. She was so groggy she had to be helped to the pedicure chair. The seat warmer was turned on, the back tilted and she continued to sleep while they worked on her hands and feet. When she awoke she had a lovely French manicure and Christmas red toes. All of her calluses had disappeared and the bottom of her feet felt baby soft.

She and Angel met up again when they placed them in side-by-side chairs to fix their hair and makeup. When they exited the salon, Hunter was standing there with a bag full of books from Barnes & Noble.

"What did you get, honey?" asked Debra, greatly relieved to see him. Hunter fished in the bag and pulled out a few books. "I got one for you, one for Angel and a couple for me," he replied.

"Let's see!" said Angel, picking them up one by one and reading the title out loud. "The Victor", Dad's new book.... "Hind's Feet on High Places"... "The Velveteen Rabbit"...and "Guess How Much I Love You"."

Hunter looked at his mom. "The last two are for you to read to me afterwards," he smiled.

Debra kissed him on the cheek. "Thank you," she whispered.

"What next, Hunter?" asked Angel. She felt (and looked) like a million bucks after the 2 hour beauty treatment.

"Clothes shopping and then lunch!" he replied. For the first time in many, many years, Debra got to experience the absolute decadence of shopping for fun at leisure. She and Hunter held hands as they walked in and out of shops and she tried on quite a few dresses before he picked out one that he felt was just right for both of them. With their packages in hand, they returned to the limo and it sped off to their next destination. They exited the limo and found themselves in front of the Azalea Inn Tea Room.

Angel began to jump up and down. "I've *always* wanted to come here!" she squealed.

They were all shown into Karen's exquisite tea room with its rich dark antique furniture and fresh flowers and given fun hats to wear (except for Hunter). First was a multi-tiered silver serving set with an assortment of fresh fruit and tea sandwiches (cucumber, egg salad, and a miniature roast beef on Yorkshire Pudding). Next came the homemade scones with real clotted cream and raspberry jam. They ate off beautiful china with delicate little cutlery and Debra couldn't help but marvel at her son who even managed to crook his pinky while drinking his vanilla tea out of a china cup without spilling. A harpist played classical music and for an entire hour all they did was eat, drink and pour their hearts out to one another. The food was a delight but even more nourishing to Debra's soul was the deep and heartfelt conversation she had been able to have with her son after so many years. The scones were followed with a Trifle of lady fingers, whipped cream, strawberries and raspberries. They were stuffed to the gills as they gingerly lumbered out of the Tea Room to the waiting limo. It was late afternoon and Debra felt a shadow creep over her heart as she realized that the day was almost over.

"What next?" she asked, trying to keep her voice light.

"Home," Hunter said giving her a grin. "I want to play a game of hoops with dad, will you be my cheering squad?"

"Oh, Hunter! That would make Danny *so happy!"* she exclaimed. The idea of seeing the two men she loved most in this life playing together as a regular father and son thrilled her more than the day spa, shopping and high tea put together.

The limo arrived home and Hunter bounded out of the car and upstairs to change into more appropriate clothing. Her husband Danny stood on the sidewalk, mouth agape, hands on hips, staring at the gaping open door.

"Was that Hunter?" he asked his wife. "Is he okay?"

"He's marvelous, Danny!" Debra said, hugging her husband. "God gave us a very special gift of one day together as a normal family. He wants to play basketball with you!"

"He wants to what?" repeated her husband, eyebrows climbing high into his hairline.

Debra kissed his cheek. "Just go with it and enjoy yourself!"

Hunter arrived moments later in a t-shirt and shorts and carrying a basketball. He tossed it to his dad. "Let's play one on one!" he challenged.

Still in shock but heeding his wife's advice, Danny began dribbling the ball, the grin on his face spreading wider and wider as he beheld his son crouching and ready to give him a real challenge.

They dribbled, shot baskets, and feinted around each other for the better part of an hour until they were both dripping with sweat. Debra and Angel both kept their promises and made up impromptu cheers for Hunter every time he scored a basket. When the game came to an end, it was 32-20 with Hunter as the winner. Danny was breathing hard but the look of sheer joy on his face was priceless. He drew Hunter close to him, hugged him and planted a kiss on the top of his head.

"I'll never forget this time with you," he said, his eyes filling with tears.

Hunter threw his arms around his dad and held him close. "Thank you," he said, his face buried in his shoulder.

"Okay, boys…time to clean up!" Debra announced. The four of them went into the house and Angel helped Debra to fix a wonderful dinner as the men took showers. For the first time that day, Debra was able to concentrate on cooking instead of worrying about Hunter. They all sat down to eat together and had steak, fries with honey mustard, cooked vegetables and ice-cold root beer.

Night finally came and Debra sat on the edge of Hunter's bed, stroking his blond fuzzy head. He took her hand in his and looked deeply into his mother's eyes.

"I hope you had a wonderful day, mom. You truly deserve it and so much more," he whispered, his eyes becoming sad. "Tomorrow when you wake up things will be back to the way they were before."

"Oh," said Debra sadly. She had so enjoyed her son's company this day and being able to talk with him. She was really going to miss hearing him tell her that he loved her.

Hunter took her face gently in his hands and leaned his forward upon hers. "Even if I can't say the words, mom, know that I love you and dad more than anything and that I'm grateful God gave me to you. I'm glad we were able to have this one day together,"

Debra sniffed, the tears starting to slide down her cheeks. "Why just the one day, my son?"

Hunter cocked his head as if listening to a voice she couldn't hear and then he hugged her close as he answered. "To give you strength for the journey ahead," he whispered.

Debra nodded, grateful to have gotten a day's worth of beautiful memories that she could always treasure in her heart. She tucked Hunter into bed and curled up next to him, wondering what the morning would bring.

When she woke up she was still beside him. "Good morning, Hunter," she whispered, kissing him on his forehead. Hunter opened his eyes and looked at her but it was not the same look he had given her yesterday. It was the look she had seen for many years and it made her heart ache. "Can you say good morning?" she asked. Hunter just smiled at her then rolled out of bed to go to the bathroom. Debra sighed and followed him; ever the vigilant protector, to make sure nothing went into his mouth that would choke him. She wondered if the previous day had all been just a dream until she caught sight of her nicely manicured hands and feet. She glanced at Hunter's nightstand and saw the books he had gotten for her the day before. She opened up "Guess How Much I Love You" and found that it had been signed on the inside cover.

"For Debra – strength for the journey ahead…Jesus."

CHAPTER TWENTY-EIGHT
"Woulda, Coulda, Shoulda"

Jeremy loves the Lord. He is always sharing the Good News with others and inviting them to church but it wasn't always that way. In his youth he did many things that he wished he could do over. These are his stated wishes: "I wish I had never tried drugs; I wish I had gone to college; I wish I had made better choices; I wish I could have told Adam and Eve not to eat the forbidden fruit; I wish I could have walked with Jesus; I wish I had more money and that the world was a better place. I wish I lived at the beach because it gives me peace; I wish I could talk to Moses. I wish I could go back and know what I know now."

"Woulda, Coulda, Shoulda"

Jeremy drove home from church that morning deeply disappointed in himself. It was one of the rare times when he had not been able to coax someone who desperately needed Jesus to go with him. He went into his home and sat on the couch, holding his head in his hands; wishing for the millionth time that he could have a complete "do over" of his entire life.

*So many wasted opportunities...so many bad choices; his life would have been so different if only...*He shook his head with regret and laid back, closing his eyes with a weariness that was not of this earth and shut his eyes.

He was awakened gently by the sound of crashing waves. Jeremy sat up and looked around. It was his place but the sounds weren't right...he got up and went to look out his window. Instead of the usual scenery he found himself looking out a glass slider at a beautiful beach. *This sure is some dream!* He couldn't help thinking to himself. *Might as well enjoy it while it lasts...* He opened the slider and found stone steps leading from his door straight down to the white sands of the beach. He grabbed a sweatshirt off the peg and practically skipped down the stairs.

The ocean beckoned to him with its sparkling aqua water and sun diamonds. The sand felt warm upon his feet. He curled and uncurled his toes in it, enjoying the powdery grains. Suddenly he noticed an empty beach blanket and picnic hamper. He looked up and down the coastline for the owner but saw absolutely no one. He walked over to it and found a note. Two words were written on it: *"For Jeremy"*. He felt a chill run down his spine. He sat upon the blanket and opened the lid; inside were all his favorite foods as well as a bottle of wine…the sound of rushing water made him look up and when he did his jaw hung slack. The tide wasn't being sucked out to sea like the forewarning of an impending tsunami but it was coalescing and dividing in two.

"No way…" he gasped under his breath. It was like watching a reenactment of the Ten Commandments. The ocean parted down the middle with the setting sun in the center and off in the distance he saw a figure walking towards him on the exposed ocean bed. *This sure is some dream!* He remarked to himself in awe. The figure arrived and stood before him.

"Let me guess," he grinned up at him. "Charleton Heston, right?" The tall man stared at him with a perplexed grimace on his bearded face. Jeremy's smile faded; evidently his "dream character" didn't have a sense of humor.

"No…Moses," corrected the man in a heavy middle-eastern accent, tapping his chest. "Charleton Heston couldn't make it!" This elicited a guffaw of laughter from him at his own joke. Jeremy paled; he wasn't sure whether to laugh along or high tail it outta there…he pinched himself, hoping it would wake him up. It didn't.

Moses' face turned serious. "Are you ready to meet the Master?"

Jeremy's heart began to flip flop. "Master?" He grew clammy and then his attention was drawn by the sight of a tall man walking towards him between the massive walls of ocean water on either side.

"Is that who I think it is?" he pointed, panic beginning to rise.

Moses sat down beside him and put a calming arm around him. "Peace, my son; you are well loved; you have nothing to fear."

As the figure continued towards them, Jeremy tried to make nervous small talk. "Y'know, I've *always* wanted to meet you!" he said.

Moses nodded at him and smiled. "That's why I'm here."

"What was it like…y'know, experiencing the Exodus and God's miracles?" He hoped Moses wouldn't find the question too intrusive.

"I am unable to adequately put into human terms my experience with the Almighty," he replied softly, his brown eyes intense. "I cannot improve upon what is written in His Word but I can tell you this…"

"What?" breathed Jeremy, leaning forward, all ears.

"The Israelites were a great, 40 year pain in the tushie!" he exclaimed. They stared at each other for a moment and then Moses burst out laughing again. Jeremy was so taken aback that he didn't immediately notice the tall figure was now standing next to him.

"Peace be unto you," said the deep and utterly masculine voice of the Savior. Jeremy and Moses each prostrated themselves; they could not have done otherwise…it was a natural reaction to being in His Holy presence.

Jesus gentle hands grasped Jeremy by the shoulder and gently lifted him upright. Tears were streaming down his face; words he had longed for years to speak fighting to escape his constricted throat. Jesus waited patiently, his brown eyes twin pools of fathomless love.

"Speak, my son." He said.

As if on command the words began to pour forth. "Lord…I am so not worthy of your presence and your time…how can I ever thank you for all You have done for me? I only wish that my life had been different so that I could have served you longer and better,"

"That is why I am here, Jeremy," Jesus replied. "Your heart is full of regrets; you dwell too much on the time and opportunities you think you have wasted but I am here to tell you that your life…every day, every minute; every second of it has been in the palm of my hand since the moment you first drew breath." Jesus sat down beside him, opened the basket and withdrew bread and wine. He tore it into two pieces and handed one each to Moses and Jeremy.

"Aren't you having any, Master?" Jeremy asked.

Jesus shook his head. "I will not partake of the fruit of the vine until they day I drink it with you in My Father's kingdom," he reminded him. Jeremy blushed; feeling foolish. *How many times had he said those very words during communion and here he was asking the author of the Bible why he wasn't drinking wine!* "Eat and behold!" commanded Jesus.

Jeremy ate the bread and drank the wine and watched as the clouds spread across the sky like a vast canopy. Images began to appear on them as if an enormous movie projector had been turned on. At first they were blurry then they became clearer and Jeremy felt a lump begin to build in his throat when he realized the images were of him and his past life. Terror began to wrap its fingers about his chest.

"Fear not," Jesus calmed him, laying a gentle hand upon his shoulder. "These are not images from thy past but images of what might have been were you able to go back and do thy life over again as you now feel you should have," he explained.

Jeremy relaxed and sat back cross-legged, watching the scenes play out before him. He saw himself as a young man, getting good grades, turning down drugs and alcohol and going to college as he had always wanted to do. He saw himself graduating, going into the workforce and becoming greatly successful. He was wearing nice clothes, dating beautiful women, had money to burn and lacked nothing. His alternate life continued to play out before him…going from one success to another, marrying, raising a family and then finally he was an old man, alone, on his death bed."

"What do you see?" Jesus asked him.

"My life as it should have been…not wasted on drugs and lousy decisions." Jeremy moped.

"Do you see anything missing?" Jesus continued. "Let me play it again for you, in more detail."

Jeremy watched it over again but this time he began to notice what Jesus had hinted at. There were no scenes of going to church, saying prayers for the lost or witnessing to others. There was nothing of God in his life at all. Finally it came to where his older self lay upon his deathbed alone…devoid of any spiritual relationship to God…terrified of what lay beyond death's imminent door but too proud to call out for mercy. Jeremy turned to Jesus, his eyes swimming as he began to comprehend.

"Now let me show you how I view thy life," said Jesus. Jeremy looked again up at the clouds and watched his actual life play out before his eyes but this time he was able to see what was happening in the spirit world as well. It was plain to see that all his bad choices: drug abuse, etc., had all worked together to bring him to his knees to Jesus for salvation and restoration. He watched with trembling heart the many lives he had touched for the kingdom of God. Souls that would never have been won had it not been for all he had suffered. Many of the people he recognized and remembered but there were so very many more that he had not even been aware of. When it was over he was weeping uncontrollably.

"All things…*all* work together for the good for those who love Me," Jesus reminded him. "Had you lived the life you thought you should have, you would never have felt need of Me. You would have lived a successful, prosperous life as far as the world was concerned but you would have lost your soul."

Jeremy wiped his tears with the sleeve of his sweatshirt and let out with a long shuddering sigh. "I still wish I could have gone back to the garden and told Adam and Eve not to do it," he grinned, trying to make light of his emotional outburst.

"Come and walk with me," Jesus said, standing up and holding out his nail-pierced hand to help him up. Jeremy gulped;

the tears threatening to spill again at the reminder of what his Redeemer had suffered for him. They walked upon the shore, the waves playing chase with the seagulls. As they walked Jesus spoke softly to him, his arm about Jeremy's shoulder.

"Even sin had a part to play in our divine plan," he explained. "Even if Adam and Eve had not sinned, there was always the opportunity for their progeny to do so at any time and the world would have become even as it is today anyway. Do you not see the infinite wisdom of the Father, Jeremy? At of all things, He shall have a people called by His name who through the exercise of their own freewill shall have given their souls to Him. Once regenerated, they shall live eternally with Him, loving Him freely but with no more capability or temptation to commit sin."

Jeremy nodded; he had never thought of it before but it made perfect sense.

Lift up thy head and behold," said the Savior.

Jeremy looked up towards where Jesus was pointing and saw a multitude of people in the clouds above him; all were clothed in glowing white garments.

"Were it not because of thy former life and all you have done since then to make restitution, none of those you see there in heaven would be there." Jesus then bent down and plucked a Sand Dollar from the sand and placed it into his palm, closing his fingers upon it.

"Never regret the life you have led, my son," whispered Jesus…beginning to fade from view. "For in it led you straight to Me. *Those who are forgiven much love much.* You may be poor with regard to material things but you are rich in good works. Now go forth and continue bearing fruit for the kingdom…time is short!"

CHAPTER TWENTY-NINE
"A Sword Shall Pierce…"

I'm sitting bedside with my daughter in the ICU unit as she recovers from her third open heart surgery. The ironic part is that it is almost eleven years to the day that our son Chase was here. Both, Chase and Kacy were born with a congenital heart disease. One nurse called it a scrabbled egg heart. Chase fought for two and a half weeks before he left this world. Two days prior to loosening him I had a miscarriage. Our world has changed forever.

I saw a falling star the other morning on my way to take Kacy to the Mema house. I remember wishing to God to let my Kacy live a long healthy life; then I realized that was the desire of my heart. My wish would be to be strong through these trails that God has allowed us to go through so that our tests could become a glorious testimony so that I will be able to help others who are lost and hurting in the same way. Then to stand before God and hear Him say: "Well done my good and faithful servant". Then to see those that are in heaven because we stood strong and trusted in God no matter what came…that is my wish.

"A Sword Shall Pierce …"

Christy sat besides the sleeping form of her youngest daughter, listening to the soft but steady *beep, beep, beep* of the heart monitors and whooshing of the respirators. Even when she wasn't in the hospital she could still hear the sounds of the ICU playing in her head; it seemed to be an ever present melody of sorrow. Her large warm hand caressed the tiny face and hand of her daughter. She closed her eyes in prayer; willing that some of her own physical strength and health could flow from her aching heart down through her arms and hands and out her fingertips to the fragile form of her little girl.

She was so tired and weary. Weary of the constant heartbreak; weary of less doctor visits and hospital stays. Weary of losing her children. Hot tears coursed down her cheeks as she fought the familiar battle to bless God instead of question Him.

She felt a gentle hand upon her shoulder and looked up to see a young doctor standing behind her. When she turned to look her heart got a shock. The young woman bore an eerie resemblance to her. They locked eyes for a moment and Christy could feel her heart starting to pound. The doctor smiled sweetly at her and motioned for her to follow her.

"I can't leave my baby," Christy whispered, reluctant.

"Everything will be fine, do not worry," replied the doctor. She gestured behind her and into the ICU unit stepped the most magnificent being Christy had ever laid eyes on. He was 12 feet tall, glowing with a soft golden light and had wings…the room began to spin.

"All is well," whispered the voice of the Angel, touching her. The room stopped spinning and an overwhelming peace and joy flooded her soul. He helped Christy to her feet and stood next to the bed of her daughter, laying a gentle hand upon her tiny chest. The beeping of the heart monitor grew stronger and more regular and the baby's color turned a healthy pink. Tears sprang into Christy's widening eyes. *Was he healing her baby?*

"Come," coaxed the doctor, wrapping her arm about Christy. "She will be fine while you are away. Let's get you something to eat."

Christy allowed herself to be led away but her head still swiveled round to ogle the Angel. He gave her a reassuring smile and peace flooded her soul again. As they walked down the familiar hospital corridor; her mind was consumed with questions until they came to the public dining room.

"Stay here, I'll get you something to eat," said the doctor. Christy stayed put but she couldn't tear her eyes away from the young woman. She seemed so incredibly familiar and Christy had to fight the urge to hug her. It was very strange. The woman returned with a tray of food and it was then that she saw her name badge. It had two initials on it: K.C.

She stared at her; wondering if she was dreaming, going crazy or both. It just couldn't be....

"Hungry, mom?" The doctor slid a hot sandwich towards her. A thrill went down Christy's back. She grabbed the young woman's hands and leaned forward.

"You called me mom!"

The doctor grinned at her; she smiled just like her husband Ken!

"So I did!"

"K.C.?"

"Yes? I thought the name tag would be a sure giveaway but you were a bit slow on the uptake." She grinned again and bit into her sandwich.

"But how can you be my daughter? You're still a baby in ICU!"

"Yes, that is me also," replied the doctor. "Time is only linear in the earthly realm, mom…it has no meaning here."

Christy paled. "Where is here?"

"Eternity!"

Christy held her head in her hands, feeling dizzy again. *Maybe she had fallen asleep in ICU and was just having a very weird dream...*

K.C. took her hands and held them gently, then kissed them. All Christy could do was stare at her. She was beautiful…

"Are you really a doctor?"

K.C. nodded with pride. "Pediatric heart surgeon; the youngest ever and I owe it all to you…and Chase of course."

"How?"

"You will tell me many stories as I grow up; about the brother I lost and the other babies, as well as my own health struggles. It gave me a passion to become a heart specialist so I could help others. Mom…" her eyes became intense. "I will save hundreds of babies that are just like me."

A lump filled Christy's throat; her eyes welling. The tiny, fragile baby back in ICU would someday grow up to become this lovely young woman and a heart surgeon!

Just at that moment, a small group of children approached their table; their arms outstretched yelling "Mommy! Mommy!" They bowled into her, hugging, kissing and laughing all at once. They had each brought her a beautiful rose, each a different color. Christy had no need of explanations this time; she knew intrinsically that these were all the babies she had lost. The youngest of the boys she knew to be Chase. All the children had reddish brown hair and blue eyes and either looked like herself or her husband, Ken. She smothered each one of them in her arms; kissing them profusely while K.C. looked on. One by one they told her the names she had secretly given them in her heart and with each embrace she felt the deep wounds of loss soothed as if with balm. Now that she could see that they were all alive and real (though beyond her mortal reach); the loss did not feel so keen.

K.C. quieted them down. "Okay everyone, time is up! Before I take mom back to ICU we're all going to pray for her!"

Christy balked…she didn't want to be parted from her children after having only just met them. K.C. put her arms about her shoulders and gave her a motherly hug. "Don't be sad," she cooed, laying her forehead against her mom's. "We will all be together here in eternity but you still have some work left to do,"

"That's right," interjected a masculine voice behind them. A thrill went through Christy's heart at the sound of it. She turned around, already knowing who she would find. Blazing like the noonday sun and with eyes that pierced her very soul stood her Redeemer. She fell instantly to her knees and covered her face with her hands, trembling despite the waves of love washing over her.

"Peace be unto you, my daughter," He said, lifting her to her feet. She felt his hands rest upon her shoulders. Warmth from his fingertips flowed through her entire being like warm honey. She opened her eyes and caught her breath. There were no adequate words in the tongues of men or angels to express what she saw in her Savior's eyes…

“I know thy heartache and sorrow,” He said, wiping the singular teardrop that escaped from her lashes. “I feel every pierce of thy heart but know that it is working for thee an eternal weight of glory. Those whom I trust much also suffer much and so it is with thee.”

Christy nodded, understanding still unable to speak she was so overwhelmed. Jesus continued. “If you can persevere to and still raise thy voice to me in praise despite all thy heartaches you shall indeed receive the words you most long to hear from Me…well done my good and faithful daughter…”

Jesus bent forward and placed a gentle kiss upon her forehead. “Have faith as a little child, my beloved, it is the only thing which pleases Me.”

The next thing Christy knew she was back in the ICU sitting in her chair. She thought it had all been a dream until she spotted the vase of multi-colored roses…the same roses her lost children had brought her but now they all had long spiny thorns on them; a reminder of the fallen world she lived in. She was alone again with her infant daughter who was cooing in her bed.

“Hey there baby-doll,” Christy whispered, caressing her daughter’s warm cheek. Kacy opened her eyes and gave her mom a delighted smile.

“Ma-ma!” she squealed.

CHAPTER THIRTY
"A Wink and a Smile"

My wish is for my baby sister, Dolly. She lost her eye when she was one year old and is having surgery on the other eye. She is now 60 and has had a lot of bad luck in her life. Despite two bad marriages and all her other trials, Dolly has always had a very big heart and given generously of herself. My wish is for her surgery to go well so she can continue to see out of her eye.

"A Wink and a Smile"

Dolly awoke slowly from the anesthetic and her hand immediately went to the eye that had been operated on. A large gauze bandage covered it. It was a full moment before she realized that she was looking at the hospital ceiling.

Well now how can this be? She wondered. Her hand went to the eye that had been gone since infancy, feeling it tentatively. She closed the lid and reopened it and then gasped when full realization hit her. *Her eye was there!!!* She searched around the room and her eye lit upon a tall handsome stranger. She did a double take.

"Hellooooooo Dolly!" he said with a big grin and then added: "I've *always* wanted to do that!"

"Who are you?" Dolly gaped.

The stranger helped her to sit up in bed. He was dressed like an orderly and was wearing white. "Would you like to go for a little stroll around the hospital grounds?" He asked. "They are exceptionally lovely."

"I-I suppose so," blushed Dolly as he helped her into a wheelchair and laid a soft warm blanket over her. "Are you sure it's quite alright? Shouldn't we ask my doctor first?"

"The great physician has assured me that it is perfectly alright for you to see the gardens. Are you ready?"

Dolly nodded and continued to gaze about her in wonder as they wheeled down the stark white corridors. People were everywhere but seemed to be in no hurry. Couples strolled hand in hand with blissful looks on their faces, mothers cuddled children, and children ran up and down, giggling out loud in glee. It was the happiest hospital she had ever been in. It did her heart good to see so many people smiling and laughing. The orderly rolled her out into the glorious sunshine and into the most breathtaking gardens she had ever seen (or smelled for that matter). Wisteria was in full bloom and filling the air with perfume. The path meandered on as far as the eye could see, into one garden after another; each more glorious than the previous one. Butterflies flitted everywhere, bees hummed and the breeze carried the smell of roses, sweet peas and orange blossoms. They rolled along for what seemed hours and then finally they paused beside a lovely lake bordered by Weeping Willows and filled with graceful white swans.

It was so beautiful that Dolly wanted to weep out of her unbandaged eye and then remembered that she had wanted to ask the orderly how the doctors had managed to miraculously give her sight.

She twisted her head around and found him standing at her side, gazing down at her with love shining out of his eyes. She suddenly recognized who He was and began to tremble.

"Fear not, Dolly," He said, squatting next to her and patting her hand. "Do you like the gardens?"

Dolly nodded yes…too amazed and dumbfounded to speak.

The man smiled, pleased with her response and straightened. "I'll take you back now," He said, turning her about. A million questions flooded her mind that she wanted to ask Him but none of them would make it past her lips. She kept stealing looks at Him as he wheeled her back and seemed amused at her constant stares.

They were finally back in her room. He assisted her back into bed, cupped her cheek and laid a gentle kiss upon her forehead. The sensation of warm honey flowed from His kiss throughout her entire body, thrilling her.

“Fear not, dearest daughter,” He said, giving her a wink and a smile before fading from view. “Your eye will be completely whole. Be blessed.”

Dolly waved goodbye to Him; an enormous grin of delight upon her face.

CHAPTER THIRTY-ONE
"Cowboys and Roses"

Lauren is 24 years old and recently lost a baby. Her wish was to see what the baby would have looked like but I thought I'd throw a little southwestern fairytale in there for good measure!

"Cowboys and Roses"

It was another ordinary day at the fast food restaurant and Lauren had been on her feet most of the day taking orders at the front counter. Her back was aching and her calves were knotted from standing in one place for so long but she was very grateful for the job. She was just about ready to end her shift when a customer stepped into her line. She looked up to present her professional smile and felt her jaw drop open in awe while her eyes went up to ogle the tall, handsome cowboy who stood before her. He gave her a lopsided grin and tipped his hat at her.

"Ma'm!"

"Welcome, may I take your order please?" she managed to remember.

The cowboy glanced up at the menu board behind her and stroked his brown moustache for a moment, considering his choices. "Mmmmm," he said, taking his time. Normally Lauren would be tapping her foot or fidgeting, wanting to end her shift and get out of there but at the moment she was in no hurry to rush him along. She wanted to look at him as long as possible.

"Think I'll try one of those Texas Toast Bacon Cheeseburgers," he drawled, fishing for his wallet in the back pocket of his jeans. He gave her a wink, "...being that I'm from Texas and all."

"Would you like some fries or a drink with that, sir?" Lauren gulped. His flirtatious wink had made her knees go weak.

"Diet coke and small fry...gotta watch the figure!" he chuckled, patting his flat stomach.

Lauren rang up his order. "That'll be $9.45" she smiled.

The man handed her a ten dollar bill then leaned on the counter with both elbows. "You're not wearing a wedding ring." He observed. Lauren's heart skipped a beat.

"Nope!" she replied, smiling at him shyly.

This made him grin broadly. "Well then…when do you get off?" he asked.

"Right now!" she said, handing him his change and meal. She closed out her register and stepped away from the counter.

"Care to share with me?" he grinned. "I'll reserve that table over there for us!"

"Okay," replied Lauren. She went into the back and clocked out. Her friends were all nudging each other and giggling behind their hands. They had seen the cowboy too.

Lauren made her way out to the table and sat down. She found the Texas Toast Burger already split in two with half of the fries.

"Howdy!" she smiled, sitting down.

"What's your name?" asked the Cowboy.

"Lauren…what's yours?"

"Henry," he replied. "Well, Lauren…if you don't mind I always like to say grace before I eat."

"Me too, Henry!" she replied. They bowed their heads and he said grace. Despite the fact that she had finished her shift, Lauren and Henry lingered long after their meal and talked for hours about everything. The next thing they knew, it had gotten dark outside.

Henry stood up and extended his hand to take Lauren's into his. He bent over and gave her a little kiss on the top. "Well, Lauren. I can't remember the last time I enjoyed myself this much. May I call on you again while I'm in town?"

"Sure!" Lauren smiled, blushing. She grabbed a paper napkin, scribbling her email and phone number on it and handed it back to Henry.

He tucked it into his pocket and tipped his hat at her again. "I best be getting along but you'll be hearing from me!"

The moment he left Lauren was surrounded by her friends at work; they were all talking at once. "He kept you here for hours!" "What did you guys talk about?" "Where's he from?" "He's so handsome!"

"Okay! Okay!" Lauren giggled, shooing them away. "His name is Henry and he's from Austin, Texas and he owns a ranch! I'm going to go home now!" She picked up her purse and headed to her car and drove home.

Henry called her the following day and asked her out on a real official "date". He was going to take her to fancy restaurant. The moment she hung up the phone she dashed out the door to Brier Creek Mall to find a nice outfit. She came back hours later with a new dress, shoes and faux pearl necklace. For the rest of that day, she fussed over her hair and makeup then waited by the front door for the doorbell to ring.

Henry was right on time. When she opened the door Lauren couldn't help but gasp. He was in a crisp white button down shirt and black woolen pants with a jacket to match and red tie. The cowboy hat was gone and she ogled his golden blond hair. Henry took her admiration in good stride and offered his arm to her.

"Don't you look a picture!" he remarked. She was wearing her new black cocktail dress, pearl necklace and matching shoes. She felt like a queen as he escorted her to the waiting limousine.

"Is this yours?" she asked, ducking inside. A bottle of sparkling cider was chilling in the champagne bucket.

"Naw," Henry grinned, popping the seal and pouring her a class full into a champagne flute. I just rented it to drive me around while I'm on business here. It's just as cheap as a taxi but a lot nicer and I don't have to worry about getting lost. It also comes in handy to take beautiful women out on dates!" he grinned. Lauren's face flamed red at the compliment.

They arrived half an hour later and spent the next few hours eating, talking and laughing. When he took her home that night he gave her a kiss on the cheek and left her with a single long-stemmed red rose.

For the next two weeks they were inseparable. Henry took her out every day that she didn't have to work and each night he left her with a kiss and another long-stemmed red rose. They grew very close in the space of two weeks and she was dreading the day when he would leave. Lauren felt like she had found her soul-mate and the thought of him flying back to Texas without her was killing her. Finally the day of his departure dawned and they were bidding each other goodbye on her doorstep. Lauren felt like crying.

"It pains my heart something awful to leave you like this," Henry said, his voice husky with emotion. "I don't suppose I could ever talk you into coming to Texas?"

"Yes you could!" Lauren answered; her heart leaping. "As long as you married me first!" she slapped her hand over her mouth and giggled. She hadn't meant to blurt it out like that.

Henry stared at her for a long moment. "Are you serious?" he asked her, his blue eyes intense. "Would you really marry me after only knowing me two weeks?"

Lauren nodded. "Yes…all you have to do is ask me," she replied. A smile like sunlight broke over Henry's face. He got down on one knee and with her hands in his…proposed.

"Miss Lauren…I love you like crazy. Would you be my wife and live with me on my ranch in Texas and be the mother of my children?"

"Yes! Yes! Yes!" cried Lauren hopping up and down with joy.

Henry stood up and took her into his arms, kissing her for the first time on her lips. "Let's go tell your family!" he suggested. Lauren brought him inside and began to ring everyone up to tell them the good news. After the initial shock they all began to congratulate her and inquire about her wedding plans.

"We're going to fly to Texas and meet his parents first for the holidays!" Lauren informed everyone. When she finally hung up the phone she was exhausted but elated. Henry held out his arms to her and wrapped her in a tender embrace.

"Get yourself packed, little darling. We'll go pick out the engagement ring in Texas!"

Six months later, after a large and beautiful ceremony, Lauren and Henry were married. They honeymooned in Hawaii and three months later she found out she was pregnant with a boy. When he was born he looked just like his daddy; fair-haired with blue eyes. They made their home on Henry's ranch and together they raised a family of three boys and two girls and Lauren never had to work at a fast food restaurant again.

CHAPTER-THIRTY-TWO
"At the Master's Feet"

I have known Kathy since we were both in our early 20's. Kathy is the most faithful, long-suffering child of God I have ever known. All her life, all she ever wanted to do was to serve God as a medical missionary in India, helping the poorest of the poor. Instead, 20 years ago, she contracted Lyme's disease which went undiagnosed for over 15 years. The disease has made it impossible for her to work a job or have any kind of normal life. She has never been married nor had children and still lives with her mom who was recently diagnosed with cancer. Despite her complete isolation (now going on decades); Kathy remains cheerful, upbeat and faithful. She has thrown herself into Bible Study and reading is the only pleasure left to her. This is my wish for Kathy and this book would not have been complete without it. If you feel so inclined, please pray for my friend and all the people in this book who are hurting in one way or another.

"At the Master's Feet"

It was noon and Kathy woke up slowly. The medication she took to dull the constant pain made it impossible to wake up any earlier. She opened her eyes to find large male feet in a pair of sandals on the floor directly across from her. Her gaze traveled up, up, up…her heart thumping; until they froze upon the face of Someone she had never thought to see on this side of heaven.

"Kathy" He said, offering His hand to her. Unable to tear her eyes from His beloved face, she put her small hand into his large warm one and felt a thrill run through her body. She felt lighter, wide awake and completely free of pain.

"Come," he beckoned, opening her bedroom door.

"Is this my time to-to…uh you know…?" she couldn't quite say the words.

Jesus looked at her. "No – not yet," He answered.

Kathy nodded and followed him through the door. She suddenly found herself standing in a dwelling made of stone. There was a bustle of activity as men and women rushed to and fro, carrying baskets of dates and figs and large clay pitchers. A dark-haired woman with a flustered look on her face was pointing and directing all her servants while at the same time, kneading dough and minding a spit upon which a lamb was slowly roasting. Kathy looked about her in awe realizing that somehow she had gone back in time and was seeing a familiar scene from the Bible played out before her very eyes. She looked down at herself and found that she was no longer wearing 21st century sleepwear but long flowing robes of hand woven linen and her hair was down past the small of her back but covered in a veil. She no longer felt any pain or exhaustion; just a sense of wonder and awe. She went off to do a little exploring and found a middle-aged man pouring wine into vessels and talking to some other men.

"Yes, it is just as you have heard." He was saying. "I wasn't asleep or unconscious…I was in Abraham's bosom. I saw and heard things that I can't even begin to describe to you. I saw our Patriarchs, Isaac, Jacob and Moses and I even saw the gulf fixed between Sheol and Abraham's bosom with our rich neighbor on the other side who died shortly after I did. He was begging for someone to go to his brothers and warm them but Moses assured him that none would listen…" at that moment he turned and noticed Kathy standing there with her mouth agape. *So the story of the rich man and Lazarus wasn't a parable…* she had been thinking. To her surprise Lazarus opened his arm and beckoned her closer.

"This is my sister, Mary," he said to the others, meaning Kathy. "She can vouch as to the validity of my death. Isn't that so, sister?" Kathy wasn't about to contradict a biblical character and ruin her daydream so she just nodded her head up and down in agreement. Lazarus gave her a brotherly hug and she took that as her cue to go. She moved on to other rooms of the house which were still bustling with activity as more and more guests flowed into the house. She eventually wound up in the room where Jesus was reclining and decided to sit down at his feet. He offered her some warm pita bread and hummus. Kathy was hesitant to eat it. It had been years since she had deviated from her simple and wearisome diet of plain chicken, oatmeal, and peanut butter. The thought of putting anything else into her stomach and what it might to do her later was terrifying.

"Do not fear," He comforted her. "Eat."

Kathy popped it into her mouth and closed her eyes with pleasure. It was delicious if only because it was such a complete change of venue but mostly because it had come directly from her Savior's own hand. *Might as well enjoy myself while I'm here!* She thought to herself and began to help herself to everything with relish. While she ate Jesus lay reclined on the cushions that were spread across the floor and Kathy followed suit, not knowing what else to do.

Then He began to speak to her and tell her stories. Stories that had never been recorded in the Gospel accounts. Kathy was transfixed not only by His words but by His face and eyes as well which never left hers. Eyes that were deep, bottomless wells of infinite love. All else in the room faded away into insignificance as He spoke.

"Master!" came an irritated voice from across the room. All activity in the room paused to stare at the lady of the house who stood sweating with her hands upon her hips in exasperation. To make matter worse she was glaring at Kathy as if she had committed a grievous social faux pas. A weird feeling of déjà vu came over Kathy. The woman continued, pointing an accusing finger at Kathy. "Do you not care that my sister has left me to do all the serving alone? Tell her to help me!"

"Martha! Martha!" Jesus said, shaking his head and laying his hand upon Kathy's shoulder protectively. "You are worried and bothered about so many things but only a few are necessary; really only one, for Mary has chosen the good part which shall not be taken from her!"

Suddenly Kathy found herself back in her bedroom, in her bed clothes with her Bible open upon her lap. She blinked a few times then looked up and was amazed to still see her Savior sitting there. He was looking upon her with such love and compassion it made her want to weep.

"My daughter," He said, cupping her trembling chin in His warm hand. "All thy life you have grieved the fact that you have been unable to serve Me as a nurse in a foreign land but I am here to tell you that I have chosen the way of Mary for you. Do not regret the long years of pain and isolation for in them you have been given the gift of sitting at My feet and learning of Me. There is no greater sacrifice I could ask or gift I can bestow than this. In all thy trials you have proved thyself a good and faithful servant and in thee I am well pleased."

Kathy bowed her head, overwhelmed; tears dripping from her eyes. When she lifted her head again He was gone but she could still feel His presence in the room. No matter what lay ahead in the days to come, she knew she was in the center of His perfect will…and that was enough.

CHAPTER THIRTY-THREE
"A Force to be Reckoned With"

Emma Jewel was born in June of 2007. As a result of a defective chromosome, she is still unable to sit up by herself, walk or even speak. Due to the fact that her specific condition is still undiagnosed, insurance companies will not cover medical equipment or therapy necessary to help her to develop physically and become self-sufficient. Despite all this, her parents have invested much of their own time, effort and money into helping to improve the life of their precious daughter. They have found a physical therapy center that has had much success with children like Emma and which had led to her improvement but the sessions are very expensive. Her father has designed several pieces of equipment for Emma's special needs to help motivate her to move on her own, as well as created a website which would bring awareness to Emma's plight as well as others with special needs. Her mother, Hannah recently released a Christmas CD "Merry Christmas" and with the proceeds will help to fund little Emma's needs. She also has a video on YouTube where she sings about her daughter as "God's Gift" which is breathtakingly beautiful. In it you will get to see images of Emma first hand. The link for the video and Emma's website appears at of this story.

"A Force to Be Reckoned With"

The beautiful brunette walked haltingly but gracefully to the podium. The large ballroom hushed politely, all eyes upon her in expectancy as she arranged her notes and bottle of water. The event had been sold out months in advance. The vast crowd was a mixture of physician's, insurance executives, political figures, pastors and families.

"Good afternoon!" smiled the young woman warmly, her gaze passing over the crowd. This was not the first time she had spoken to a large number of people. As an international ambassador for those similarly afflicted, she had almost become a celebrity and tickets to her gatherings were sold at a premium. In the past five years she had appeared before many crowded ballrooms, church assemblies and even testified before Congress which had resulted in legislation that had brought not only national attention to those with her affliction but the needed change in insurance policies so that parents of children would not have to bear the burden of providing necessary equipment and therapy alone. Tonight, however, would be a little different and she trembled with excitement at the thought of what lay ahead.

"Good afternoon," murmured the hundred of attendees back to her. She enjoyed a wonderful rapport with her audiences who had come to be like an extended family to her. For the next forty-five minutes she spoke eloquently about the medical research that had been conducted and the therapies which had resulted for people with her condition and the progress that had been made in the years since she was born. She then concluded with a brief summary of the funds that had been raised for her nationally recognized charitable organization. Then she switched gears. When she had completed her presentation the crowd broke into spontaneous and enthusiastic applause. She had to raise her hands to get them to quiet down.

"I hope you will indulge me for just a few moments on a more personal note," she said, nodding offstage to the technical crew. The lights dimmed and the large projection screen to the right lit up. "As you may all be already aware, this effort started out with just a small handful of dedicated people who refused to give up on me," she continued, her blue eyes focusing on two people in the front row. "Not only does this charity and all whom it benefits owe them a debt of gratitude, but I do as well. With that in mind, I would like to show you this video of the two most important people in my life: my parents…A.T. and Hannah Jane Snoots who are celebrating their 25th anniversary today! Were it not for their dedication, determination and selfless devotion to me, and their desire to see that I live life to my full potential…I would not be standing before you today as I am but would rather have been consigned to live my life in some forgotten corner, alone, helpless and completely dependent upon others for my most basic needs. Mom and dad…this is for you!"

The crowd's eyes turned to the screen and up came the music video that her mom had made for her when she was just a toddler to help raise money for her therapy. Throughout the large hall, the beautiful voice of her mother's younger voice wafted like a soft breeze as she sang the anthem song for her charity, "God's Gift". Pictures of Emma in her youth passed across the screen, her large blue eyes staring at the crowd, beckoning, entrancing and uplifting them. When it was over there wasn't a dry eye in the house. Then…before the lights could come up, a single, beautiful voice lifted in praise and began to sing:

"Jesus loves me! This I know,
For the Bible tells me so;
Little ones to Him belong,
They are weak but He is strong.
Yes, Jesus loves me!
Yes, Jesus loves me!
Yes, Jesus loves me!
The Bible tells me so.

Jesus loves me! He who died,
Heaven's gate to open wide;
He will wash away my sin,
Let His little child come in.
Yes, Jesus loves me!
Yes, Jesus loves me!
Yes, Jesus loves me!
The Bible tells me so.

Jesus loves me! loves me still,
When I'm very weak and ill;

From His shining throne on high,
Comes to watch me where I lie.
Yes, Jesus loves me!
Yes, Jesus loves me!
Yes, Jesus loves me!
The Bible tells me so...

As the lights slowly came up, it revealed Emma leaving the podium and walking unaided down the steps to her mother and father who were weeping with pride. She lifted them both to their feet, embraced them and together they sang the last chorus of the song as they slow-danced together:

"Jesus loves me! He will stay,
Close beside me all the way;
He's prepared a home for me,
And some day His face I'll see.
Yes, Jesus loves me!
Yes, Jesus loves me!
Yes, Jesus loves me!
The Bible tells me so."

When they were done, the crowd stood to their feet as one to give them a standing ovation, weeping with abandon. Emma's own expansive blue eyes were filled with tears as she kissed her parents.

"I will never be able to adequately express my gratitude for all you have done for me, mom and dad," she whispered despite the lump in her throat.

Hannah and A.T. cupped Emma's face in their hands, blessing her.

"You already have, my darling." Hannah whispered in return. "You already have."

If you would like to see a beautiful video of little Emma, go to this link: http://www.youtube.com/watch?v=ww_4XDDLlDM

If you would like to donate to help this little girl, a charitable website has been set up here:

http://www.hopeforemma.com/About-Hope-for-Emma-charity.html

For every "Make a Wish" book purchased from me personally, I will donate $1 to assist little Emma with her equipment and physical therapy.

CHAPTER THIRTY-FIVE
"Breath of Heaven"

"My wish is a very special wish! I miscarried about 4 1/2 months into my last pregnancy, and because of many large tumors, surgeries, and a short battle with Lymphoma, I am no longer able to have children of my own. Ultimately my wish would be to know my baby, hold him, love him, and tell him how proud I am of him, but more importantly, I wish he knew me, his mommy!"

"Breath of Heaven"

Angel stared with longing at the pregnant woman in the mall; feeling the familiar ache that seized her heart. She closed her eyes, trying to imagine what it would be like to hold a wriggling baby in her arms only to have the tears of regret flow down her cheeks.

Suddenly she felt a tug upon her smock top and looked down to see a little boy with large blue eyes staring up at her. He looked to be about three.

"Can you find my mommy?" he asked, his forehead creasing with anxiety. "I lost."

Momentarily startled, Angel squatted down next to him so they were eye to eye. "What is your name?" she asked softly. The little boy rubbed a chubby knuckle over his eyes which were beginning to well up with tears.

"Bobby," he replied, his voice rising with fear on the last syllable. Angel's heart went out to him.

"What's yours?" he asked.

"Angel," she replied with a gentle smile, digging to find a Kleenex in her purse.

The little boy's eyes went as round as saucers. "Are you a *real* angel?" he asked in wonder.

Angel couldn't help but stifle a small giggle. She took hold of his hand. "Well, let's just say that today I will be *your* angel. Now let's find your mommy. What does she look like?"

Bobby put both hands on either side of his head and squeezed his eyes shut in concentration. "I don't know," he said plaintively. "She's only been my mommy for a little while…" Then he began to cry. Angel wrapped him in her arms and patted his back to comfort him.

"It will be okay, Bobby," she cooed. "We'll find her! I bet she's looking for you too." She took his little hand in hers and together they walked to the mall security office. On the way she stopped and got him a red balloon and distracted him by telling him the story about the film called "The Red Balloon" her mother had told her when she was little. How a red balloon had become the friend of a little boy and followed him to school and then waited around for him until school was out and the adventures they had.

"When they reached mall security there was already a small knot of people crammed inside. They all turned around at once as soon as Angel and Bobby opened the door and a woman cried out with relief, dropping to her knees. "Bobby!"

"I'm sorry, mommy…" he wailed, allowing her to pick him up and laying his head upon her shoulder.

"Thank you so much, you're an angel!" the woman said to Angel. Bobby perked up and pointed at her.

"I knew you were an angel!" he crowed, smiling through his tears. "She got me a magic balloon, mommy!"

"That's wonderful, Bobby! " said the woman. She transferred Bobby over to her husband and navigated her way through a small throng of other children of various ages and colors closer to Angel. She took both of her hands in hers. "I can't thank you enough for keeping him safe and bringing him back to us!" she said in relief. "This isn't the first time he's disappeared looking for his real mom. I just can't bear to tell him that he will never be able to go back with her; she died of an overdose two months ago. Her name was Elllen."

Angel stared at her, stricken, then cast her gaze back to Bobby who was smiling at her through his tears. She pointed to the other children. "Are those all yours as well?" she asked.

The woman nodded. "I could never have my own kids and I have a lot of love to give so we adopted. They are all special needs kids, except for Bobby. He just needs a lot of patience and healing. This is the third time in a week he's gone missing. If Social Services gets wind of it they'll take him away and then his life will be disrupted again. There's no telling what kind of emotional damage that will do."

Angel stared at Bobby who was looking back at her with large solemn eyes then she looked at his adopted mother again, her brown eyes tinged with worry. "He thinks I'm a real angel, you know," she told the woman. "That may be something I can use to your benefit."

"What do you mean?" asked the woman.

"Can you let me speak with him one more time before you leave?"

"Of course!"

"Okay…give me a sec." Angel walked back to Bobby whose eyes lit up when she approached. He reached for her and at seeing his wife's nod of assent the husband let Bobby climb into her arms.

"Bobby, I have something very important to tell you. A message from your mommy, Ellen," began Angel, setting him on her lap as she sat down.

"What?" he asked, his lower lip beginning to tremble. It was all Angel could do to keep from crying herself.

"Your mommy sent me to tell you that she is okay and to not look for her anymore because she is up in heaven watching over you."

"She's in heaven?" Bobby repeated, his blue eyes filling with renewed hope.

Angel nodded, struggling to keep her voice steady despite the lump in her throat. "Yes, Bobby. She asked me to tell you that she's not sick anymore and that she loves you very, very much."

"Mommy's not sick anymore?"

"No darling, and she's not sad anymore either. Heaven is a very wonderful place and I have to return soon. Is there anything that you would like me to tell your mommy for you?"

Bobby nodded, wrapped his little arms about her neck and whispered in her ear.

"Tell mommy I love her and give her this," he said planting a little kiss upon her cheek that was becoming soaked with tears.

"I will, I promise!"said Angel, carrying him back to his adopted mother and depositing him in her arms with a teary smile.

"Thank you!" Angel told her.

"Why are you thanking me?" replied the woman. "I should be thanking you!"

Angel smiled feeling the burden of emptiness that she had carried for so long lift from her shoulders at long last. "Because now I know what God wants me to do with my life!" she replied.

CHAPTER THIRTY-FIVE
"A Dream is a Wish Your Heart Makes"

This is my true life wish fulfillment. It is not a story I wrote but describes actual events from my life about meeting my real life "Prince Charming", my husband..Michael.

"A Dream is a Wish Your Heart Makes"
(My Own Wish That Really Came True)

It was 1978, I was 18 and had never gone out on a date nor had a boyfriend. I wasn't weird looking but it seemed as though God had put a large "kiss off" sign on my forehead to keep members of the opposite sex away. I was commuting to Los Angeles daily on the public bus to attend the Fashion Institute of Design and Merchandising ("FIDM") where the chances of meeting a normal, nice Christian male interested in the opposite sex were extremely dismal. I had just become a Christian the year before and was spending my hour long commute nagging the Lord daily about wanting to go out on a date. I was feeling quite desperate!

On one particular day I think the good Lord had had enough of my "kvetching" and while 'lucky dipping' through my Bible, the following scripture jumped off the page at me. I could almost actually hear the Holy Spirit yelling the verse at me: "DELIGHT YOURSELF IN THE LORD AND HE WILL GIVE YOU THE DESIRES OF YOUR HEART!!!" At the same time, a still small voice in my head told me to write a story that would portray my wishes being fulfilled.

I went home that day, uncovered my Smith Corona typewriter and began typing away. The title of the book was: "Jesus Wave-walker, Jesus Joy-giver", a pretty lame title now that I look back on it but it turned out to be a pretty prophetic story. I put myself in as the main character and described how the Lord called me up on the phone to take me out on a date and during that date He "introduced" me to the man He had chosen for me. At this point, I must digress and tell you that the name for my future husband, whoever he was, was always "Michael". I prayed for Michael by name and even made a list of all the attributes I desired in my future mate: a good Christian, funny, handsome (to me anyway), had a large family, nice friends, a good work ethic, responsible, trustworthy, kind, handy, played guitar….and oh yes…had kept himself pure from women. Whenever I would tell my friends this last item they would shake their heads at me and whisper "Good luck!" under their breath. I finished my short story naming the character of the man he chosen for me as Michael. I then illustrated my book (drawing myself the way I wished I looked) as well as my "dream man", Michael.

Fast forward four years. I was at my 8th or 9th College and Career Church Retreat in the hopes of meeting a nice Christian boy. In the past 4 years I had left FIDM, gotten a job and moved to Orange County, met my first love, Barry, (who had died 4 months previous from a brain aneurism) and was still grieving even though my feelings for him had been unrequited. I was friends with a house full of Christian men but was still being treated like one of "the guys". I was quickly becoming resigned to the fact that I was going to die an old maid when I looked across the crowded room of the retreat's dining room and saw a face that caught my eye (just like that verse in the song: "Some Enchanted Evening in South Pacific). He was pretty handsome and I remember thinking that he was probably too stuck up to talk to me! The next thing I knew, he was sitting next to me.

We exchanged polite smiles and introduced ourselves.

"Hi," I said. "My name is Marlayne."

"I'm Michael," was his reply.

My ears perked up but I said nothing about his name for fear of scaring him away. *Interesting*, I thought. We talked politely for a few minutes then said our goodbye's when breakfast was done. From that moment on I was his shadow. We ended up talking for hours about cartoons, my first love then his first love;

the fact that I was a Messianic Jew and on and on until the stars came out and it was time to go to our respective cabins. It had snowed that weekend (despite being April) and we threw snowballs at each other the next day. I didn't even mind when he put his arm around me and kissed my forehead (which normally would have scared me off). The last day of the retreat I was starting to fret because Michael still had not asked for my phone number. After Sunday morning's Bible study we would all be going our separate ways and if he didn't ask for my phone number I would probably never see him again. With that in mind, I asked to see his Bible. He handed it over to me and I wrote my name and phone number inside the front cover and handed it back reasoning that I rather come off as forward than die a spinster.

The following day, back at home I told my roommate about meeting Michael and how we had hit it off. As I left our apartment to visit Barry's parents, I gave her some very specific instructions: "Now, Theresa, if a guy by the name of Michael calls… don't say anything to him but call me at the Henriot's house and let me know." She agreed and to my delight while I was having dinner with Ruth and Al, she called and sang out: *"Michael caaaalled!!"*

I was ready at that moment to call him right back (impatient person that I am) but I distinctly felt the Lord instructing me to wait an entire day. If you know me at all you would know what absolute torture this was but I obeyed and waited.

The next day I called Michael back and in a very nonchalant voice said: "Hi! I heard you called yesterday." (Little did he know that I was jumping up and down for glee at that moment.) Michael then asked me out on a date for the following weekend with his sister, her husband and another couple to go to Westwood to see the re-release of Fantasia. I went right out and bought myself a whole new outfit for the occasion and when I opened the door of my apartment the following Saturday and saw Michael standing there I couldn't help but think "Oh my… is he ever handsome!"

After the movie we went to Hamburger Hamlet for dinner as a six-some. Little did I know until several years later that something very unusual took place during that date while I was in the ladies room. His sister's friend, Tina, who had never laid eyes on me until that night had turned to Michael's sister, Debbie and asked her: "Well, what do you think of Marlayne?"

"She seems nice," had been Debbie's polite response.

"Well that's Michael's future wife." Tina informed everyone. Michael was instantly incensed. He couldn't stand this girl and how opinionated she was, so the fact that she had just said this to him instilled the exact opposite reaction. *NO WAY NOW!* Were his thoughts at the time but God had other plans.

We dated for the next four years but 9 months into our relationship I finally got up the courage to show him my story with his name and face in it. It was a good thing I had waited until he was really "hooked" because if I had shown it to him early in our relationship he would have high tailed it for the hills! Almost five years after we met we were married. I put my prophetic story on display at our reception so everyone could see how God had brought us together – and haven't seen it since. It simply disappeared.

My list? Oh yes, Michael fulfilled everything I had put on my list, including the last item!! That was 24 years ago and we are still happily married. Michael and I were recently discussing that story and my history of other men avoiding me like they had seen a giant "kiss off" sign plastered on my forehead when Michael said one of the sweetest things to me I have ever heard:

"Well, honey, I didn't see the words: 'kiss off' on your forehead…" he reassured me, planting a tender kiss on said spot. "I saw the words: *KISS HERE*."

THE END

SPECIAL NOTE

If you would like to know the God of the Universe who loves you and gave His only begotten Son to reconcile you to Himself; all you have to do is to ask Jesus into your heart. Don't wait…time is running short and He is returning soon.

Marlayne Giron
Email: thevictorbook@sbcglobal.net
www.thevictorbook.com

Marlayne Giron is a wife and mother living in Southern California. She is also the author of:

The Victor
A Tale of Betrayal, Love, and Sacrifice

The Victor is available at Amazon in perfect paperback or Kindle format as well as Borders Books and Barnes & Noble

ENDORSEMENTS

ꙮ

"I was totally blown away when I read my wish story! It touched me so much tears of joy flowed down my cheeks. It was more than what I expected. You will be amazed at the inspirational God-given messages through the writings of this awesome author. (Message received from my wish -- TRUST THE SON!)" – **Martha Ray Winders (Something New Under the Son)**

"Tears began streaming down my cheeks from the very moment I began reading my wish story! This author has been blessed with a gift that could only come from God Himself, and I was truly blessed by her God-given talent!" – **Gail Watts (Waterfall Blessings)**

"When I read my story, it brought tears to my eyes. It was as if Marlayne had peered into my mind. The Holy Spirit had to have revealed my thoughts to her, for her to have that much insight into my life, because we have never met. This short story has deeply moved me to continue my work. I guess you never really know how you have affected people you briefly encounter, until you read something like this." – **Jeremy Baldwin (Woulda, Coulda, Shoulda)**

"I have read many things in my life that have touched my heart, but nothing like what Marlayne has written. I keep my wish fulfillment story by my bed with my daily devotional and my Bible. Every night when I read it, tears flow. This is such a blessing." – **Ronnie Jackson (Appointment with Destiny)**

"Marlayne: All I can do is cry.....it is the most beautiful story; more than I could have imagined, though the stories I had read on your site were so inspiring I knew that the people you had written them for must have been thrilled.   I just had let you know that I am bawling my eyes out. What a wonderful gift you have given to me, to Emma, to the family, and most of all to the Lord for as you have given to us, you have given to Him. Thank you! Thank you! Thank you!" **- Susan Smoots ("A Force to be Reckoned With)**